The Detective Matt Jones Thriller Series

"Ellis keeps everything in focus while building a staggering momentum."
—*Booklist*, Starred Review, *City of Echoes*

"Only really good writers can make you feel so strongly. *City of Echoes* is another bravura effort from the talented Robert Ellis."
—*Mystery Scene* magazine

"*City of Echoes* is an absorbing and entertaining read from first page to last and documents novelist Robert Ellis as a master of the genre."
—*Midwest Book Review*

"*City of Echoes* is a Best Book of the Month."
—Amazon.com

"Ellis eases new readers into the second Matt-centric novel. Having previously suffered betrayal, Matt has good reason to be paranoid, which results in a gleefully tense sequel. His relationships are complex . . . the mystery is straightforward. A persistently gripping thriller with strong characters."
—*Kirkus Reviews*, *The Love Killings*

"With an early focus on the possible murders, Ellis' series entry is more thriller than mystery. The author works this to great effect as the story reveals the burden of unearthing evidence. Ellis generates an impressive amount of suspense. Solid entertainment."
—*Kirkus Reviews*, *The Girl Buried in the Woods*

PRAISE FOR ROBERT ELLIS
City of Fire (Lena Gamble, Book 1)

"Los Angeles under a cloud of acrid smoke . . . Robert Ellis's *City of Fire* is a gripping, spooky crime novel."
—*The New York Times* Hot List Pick

"*City of Fire* is my kind of crime novel. Gritty, tight, and assured. Riding with Detective Lena Gamble through the hills of Los Angeles is something I could get used to. She's tough, smart, and most of all, she's real."
—Michael Connelly

"*City of Fire* features a tough but deeply flawed protagonist, a tantalizingly complex plot, fully realized—and realistic—characters, and most of all, a palpable intensity. And if that weren't enough, the bombshell plot twist at the novel's conclusion makes this an absolute must read for thriller aficionados."
—*Chicago Tribune*

"I just discovered Robert Ellis. This book is terrific."
—Janet Evanovich, *People* magazine

"This book is fast, gruesome, and twisted, like a scary Jodie Foster movie. Ellis makes it easy to be terrified."
—*Library Journal*

The Lost Witness (Lena Gamble, Book 2)

"Scorching. Deliciously twisted. Nothing is what it appears to be. Ellis succeeds masterfully in both playing fair and pulling surprise after surprise in a story that feels like a runaway car plunging down a mountain road full of switchbacks."
—*Publishers Weekly*, Starred Review

"Ellis serves up a killer crime tale with riveting characters and relentless twists."
—*Booklist*, Starred Review

"Ellis's elaborate puzzle is a nail-biter to the final page. Great LA settings enhance this high-speed thriller. Recommended for all popular collections."
—*Library Journal*

"Ellis piles on the Hollywood atmosphere and procedural detail, and the end revelation is expertly timed and genuinely shocking."
—*The Guardian* (UK)

Murder Season (Lena Gamble, Book 3)

"*Murder Season*: a terrific sick-soul-of-LA thriller. Before you can say *Chinatown* we are immersed in a tale of mind-boggling corruption where virtually every character in the book—with the exception of Lena—has a hidden agenda. Ellis is a master plotter. Along the way we meet wonderful characters."
—*Connecticut Post*, Hearst Media News Group

"Within the space of a few books, Ellis has demonstrated that rare ability to skillfully navigate his readers through a complex plot filled with interesting, dangerous and surprising characters."
—Bookreporter.com

CITY OF STONES

A DETECTIVE MATT JONES THRILLER

BOOK 4

ALSO BY ROBERT ELLIS

The Girl Buried in the Woods

The Love Killings

City of Echoes

Murder Season

The Lost Witness

City of Fire

The Dead Room

Access to Power

CITY OF STONES

ROBERT ELLIS

A DETECTIVE MATT JONES THRILLER

BOOK 4

This is a work of fiction. All names, characters, places, organizations, and events portrayed in this novel are either products of the author's imagination or are used fictitiously.

CITY OF STONES

Copyright © 2021 by Robert Ellis.
Los Angeles, California

ISBN: 9798727884973

All rights reserved.

No part of this book may be reproduced in any form or by any means without express written permission from the author or his legal representatives, excepting brief quotes used in reviews. For more information, visit: https://www.robertellis.net/

Cover design by Elderlemon Design

1. Detective—California—Los Angeles—Fiction. 2. Young women—Crimes against—Fiction. 3. Young Men—Crimes against—Fiction. 4. Murder—Investigation—Fiction. 5. Mass Killings—Fiction. 6. Los Angeles (Calif.). Police Dept.—Fiction. 7. Los Angeles (Calif.)—Fiction. I. Title.

First Edition: June 2021

10 9 8 7 6 5 4 3 2 1

To Neil Oxman

ONE

It was late January in Los Angeles—a quiet afternoon on the lawn inside the track at the Police Academy—and even though the sun was out, the sky a pregnant blue almost as dark as the uniform he was wearing, Matthew Trevor Jones stood on the temporary stage fighting off the shivers and counting the minutes before he could go home.

He didn't want to be here. He wasn't ready to see people yet. He wasn't close to being ready.

He was still living in a time warp, still twisting in the blur of what had happened to him over the past two weeks. What Lieutenant McKensie, his supervisor at the Hollywood station, was calling his "disappearance."

He glanced at the award he had received today. Then down at his partner, Denny Cabrera, clutching his own award but still living at the rehab facility and still unable to get out of his wheelchair.

It didn't seem like the right day for a celebration. The wounded remained wounded. And the memories of their last case—and all the nightmares that went with it—still had a firm grip on their backs and would be following them around for a long time.

Matt took a deep breath and exhaled.

His gaze swept past the police commissioners seated beside Chief Logan and Lieutenant McKensie. The governor of California, James "Jimmy"

D. Hayworth, stood at the podium finishing up his speech. Seated behind him, Matt could see the governor's front man and personal attorney, Alan Fontaine, along with Lisa Hayworth, the woman most people believed would become First Lady a year from November. Matt had stopped following politics at some point during his tour of duty as a soldier in Afghanistan. Still, from listening to the radio in his car and spending time on the internet, he couldn't help but notice that if the governor ever announced a run for president, he had the clout and the record to already be considered a shoo-in.

Matt turned back to the front of the stage. He wasn't listening to the governor's speech. Instead, he was looking across the grass at the stands filled with cops and cadets and city officials. Even his shrink from the LAPD's Behavioral Science Services, Dr. Julie May, had shown up and was sitting beside the media and a section reserved for the twelve men and women readying their bagpipes and waiting for their cue. Matt guessed that Dr. May was furious with him for skipping out on his appointments over the past two weeks. For not even calling to let her know where he was or why he wouldn't be in to see her.

But what if he had checked in? What would he have said to her?

I'm somewhere in Malibu . . . I think I am, anyway . . . Somewhere near there . . . I'm not really sure . . . Someplace where the rich and famous go when they're having work done and don't want to be seen . . . My face is wrapped in bandages, and I can't really think . . . I'm not sure what to say about it . . . I don't know where I am . . .

If he really tried to focus—really, really tried—Matt could see his uncle, Dr. George Baylor, the brilliant plastic surgeon turned serial killer, bleeding through the nightmarish gloom. Dressed in a smock and issuing orders to a handful of assistants as the medical procedure moved from the cuts peppering Matt's entire face to the scars from the four bullet wounds he'd received just two and a half months ago to his shoulder, upper chest, and gut. He could see the shadowy figures weaving in and out of his mind through the dark haze. He could still hear the doctors speaking even though none of their words registered or made any sense. And then there was that IV in his arm. The one delivering drop after drop of an unknown sedative from an unlabeled bag.

He could remember staring at it. Staring at it for hours.

Twilight anesthesia, his uncle whispered into his ear after a number of days seemed to have passed.

You will remain semiconscious, Matthew. And you will have little to no memory of what has happened to you or even where you are. No recollection of anything until you've begun to heal and we deliver you home.

His cell phone started vibrating in his pants.

Matt's mind rocked to the surface. Although the ringer had been switched off, the governor's wife had noticed and was looking at him. When she turned away, Matt dug the phone out of his pocket and gave the face a casual but quick glance.

It was another reporter. This one calling from the *Los Angeles Times*. Someone named Ryan Brooks, whom he only knew from reading the newspaper on the web. Matt grimaced. It wasn't just the timing of the call that made him so livid. Brooks had to know what was going on today. Three reporters from his own newspaper were sitting in the media section right across the lawn.

Who did Brooks think he was? And how did he get his cell number?

The call seemed so rude. So insulting. So typical.

Matt switched off the phone and slipped it back into his pocket. When he looked up, he could see the governor's wife gazing at him again. But something about this time seemed different. She was sizing him up from head to toe with those brown eyes of hers. And he could see her wheels turning. She was measuring him and thinking about him. When she reached his face, her eyes met his and she flashed a gentle smile.

Matt smiled back, then turned away.

Lisa Hayworth had to be twenty years younger than her husband. And as Matt thought it over, probably no more than five or six years older than him. But even more confusing, she didn't seem like the kind of woman who would look at a man the way she had just looked at him. The more Matt thought it over, the more he thought Lisa Hayworth came off just like most people in politics. With light brown hair cut above the shoulders and bangs that framed what appeared to be an intelligent, even pleasant and friendly face, her sturdy build seemed as if it fit some kind of bureaucratic mold.

He shrugged it off. But when he turned back, he found her openly staring at him now.

The governor's wife.

A wave of confusion and embarrassment came and passed. Then Matt offered the woman a simple nod and glanced back at Dr. May sitting in the stands.

Obviously, everything that he thought had just happened hadn't really happened. The governor's wife was looking at him the same way anyone else would look at him. Obviously, Matt was making it all up in his head and needed more downtime. A lot more downtime. As he imagined Dr. May would have put it, "I'm sorry, Matthew, but you have a lot to process. You're not ready to see people yet. You're still living in that time warp, still twisting in that blur . . ."

TWO

Matt wheeled Cabrera away from the temporary stage to a quieter spot on the other side of the track beneath the trees. The media had stormed the governor as soon as he finished his speech and stepped down onto the lawn. As Matt watched and listened to the banter from a distance, he could tell from the expression on his partner's face that he was amused by the spectacle as well. Every question by every member of the media was exactly the same.

Are you running for president, Governor? Why won't you answer the question for us, sir?

Hayworth seemed to be enjoying himself, waving the reporters off and laughing as each one tried to get an answer that would never come. At least not today. Not this far away from Election Day.

Matt spotted a folding chair by the stage and dragged it over.

Cabrera turned and watched him setting it up. "The cuts on your face look like they're healing pretty well," he said. "So where have you been for the past two weeks, Matt? Who did the mending?"

Matt sat down, leaned back, and crossed his arms over his chest. "I can't answer that," he said finally. "You know I can't."

Cabrera shook his head. "I know you can't either, because I knew the answer to the question before I asked it. I know exactly who you were with.

So does Lieutenant McKensie. Baylor fixed your face."

"Okay," he said quietly. "Okay, then let's move on."

"Let's move on," Cabrera repeated. "Are you sure about that? Baylor's a serial killer. You're supposed to be a police officer. You have an obligation. It's your duty—your job to do what's right."

Matt looked down at the lawn as he mulled it over. "It's complicated, Denny."

"It's black and white, Matt. Even if he is your uncle. God knows why you don't want to see it the way it really is."

Matt shrugged his shoulders and looked up. Alan Fontaine had broken away from the crowd and was running toward them as if he had a mission. By the time he reached them, the lawyer was gasping for air and leaned over with his hands on his knees.

"The governor," he said, still trying to catch his breath. "He wants to know if it would be okay to get a picture with you guys."

Matt glanced at Cabrera. When his partner nodded, he turned back to Fontaine.

"Sure," Matt said. "It's okay with us."

Fontaine smiled. "Terrific," he said. "He wants to do it himself. You know, with his phone. It'll mean more that way."

Fontaine called out across the lawn and waved the governor over. For a moment, the media appeared bewildered, then grabbed their cameras and gear and charged forward like a band of overexcited children. Matt stood up as the governor approached.

"I'm sorry for all the bother," the governor said. "I just wanted a picture of the three of us to add to my wall of honor in the office."

The media bandwagon arrived, the hot-white strobes from all the still cameras cutting through the dim afternoon light. Matt glanced at the line of video cameras beginning to shove their way in as well—everything flickering like a black-and-white movie—then turned back to the governor.

"It's no problem at all, sir."

The governor flashed a smile—the kind that Matt imagined won votes—then pulled a cell phone out of his pocket, knelt down beside Cabrera, and waved Matt closer.

"Days like this are special," the governor said under his breath as he framed the shot. "I don't get to do them enough. Not nearly enough."

Governor James David Hayworth snapped the picture. As he lowered the phone to look at his photograph and show Cabrera, Matt could see that the reporters were eating the moment up like candy. But also, Matt could tell that the governor was a sincere person. It was almost as if he didn't know the media was even there. His clear blue eyes were sparkling, his chiseled face wrought with character. Matt knew that Hayworth was a veteran, a former naval pilot who had served a generation ahead of him in what had now become the endless war in the Middle East. Matt also knew that Hayworth had been shot down, ejected below five hundred feet in the air, and somehow survived.

Matt no longer followed politics, but some things had a way of standing out. He had only heard of one other pilot who survived an ejection that close to the ground, and that was during the Vietnam War.

The governor bowed slightly and thanked them. After slipping his phone into his pocket, he turned to Matt and winked.

"I'll get these guys out of your faces," he said. "But my wife wants to talk to you."

"About what?" he said.

"She says she knows you. You grew up together. She's from Jersey."

Matt didn't say anything, thinking it over and remembering the way the governor's wife had been measuring him. He could still recall those wild thoughts he'd had as he dealt with the embarrassment and tried to understand what was going on. But now the slate had been cleaned, and he could feel his body beginning to relax. Though he couldn't place her, at least it finally made some sort of sense.

THREE

"You don't remember me, do you? You've got no clue."

She was standing ten feet away. She glanced down at Cabrera in the wheelchair, then looked back at Matt and stepped closer. While Matt struggled to sift through his past, he could tell from the glint in her eyes that she was delighted by the situation.

"Look at me," she said. "Closer, Matty. Look."

It seemed like a clue. Not many people had ever called him "Matty." Still, the memory wouldn't cut through. After a few moments, he shook his head and laughed.

"I'm sorry," he said.

Her smile widened and she gave him a look. "I'm Lisa Tillman," she said finally. "Johnny's sister."

Matt did a double take as his eyes danced over the woman's face, and time suddenly filled in all the blank spots.

"Lisa," he said. "It really is you. It's been so long."

"Almost forever," she said, still grinning.

Lisa Tillman was the big sister of one of his childhood friends. They had lived three houses down the street in Pennington, New Jersey. Matt's Aunt Abby had been a good friend of Lisa's mother, and when Matt was too young to be left alone, he usually stayed over at their house so Lisa could look after him.

It really had been a long time.

"You moved away," Matt said.

"You were still a boy. I went to college. When Dad changed jobs, the family moved to North Carolina."

"How's your brother?"

"Married with two kids. Teaching, and I think happy."

Matt guessed that Lisa had little to no idea about what had happened in Philadelphia, New Jersey, and Connecticut with the Love Killings. How much of his past he had been forced to let in and was still wrestling with. He let it go and glanced at the media huddled around the governor on the lawn, then turned back to her.

"So how did you end up here doing this?" he said.

A faint smile lit up her face again. "I'm still working on that one. How'd you end up here doing this?"

He shrugged and gave her a look. "Luck, I guess."

The media had begun to notice them talking. Three guys were heading toward them with their video cameras up and rolling. Behind them, five reporters with five photographers were giving chase. Then five more after them. Then even more.

Lisa lowered her voice as the strobe lights started flashing. "Why are they walking that way?"

Matt grimaced. "It's called the Groucho. They're mimicking the actor. They walk with their knees bent and keep their backs straight so that they can aim their rifles and fire on the move."

"But those aren't rifles."

"No, they're not. They just seem that way right now."

It didn't take much to understand that the media was about to begin feeding on them. The number of cameras and bright-light flashes, the number of people pushing and shoving and shouting questions had grown exponentially. And the questions weren't just directed at the governor's wife. Most of the reporters wanted to know if Matt had intentionally let his serial killer uncle escape.

"What was it? A family thing?" someone shouted.

Lisa squinted under the lights and tugged on Matt's arm. "I don't like this," she said. "Would you guys mind helping me to our car?"

Matt nodded, grabbed the handles on Cabrera's wheelchair, and pushed through the frenzied crowd. The parking lot was close, just on the other side of the trees. And even though Matt had driven a clear path through the center of the group, no one holding a camera or microphone seemed to get it. They were closing in and trying to block their way. When a woman poked Matt in the face with a long microphone, he batted it away and plowed forward as fast as he could.

They cut through the trees and came out on the other side. The governor's limo was idling by the curb. Still pushing Cabrera in the wheelchair at a quick pace, Matt caught the driver's eye and guided Lisa to the rear door.

She seemed upset by the commotion but turned and gave Matt a hug. "It was great seeing you," she said in a quiet voice. "It brings back a lot of wonderful memories, which I knew it would. Your Aunt Abby was a good woman, Matty. Thank you. Thank both of you."

She gave Matt a last look, then squeezed Cabrera's hand and climbed into the limo. The media was swarming from all around like bees with their stingers out. Cameras were flashing, the glare bouncing off the car's darkened glass and often directly into Matt's eyes. But even more irritating, the questions about his uncle were nonstop and appeared to be intentionally mean-spirited, the reporter's voices raised and almost shrill.

Matt scanned the parking lot and noticed two police cruisers with their LED light bars flashing as they blocked the entrance to a side road. Rolling Cabrera between the two cars, he spun the wheelchair around so that they could watch the show from a safe distance away. The governor had just stepped through the crowd, waving at them as he got into the limo and sat beside his wife. After a few minutes, the car idled out of the lot and made a left turn on Academy Road, passing Dodger Stadium and heading for the 110 Freeway.

"Sweet and sour," Cabrera said once the limo disappeared.

"What's that?" Matt said.

Cabrera shrugged. "Some things in life taste sweet, Matt. Then there's everything else, which usually tastes sour."

"Usually?"

Cabrera beamed at his newfound wisdom. Matt laughed, but in irony. He knew that his partner wouldn't be back at the murder table for at least six months, and he already missed him.

FOUR

Traffic had been horrendous, the twenty-mile drive from the academy to his house in the hills above Potrero Canyon Park taking almost two hours.

He didn't mind really.

Not when dusk was just giving in to the night. Not when the shadows had turned blue and all the lights were coming on. He could remember working with a crime scene photographer who loved to take pictures of landscapes on the side and always called this time of day *magic hour*.

Matt pulled into the carport and climbed out from behind the wheel. Unlocking the front door, he hit the outdoor lights and stepped into the living room. The house was dark inside, but through the windows to the south he could see Santa Monica and Venice Beach just beginning to vanish beneath the marine layer sweeping in from the ocean. To the east he still had a clear view of the LA Basin all the way to the tall buildings downtown. He crossed the room to the slider and gazed through the glass. The moon had just begun to rise above the horizon and appeared to be trapped behind the buildings. For several moments, he stared at it in wonder—the moon, just short of full, casting the entire city in a warm orange light.

Magic hour . . . It was good to be home.

Matt turned away finally, switching on the lights and breezing down the hall into his bedroom. After getting out of his uniform, he pulled on a pair of jeans and grabbed a sweatshirt. Then he stepped into the kitchen and poured a vodka over ice from the bottle of Tito's he kept in the freezer.

While it may have been true that the wounds on his face and right arm were healing from his uncle's work and that even the scars from the four gunshot wounds he'd received in October were beginning to fade, Matt knew from the surgeons who saved his life that the pain would be with him for a long time. He looked at his meds on the counter, then took a sip of vodka. As he thought it over and his stomach began to glow, it seemed like vodka was the right way to go tonight.

At least for now.

His cell phone began vibrating. Digging it out of his pocket, he checked the face and became very still.

It was that reporter again. The one from the *Times*. Ryan Brooks. Calling at—Matt checked the time on the phone's face—calling at seven fifteen on a cold night in late January.

Matt ditched the call, slipped the phone back into his pocket, and walked into the living room with his drink. There had been a time when he thought that if his uncle was captured or even killed, these kinds of calls would go away. But after adding it up, he'd had a change of mind—a hunch that there would always be something new to the narrative about a serial killer like Dr. George Baylor. The anniversary of an innocent person's murder, a new piece of evidence found, another body from yet another vicious killing unearthed, or worse, a reporter nosing around in Matt's past and uncovering something deeply personal that remained too painful to look at and deserved to have been left alone.

The phone started ringing again. Not his cell this time but the landline.

Matt walked over to his reading chair, grabbed the handset, and eyeballed the caller ID.

It was Brooks again. Somehow, the reporter had managed to get his home phone number.

Matt shook his head in disbelief and sat down in the chair. After resting his glass on the table by a short stack of books, he switched on the phone.

"How did you get my phone numbers?" Matt said in an exceedingly quiet and grim voice.

Brooks hesitated, then spoke quickly. "I'm not trying to hound you, Jones. I apologize if it feels that way. I really do. I don't want to bother you."

Matt grimaced, seething. "How did you get my phone numbers?" he repeated in an even more somber voice.

"You sound pissed off," Brooks said. "You have a right to be. I just wanted to talk to you."

"I figured that much out."

The reporter cleared his throat. "I wanted to talk," he said nervously. "Not about that. Not about what you're thinking."

"What am I thinking, Brooks? By the way, that's your real name, right? The one on your caller ID? You're working for the *Times*?"

"That's me," he said. "Ryan Brooks. There's nothing phony going on here, Jones. I wouldn't do that. I just wanted to talk to you."

Matt stood up and started pacing by the windows. "About what?"

Brooks hesitated again, then let out a sigh.

"I need a favor," the reporter said.

Matt stopped pacing and looked out the slider. The tall buildings downtown had lost their grip, and the moon was inching its way free and clear in the sky above the city.

"A favor?" Matt said.

"Maybe I should put it another way. I need advice. I'm researching a story. It has nothing to do with you."

Matt took a moment to chew it over. "Why me?" he said finally.

"I'd rather not talk about it on the phone. I don't mean to sound mysterious, Jones. But I was hoping we could meet tomorrow."

"I'll ask you again, Brooks. Why me?"

"I've read enough to know that you've got a rare gift for this kind of thing. From what I've heard, you're still on medical leave. I was thinking you might have some spare time. The story I'm researching is straightforward enough, but it needs a pair of eyes like yours. A detective's eyes. Someone with your instincts. Someone who can tell me if I'm on the right track or just making things up along the way."

Matt picked up his glass and took a sip. The ice had melted, the vodka losing its edge. He needed a refill.

"Okay," he said. "Okay. Where do you want to meet?"

FIVE

Matt glided down the hill on Manhattan Beach Boulevard, made a left on Ocean Drive, and turned into the parking lot. Shouldering his laptop case, he checked the meter, saw that it still had three hours left, and started up the sidewalk through the billowing fog.

Brooks's house was half a block away, and by all appearances, the journalist had it made. It looked like a California bungalow that had been modified to fit a corner lot sitting directly on the beach. Matt noted the cedar-shake siding and the massive deck fitted with seamless plexiglass windscreens. The second deck on the floor above that must have been the master bedroom.

He wondered how old Brooks was. How many years he had been writing. On the phone last night, he had sounded young, but then again, it was hard to tell because the man seemed so nervous.

Matt checked his watch. It was 9:00 a.m., and he had made it on time—the drive south a straight shot on surface streets along the coast and surprisingly easy. As he crossed at the corner, he began to relax some, listening to the ocean and smelling the salt in the air. The sun was trying to bleed through the marine layer but had only made it halfway. Still, everything Matt set his eyes on seemed to be glowing in the mist.

He gave Brooks's house another look and could see that the entrance was from the street rather than the strand running along the beach. After passing the garage, he found the wooden gate open and the space for another car empty. Stepping onto the property, he followed the brick walkway to the front door. There was a bench here with a basket filled with yellow flowers. A stroller for a baby had been parked before a privacy fence and gate between the house and garage.

Matt pressed the doorbell, heard it ring inside, and waited. He had to admit that with little to no information, Brooks had managed to hook his imagination. Last night, he'd had a second drink as he tossed it over.

What kind of story couldn't be told over the phone these days? Why was Brooks worried that he couldn't trust his own instincts and needed someone else's take? A detective's take on a story that was still being researched?

Matt rang the doorbell again, then cupped his hands around his eyes and peered through the window into the front hallway. He could hear the faint sound of a TV but nothing else.

He shook his head and returned to the door, giving it a hard knock. Then he pulled his cell phone out, found Brooks's number on the missed call list, and hit "Enter." Brooks's cell phone started ringing inside the house, but the writer didn't pick up.

Matt wondered if they might be outside on the deck. Before walking around the house, he decided to try the door handle. And that's when he felt an ice-cold chill run up his spine.

He watched the heavy door swing open with a creak. He could hear the TV—the volume low—cutting through an oppressive silence. The bad vibes ran deep and were unmistakable. It almost felt like the house had been waiting for him to arrive.

He called out Brooks's name in a loud, shaky voice that seemed to die in the eerie stillness. When no one answered, he felt his heart begin pounding in his chest.

Matt stepped inside and closed the door. Lifting his .45 out of its holster, he let his eyes wander to the right. Through the doorway he saw a study lined with bookshelves. Files littered the desktop, along with several reference books that remained open. A laptop case had been tossed on the couch.

Matt turned to his left and stepped into the kitchen, realizing that it opened to a great room and the deck and beach beyond. A small TV was on the counter by the stove and switched to a twenty-four-hour news station. Matt noticed the water simmering in a large stockpot. From what little remained at the bottom, it seemed clear that the stove had been on all night. After slipping on a pair of gloves, he turned off the burner and looked at the table. An infant's highchair stood between two place settings. Noting that it was just after nine in the morning and all the lights in both rooms were on, he glanced back at the counter. On the cutting board beside the TV, he found a baguette of French bread and two glasses of red wine that had been poured but not touched. On the other side of the stove, he saw a box of pasta and a jar of marinara sauce that hadn't been opened yet.

Something moved.

Matt flinched, his eyes reeling wildly back and forth.

And then he saw it in the corner. A cat drinking water out of a bowl before scurrying out of the room.

He tried to settle down, but the situation, the place and time, seemed more than grim and way too vivid.

Matt pulled out his cell phone, hit "Enter" again, and returned it to his pocket. When he heard Brooks's phone begin ringing from upstairs, he grit his teeth and started up the steps. Slowly, methodically, listening to the sound of the ringing become louder and the TV begin to fade into the gloom behind him.

How had Brooks put it on the phone last night?

I've read enough to know that you've got a rare gift for this sort of thing. From what I've heard, you're still on medical leave. I was hoping you might have some spare time. The story I'm researching needs a pair of eyes like yours. A detective's eyes. Someone with your instincts. Someone who can tell me if I'm on the right track or just making things up along the way.

Along the way.

Along-the-way . . .

Matt stepped onto the landing, following the sound of Brooks's phone into the master bedroom.

He found the writer on the floor at the foot of the bed. He'd been stabbed too many times to count. The knife was still in his back and looked like a chef's knife that had come from the kitchen. The white walls and white bedspread were sprayed a dark red, and the blood that had pooled on the floor beneath the body had already begun to darken.

Brooks's cell phone stopped ringing.

Matt's heart started pounding again. He took a moment to center himself. And then another because he knew where the road had to be leading.

There was grim, and then there was worse than grim.

He listened to the curtains tapping against the window frames. The sound of the ocean through the open slider. He hoped that the sun would come out today. He hoped that he would see it and feel its warmth.

He stepped around Brooks's corpse and the pool of blood, inching his way toward the bathroom. Once he cleared the corner, he spotted a second body on the floor. A young woman, no doubt Brooks's wife or partner. Her back and legs were peppered with stab wounds. And her neck appeared bruised, but in a way Matt had never seen before. Kneeling down for a closer look, there seemed to be a pattern to the bruising. Half circles on the side of her neck leading down to her chest. It suddenly occurred to him that he was staring at bite marks. The woman had been bitten.

He let it settle in. The sight of it. The idea of it.

After a while he stood up and gazed through the doorway into the bathroom. There was too much blood on the floor to enter. But even if there hadn't been, he would have given himself a time-out. A chance to come up for air.

He could see the third dead body lying in the bathtub.

Brooks's baby daughter.

SIX

Lieutenant McKensie peeked inside the bathroom. Matt knew when his supervisor spotted the dead girl in the bathtub because the big man cringed and wiped a tear away from his sharp green eyes. "Have you had time to figure out their names?" McKensie said quietly and with reverence.

"Ryan Brooks, his wife, Cindy—she's wearing a wedding ring—and their daughter, Emma."

"How old's Emma?"

Matt took a step back. "Two," he whispered.

McKensie winced. "Let's go downstairs."

Matt nodded, stepping around Brooks's corpse and following his supervisor out of the room. Once they reached the first floor, McKensie headed for the slider in the great room and what Matt assumed was an immediate need for fresh air. They stepped out onto the deck. McKensie grabbed the back of a chair, then shook his head.

"Why am I always surprised?" he said.

"What do you mean?"

McKensie glanced through the mist at the neighboring house, checked the beach in the fog, then turned back and lowered his voice. "I've been doing this a long time, Jones. A real long time. At a certain point you begin to think that you've seen everything there is to see in this world. And then . . . and then you walk into a house like this one and there it is."

"There's what, sir?"

"Something new," he said. "Something worse."

McKensie was a tough man with leathery skin and a shock of white hair. Despite his age, he was strong and built like a street fighter. Still, the punch he'd just taken seemed to stagger him.

"You shouldn't be here, Jones. Seeing this isn't good for you. Not with what you've been through over the past couple of months. When's your next appointment with Dr. May?"

"This afternoon, but I'm okay, Lieutenant."

McKensie met him eye to eye. "Really?"

Matt didn't say anything. He'd been telling the truth, or at least he thought he had. He was okay, sort of. Still mesmerized, maybe, still in shock. But what seemed so much more important right now were the three victims of this hideous mass killing. Madness was in full bloom here. The harshness of the murders could have only been committed by someone who had completely lost control of themselves. Someone who was so far gone that their insanity would be difficult to hide from others. The bite marks on the mother's neck and body. The death of an infant—

"He's gonna do it again," Matt said. "Again and again, until we stop him."

"Probably. But it's not my call, Jones. This isn't even our jurisdiction. We're in Manhattan Beach. And we need to get out of here and call it in."

"I want you to see something first," Matt said.

McKensie gave him a look but followed him back into the house and through the kitchen until they reached Brooks's study.

"I wanted you to see this," Matt repeated.

"Why? It's a home office, Jones. A study. Probably the only room in the house without a decent view of the beach."

Matt pointed at the desk. "Brooks's computer," he said. "It's gone."

"If it's a laptop, it could be anywhere in the house."

Matt shook his head. "It is a laptop. The case is right over there on the couch, but it's empty. I walked through every room, and it's not here. And look at Brooks's desk. Whoever took the laptop left the power cable and the mouse behind."

McKensie shrugged as he took in the rest of the room. A large black-and-white photograph of Brooks with his wife and daughter had been framed and was hanging on the wall above a lamp and table. Matt stepped in beside his supervisor for a closer look. The photograph appeared to have been taken at the end of the Manhattan Beach Pier on a windy day. The waves in the background were big and steep, the ocean so rough the water might have been boiling. Cindy Brooks was wrapped in a raincoat clutching her infant daughter with Ryan hugging both of them from behind.

"I get your point," McKensie said as he continued to eye the photograph. "He called you last night. He wanted you to see a story. But you're forgetting something, Jones. Something important."

"And what's that?"

"Think about what happened upstairs. Whoever did this to these people—look at them—they were a beautiful family. Whoever murdered these people is grade A out of their mind. The most likely explanation is that there's no motive at all. It was all about the killing. All about the thrill of killing."

Matt couldn't argue the point, because what McKensie had just said appeared self-evident. And that, he realized, was the complication.

He turned back to the photograph. Brooks's wife had a refined way about her and seemed very happy. She was wearing a brooch on her raincoat. Although Matt couldn't be sure, the piece of jewelry looked like it might be a replica of the Library Tower in downtown LA. He looked at Ryan Brooks with his arms around his wife. He had the same glint in his eyes that she did. When Matt looked back at the infant girl, it occurred to him that this photograph had to be more than a year old and might have been taken on the day they brought Emma home from the hospital.

It had that kind of feel to it. A moment of absolute hope and joy.

McKensie stepped over to the desk. After he slipped on a pair of gloves, he began leafing through the files.

"These books," he said. "These papers. They're all about water rights. Why do you think he couldn't talk about that on the phone? Why all the mystery?"

Matt shook his head, staring at the desktop and thinking it over. "I have no idea," he said finally. "I wish he'd spoken up."

McKensie stepped over to the doorway and peeled off his gloves. "Well, it doesn't really matter one way or the other, Jones. You're on medical leave. And even if you weren't, this isn't your case, this house isn't on our turf, and Ryan Brooks was a journalist."

"Which means what?"

McKensie pulled out his cell phone. "Manhattan Beach PD," he said. "The chief and I go back a ways, and it's time to let him know what you found. Believe me, they'll take one look at this place and run for cover."

"What do you mean?"

McKensie located the chief's number on his contact list, hit "Enter," and brought the phone up to his ear. "This one's messy like Charles Manson, Jones. And Ryan Brooks was a journalist, which complicates everything. Nobody local would get near a case like this. They'll pass it off to the FBI with the greatest pleasure and wish them luck. Then they can go back to doing what they do best around here."

"And what's that?"

McKensie shrugged. "Writing parking tickets."

SEVEN

McKensie's take on the way things would play out had been the right one.

While Manhattan Beach PD had shut down Ocean Drive and a handful of patrol units were providing security and crowd control, the department had passed on the case based on McKensie's description of the crime scene and without ever having entered Ryan Brooks's home. Two bulls from the FBI's field office in Westwood, Wayne Fresno and Benny Cook, were now in charge of the murder investigation.

Matt couldn't help feeling disappointed.

As he waited in the back seat of their car to give his statement, he could see them through the windshield. They were standing beside the evidence collection truck talking to David Speeks, the supervising criminalist from the county's Forensic Science Division. All three were nodding in some sort of agreement. Matt looked at the house behind them as Ed Gainer, the lead investigator from the coroner's office, popped out of the front door and hurried over to his van. Gainer and his crew had arrived about an hour ago while Fresno and Cook were taking McKensie's statement.

But now it was Matt's turn, and he was trying to keep his mind focused. Trying not to let his imagination color anything that he might have seen. Trying not to let the shock of what he had experienced dull his thinking.

He looked at the key in his hand. It was a key to the Brooks's home. For reasons he couldn't explain, he had noticed Cindy Brooks's key ring hanging by the front door and removed it. He didn't expect anyone would miss it, nor did he ever expect to—

He heard footsteps and looked up to see Fresno and Cook approaching. As Cook climbed in behind the wheel, Matt slipped the key in his pocket and slid over to make room for Fresno in back. Both men were in their fifties, and both had a certain institutional toughness about them. Fresno checked his clipboard as he settled in the seat.

"Pretty messy in there, huh, Jones?" he said while still leafing through his papers. "Have you ever seen anything like that before?"

Matt lowered his voice. "A couple of times, yeah."

"So we heard," Fresno said. "Why don't you start with what happened last night."

"Brooks called me. He wanted to show me something. He wouldn't say what it was on the phone."

"A story, right?"

"Something he was researching."

"So you drove down this morning. You found the front door unlocked and walked in."

It hung there. The weight of an atrocity.

Matt met Fresno's brown eyes and nodded.

Cook turned from the front seat and leaned against the dashboard. "Do you remember what you might have touched inside the house, Jones?"

"Nothing once I realized something had happened."

"And when was that?" Cook said.

"The minute I stepped into the kitchen and saw the water still boiling from the night before. It seemed pretty clear that something was wrong."

Fresno jotted a note down on the top page of his clipboard. "So you didn't leave any prints," he said.

"No. I kept my gloves on until me and my supervisor walked outside."

"Good job," Fresno said in a lower voice. "You and McKensie stepped outside and waited for us to get here. You must have had plenty of time to think things over. Do you have any idea who might have done this?"

A moment passed. Matt gave both agents a careful look but couldn't get a read off either one of them. It was almost as if their faces had turned to stone just as Fresno asked the question. A question that reeked with suspicion and potential danger.

"If I knew who murdered these people, Fresno, we wouldn't be sitting here talking about it."

Fresno shook his head like that wasn't good enough. "I'll ask you again, Jones. You got any idea who did this? Any idea who *could* have done this?"

"I know where you guys are going," Matt said. "And you're way out of line."

They were playing him, and Matt couldn't help but feel disappointed that it was now out in the open. Fresno and Cook's first impression of the crime scene had been skewed by Dr. Baylor's escape and the irony that the serial killer turned out to be Matt's uncle. Unfortunately, neither agent seemed to have done their homework. Matt knew that his uncle had nothing to do with these murders the moment he saw the knife wounds on Brooks's back. They were crude and messy, too haphazard and too hurried to be the work of his uncle or any other skilled surgeon. He could remember Art Madina pointing it out during the autopsies last October. Dr. Baylor made clean cuts on his victims because he didn't know how to do it any other way. When Matt pressed the medical examiner for a deeper explanation, Madina had said that it's in a surgeon's DNA. They make clean cuts because they're always thinking about the scar that could be left behind.

Fresno said something, but Matt missed it.

"I didn't get that, Fresno. What are you trying to say?"

"I think you're covering for somebody, Jones. And we both know who I'm talking about."

Matt grabbed his laptop case and reached for the door handle. "Have it your way," he said. "Are we done here?"

Fresno wrinkled his brow in complete disbelief. "What did you just say?"

"I asked if we're done, Fresno, because I'm not hanging around for this."

"Hey, listen, dumb guy," Cook blurted out from the front seat.

Matt opened the door and shot Fresno a look. "We're done," he said.

The agent's face balled up in anger, and Matt slammed the door shut and walked off. Slinging his laptop case over his shoulder, he could hear them behind his back.

"You got that right, Jones. We're done! And so are you! Just make sure you keep your nose out of our business! Did you hear that, Benny?"

Matt ignored them, found his car in the lot, and drove off.

EIGHT

Dr. Julie May gave Matt a long look of concern as he entered her office and sat down on the patient's lounge chair beside her desk. "Your supervisor called me, Matthew. He told me what happened this morning."

"Then you know how happy I am to be here."

She leaned toward him and removed her glasses. "But you need to be here," she said. "And you need to know that you need to be here. It's an important part of your recovery. You're not ready to work another case, and you won't be for a while."

Matt didn't say anything as he measured her from the other side of the desk. Dr. May had told him in an earlier session that her parents moved from Kanazawa, Japan, to San Jose before her birth, and he guessed that she was about his age. She had an angular face, dark silky hair cut to her shoulders, and gentle eyes that always seemed to light up the room on a cloudy day. Matt would have called her stunning, but he couldn't tell if it was the way she carried herself or the kindness she had shown toward him since they first met. He knew that Dr. May had graduated from the medical school at Stanford University and that she had a reputation in the department for being brilliant. But Matt didn't find any of that important right now. What mattered most was that he found her easy to talk to, even when the subject matter seemed too difficult to mention aloud. He liked her and trusted her and respected her, and he imagined that she felt the same way about him.

He turned and gazed out the window at the tall buildings, the sky darkening as dusk set in. The shock of the day was beginning to wane, and he felt tired and drained. Memories of finding his father with his second wife and two sons murdered just a month and a half ago were beginning to surface again. Getting to sleep would be difficult tonight.

"You're thinking about the Love Killings," Dr. May said. "It's all coming back."

He looked her way and nodded.

"Your father was lying on the floor," she went on. "He was mortally wounded, but he was still alive."

"Everybody else was dead," he whispered. "I don't want to think about it right now. It still feels too close."

"But you can't help it. Not after today. Not after seeing Ryan Brooks and his wife and their baby daughter dead."

"You're right," he said. "I can't help it."

"You held your father in your arms, Matthew. You looked into his eyes and connected, and then he passed away. Your father was gone, and you had just found him. You had just met."

Matt made another try at shutting down the memory. A memory that felt like it was tattooed to his being. He could feel sweat percolating on his forehead, his stomach churning.

"Your face is healing," Dr. May said. "Where have you been for the past two weeks, Matthew?"

He shrugged without a reply. Dr. May stepped around her desk and pulled a chair over to the lounge.

"Unbutton your shirt," she said.

"Why?"

"Because I'm your doctor."

"You're my psychiatrist."

She shook her head with the hint of an ironic smile. "I'm your doctor, and I want to see what he did to you. It's no secret who you were with. Now please, unbutton your shirt."

Matt opened his shirt and pulled it away from his jeans. Once Dr. May slipped on her glasses, he watched her scoot closer and lean over his chest. She was touching the scars and rubbing them with her fingers. After a few moments, she turned and met his eyes.

"Did you go voluntarily?" she asked in a low voice.

"I'm not really sure, to be honest with you. He came to the house. I was in some kind of a state."

Matt had never been this physically close to Dr. May before. He could smell the shampoo in her hair, the soaps and lotions she used on her skin. At one point he could feel her breath on his chest and her hip pressing against his rib cage.

He looked back at her fingers smoothing the scars and massaging them as she measured them. For almost five minutes she didn't say a word. At some point during the examination, Matt realized that his mind had cleared, and he no longer felt drained.

She turned back to him and leaned even closer, her eyes avoiding his and taking in the scars scattered all over his face. She touched a wound on his cheek, and another on his chin—and then it was over. She got up and stepped around her desk without sitting down.

"He's very talented, isn't he," she said. "Your uncle."

Matt didn't know how to respond and remained quiet.

"You can button up," she said. "Within two years those scars will melt away, and no one will ever know that you were shot. The cuts on your face from the shattered glass will heal even faster. Are you taking your meds for pain?"

Matt nodded. "As needed," he said in a quiet voice.

She was pressing her back against the wall, standing with her legs crossed and looking his way as she thought something over. She still seemed troubled.

"As needed is good," she said finally. "Very good. Let me ask you one more thing. Since you walked into Ryan Brooks's home this morning, how many times have you thought about your father?"

Matt stood up, unfastened his jeans, and started tucking in his shirt. "A couple," he said.

"Only a couple?"

"Four or five times maybe. But that's it."

Dr. May rolled her desk chair out and sat down, still appraising him and still showing concern.

"Well, you're lucky that Ryan Brooks and his family lived at the beach. You're lucky that the FBI has stepped in and taken over the case."

"They're incompetents, Doctor. They're never gonna make it to the finish line. They're already on the wrong track chasing ghosts."

"You're the one chasing ghosts, Matthew. That's what you need to understand. What you experienced this morning could trigger a setback. Too many setbacks and you could become lost. The kind of lost that's hard to find your way back from."

NINE

Matt took one look at the stream of headlights on the Harbor Freeway and realized that the twenty-mile trek from downtown to his house on the Westside would turn into a two or three-hour ordeal. The Hollywood Freeway looked even worse. All he could see was a river of brake lights on their way to nowhere.

He decided to give it some time and drove three blocks west. After making a right turn at the light, he found a place to park and grabbed his leather jacket. The night air felt particularly raw, the cloud cover in the sky above thick and billowing like it might rain. Hurrying down the narrow alley, he stepped into the Blackbird Café and felt better before the door even closed.

That's the way it often seemed to work here.

Everything about the place exuded warmth. The books on the shelves, the art on the walls donated by patrons, the windows and terrace with a view of the entire city, the classical music set at just the right volume so as not to crowd out the quiet conversations one might have in a reading room.

Matt loved it. But it was more than just the relaxed setting or even the fact that Lena Gamble had been the one who first discovered this place and brought him here. The Blackbird Café made the best cup of coffee he had ever tasted, and he was more than ready tonight.

He ordered a cup of the house blend with one sugar. Entering the main room and relieved to see a number of empty tables and booths, he chose a spot by the windows on the far side. For several moments he let the steam rise from the cup into his face and savored the brew's aroma. And then he settled back in his seat and took a first sip. The coffee was rich and strong and just what he needed. He could feel his mind coming back to life as he watched the long line of jets flying below the clouds in the southeastern sky on their final approach to LAX.

From here it all seemed so peaceful. He gave his coffee a light stir, took another sip, and let his mind wander.

He believed that Dr. May had his best interests in mind, but he also knew in his bones that her warning had come too late. The moment he had first laid eyes on Brooks and his family, the case had become a personal obsession. He also believed that he owed it to Brooks and his wife and child to find the killer and end this.

He remembered the sound of the writer's voice last night. Brooks had been nervous. While it may have had something to do with the way the call began—Matt had been rough on the reporter, thinking he was being hounded—in the end Brooks definitely wanted Matt's take on something. A detective's take. Something that he didn't want to talk about on the phone.

It occurred to Matt that he may have been misreading Brooks from the very beginning. Had the writer been nervous? Or had it been something else? Could it have been fear, or even terror? Was Ryan Brooks murdered because of something he knew?

But even more disturbing, how could Agents Fresno and Cook, even Matt's supervisor, Lieutenant McKensie, ignore the possibility that there might be a reason for the killings? Charles Manson, Dr. Baylor, helter-skelter—how could they be so sure of themselves? After all, their take on the murders had been based on little more than a glimpse. A mere walk through a bloody crime scene and what had become an all-too-real house of horrors.

And what about Brooks's computer? Why was it missing? Why didn't that seem to matter to them? Why couldn't they see what appeared to be so obvious?

Matt realized once again that he was wrestling with "the complication."

Though he still may have only been a rookie, and though his experience working as a homicide detective amounted to three cases that began just this past October, his mentor at the Police Academy had spoken about the problem many times.

Every murder case had a complication, his mentor used to say. A fork in the road of its basic logic. This was the moment when a detective either lost or found his or her way. Would the detective follow only the most obvious leads? Or would he or she use their imagination to see past the way things appeared and dig up what was really underneath? Would the detective have the patience to hold off making any conclusions until the layers were peeled back one by one and what was hidden below finally became self-evident?

Matt dug his cell phone out of his pocket, found Art Madina's number at the coroner's office, and hit "Enter." When the medical examiner picked up after a single ring, Matt checked the room before speaking, noted a man looking at him two tables away, and lowered his voice.

"When are the Brooks autopsies scheduled, Art?"

"I thought you might be calling," the ME said. "They're done. They're being stitched back up right now."

Matt glanced at his watch, surprised. "Why so fast? Who moved them to the top of the list?"

"Brooks was a journalist, Jones. Everyone wants to know what happened, ASAP."

"Who performed the autopsies?"

"I did Brooks and his wife. Deb DiMarco handled the infant."

Matt checked the tables again. The man whom he had thought might be eavesdropping was leaving his table and heading for the door. Matt pressed the phone against his ear.

"Was there anyone with you?" he asked.

"You mean from the FBI?"

"Yeah," Matt said. "Fresno and Cook. Were they there?"

Madina paused. Matt could hear a door closing over the phone. After a few seconds, the ME came back on.

"Sorry," he said. "They didn't show up, Jones. They said they'd be here, but it never happened."

Matt pushed his coffee away as he thought it over. Fresno and Cook were no-shows. Why should he have expected anything different?

"Did they call? Did they say why they couldn't make it?"

Madina cleared his throat. "They're gonna stop by tomorrow morning at ten."

"Ten?"

"Between ten and twelve. That's what they said."

Banker's hours . . .

Matt let it go. When he saw a woman walking into the room from the terrace, he turned away.

"Is there any way we could meet, Art?"

"Officially? I don't think so. This is the FBI's case now."

"What about unofficially?"

Madina didn't answer the question right away. Matt imagined that he was weighing the risk.

"I'll be in at seven," he said finally.

"See you then."

TEN

Matt checked the clock on the dash as he finished off a breakfast burrito from the Jack in the Box across the street and washed it down with take-out coffee that had turned lukewarm in the paper cup. It was 6:50 a.m., and he had just seen Art Madina pull into the lot at the coroner's office and enter the building. Matt had been parked there for half an hour or so but decided to give the medical examiner a few minutes to unpack his briefcase and settle in.

Although Madina had been good to him in the past, Matt wondered why the ME was willing to take a risk and do him this favor. He'd thought about it last night when he realized that no matter how much he tried, sleep was never going to happen. All of the images from the Brooks crime scene had come to life in the darkness and taken over his bedroom. At a certain point, the memories became so vivid, he turned on every light in the house and moved to the couch in the living room.

His eyes rocked back to the clock. It was 6:51 a.m. Only a single minute had gone by, and he couldn't take it anymore. He tossed the burrito wrapper in the bag, took a last sip of coffee, and grabbed his laptop case.

The early-morning air still had a bite to it. Crossing the lot, he was well aware of his surroundings and hoped that he wouldn't run into anyone he knew. He found the front doors still locked. After the guard buzzed him in, he stepped up to the counter and handed over his ID. There could be no doubt that the guard's eyes lingered over his face as he passed back the ID.

"Dr. Madina's expecting you, Detective?" the guard asked.

"Yes, thanks," Matt said. "I've been here before."

Spared the usual sights, sounds, and foul odors coming from the operating rooms and storage freezers in the basement, Matt walked down the hall and found Madina standing beside his desk.

"Thanks for seeing me," he said.

Madina checked the hallway and closed the door. "In case you're wondering, your uncle shouldn't be considered a person of interest this time around."

Matt nodded. "It was too reckless," he said. "Too random. I knew it the minute I saw Brooks on the floor."

"Yeah, well, Fresno and Cook still don't get it."

"They don't want to get it, Art."

"And that's why I agreed to walk you through this. We've got a problem."

Madina motioned Matt over to a large flat panel monitor on the wall, then sat down on a stool before his keyboard and began paging through images from the crime scene and three autopsies. Matt slid a notepad out of his bag and found a pen.

"Brooks was stabbed thirty-seven times," Madina said. "We counted twenty-three wounds on his wife."

"What about their daughter?"

The ME gave him a look. "Do you really need to know?"

"Probably not," Matt said. "But how many?"

"Let's put it this way. She was only two and small for her age. She weighed just under twenty pounds. The only wound that mattered was the first one."

A long moment passed as Matt saw an image of Emma on the monitor and had to look away. He thought about Dr. May and the warning she had given him yesterday afternoon. He thought about the idea that her concerns came half a day too late.

Madina highlighted a photograph of the master bedroom before it had been processed. Matt's eyes went straight to Brooks lying on the floor with the ten-inch chef's knife in his back.

"You were the one who found them," Madina said. "You were there, Jones. I see three murders by one killer. How do you think he pulled it off?"

Matt took a moment to clear his mind. He had been tossing it over since he turned on the lights and made the move to the couch last night.

"I think Cindy Brooks was upstairs giving their daughter a bath while Brooks made dinner in the kitchen. The killer could have been known by the writer, but maybe not. Either way, an attempt was made to subdue Brooks in the kitchen—"

"His nasal passages were inflamed," Madina said. "Same with his lips and mouth."

"Pepper spray?"

The ME shrugged. "That was my first thought, but we won't get the results back for a couple of weeks."

"Okay," Matt said as he thought about it. "Okay. So it wasn't a lethal attempt to subdue him but enough for Brooks to know that he and his family were in immediate danger. All he's thinking about is protecting them, so he runs out of the room. The killer grabs the knife off the counter, chases Brooks upstairs into the bedroom, then strikes before he can reach his wife and daughter."

Matt could see it in his head, a hideous shadow without a face shimmering through the doorway and plunging the knife into Brooks's back. Once the writer collapsed onto the floor, his wife probably turned to save Emma and took a blow in the back as well. And then the world would have stopped spinning—everything crazy, everything wrong and upside down—as the killer stepped over his prey and entered the bathroom.

And that's when the crying would have stopped.

Madina shook his head and sighed. "That's the way I see it as well," he said in a low voice. "The killer incapacitated these people. Once they were down, he came back and stabbed them over and over again."

"Like he was out of control," Matt said.

Madina met his gaze. "Like he couldn't stop, Jones."

Something deep inside Matt's gut pinged. "What about Cindy

Brooks?"

Madina opened another window on his computer. Four images of Cindy Brooks were included. Two from the bedroom as the coroner's investigator turned her body over, and two from the operating room during the autopsy.

"Her clothing had been pulled away from her waist and thighs," the ME said. "I listed the damage to her genitals from that night as slight to possibly none. No semen was found, but that's not unusual in cases like this."

"You mean the killer was shooting blanks?"

Madina opened yet another image, this time a close-up of the bite marks on the victim's neck and upper chest. "Or he saved it for later. Imagine what was going on in that bedroom when he got to her. When he was so overwrought and jacked up that he started biting her. Stabbing her. Killing her."

Matt remained silent.

As Madina's words began to settle in, he couldn't help wondering how or why his imagination seemed to sketch the unknown with such gruesome and horrid details. And yet it still came back to the complication this brutal crime had conjured up. The fork in the road. The point where a detective either lost or found his or her way.

The killer was obviously a monster. Still, Matt couldn't let go of the idea that this monster had come out of the dark for a reason.

ELEVEN

The *Los Angeles Times* **had moved** out of downtown to a new building in El Segundo across the 105 Freeway from LAX on the Westside. The building was big and modern, and with rush-hour traffic heading east, Matt made the early-morning drive across town in less than an hour.

He pulled into the visitor's lot and found a place to park. As he walked to the entrance, he tried to come up with the right words to get past the front desk in the lobby. He didn't think he could use his badge, and he guessed that claiming this was an official visit would blow up in his face.

He stepped through the glass doors and spotted a young woman seated beside a guard at the reception desk. The moment they looked his way, Matt knew that he wouldn't need any story at all. Both of them recognized him in an instant. Why he was here wouldn't require an explanation.

Matt noted the sad glint in the woman's eyes and watched her enter four numbers on the telephone keypad just before he arrived at the counter. She had someone on the line. When she finished and Matt began to say something, she waved him off and pointed across the lobby.

"Do you see the elevators to the right of the coffee bar?" she said.

Matt followed her gaze and nodded.

"You want to go to the fourth floor, Detective. A woman named Kate

Berman will meet you there."

"Who is she?" Matt said.

The receptionist took a moment to collect herself. "Ryan's editor," she said finally.

"Are you okay?"

She nodded even though it seemed clear that she wasn't. "Thank you for asking," she said. "You better get going."

Matt wondered how a single moment, a single abhorrent act, could change everything. As he crossed the lobby, he looked at the people he passed and saw the same thing on every one of their faces. They were mourning the loss of Brooks and his family. The elevator he shared with two men and a woman appeared to underline that somber feeling of despair. He thought about the size of the building again. It was big, but not much different than a large high school. If he had to guess, he would have said that there were seven to eight hundred people working there. A small-enough number to support the idea that almost everyone knew each other and shared some sort of bond. As he mulled it over, he imagined that Brooks's passing felt like the loss of a beloved family member.

The elevator doors opened, and as Matt stepped out, he found a middle-aged woman with dark hair and a pleasant face waiting for him.

"Detective Jones," she said. "I'm Kate Berman."

Matt nodded in greeting.

"I'm not here in an official capacity," he said.

"Then why are you here?"

"Ryan called me the night before and wanted to meet. I'm trying to understand what happened. I thought it might help if I spoke with someone who knew him."

His explanation seemed to agree with her, and she led the way onto the main floor—a large, open space filled with more than fifty ultramodern workstations. As they stepped down an aisle, Matt glanced at the flat panel monitors hanging from the ceiling and realized that they outnumbered the workstations. But what struck him most about the floor was that he didn't notice any walls or partitions. The people working here could see each other and talk.

"Everyone's heartbroken," Berman said. "Ryan was a favorite around here. A young man with a bright future. A new father with a new bride."

Matt didn't say anything. He thought that Berman might be leading him to somewhere more private. Instead, she stopped beside an empty workstation and turned to him. Matt glanced at the backstop behind the computer and noted Ryan Brooks's name.

"Why did he want to meet?" Berman asked.

There were a handful of people working within earshot. Matt saw a man at a workstation one aisle over whom he thought was listening. In the end Matt decided to ignore it because he didn't think he had much choice. But even more, he had been lucky enough to get past the lobby.

"Do you know why he wanted to meet?" Berman repeated.

"He didn't say. He was working on something that he wanted me to see. He wouldn't talk about it on the phone."

Berman frowned. "That doesn't make any sense, Detective. Ryan was a feature writer. Why would he need you?"

"That's what I'm trying to understand. I found files on his desk, more than a handful of books left open and marked. They were all about water rights. Could that be it?"

She shook her head. "Now you're making even less sense. Ryan's next piece was for the Sunday magazine section. The Oscars are coming up. He interviewed the nominees for Best Director and was supposed to turn in his work today."

Matt took a step back, trying to hide the disappointment he knew was showing on his face. He glanced at that man working one aisle over again, caught him staring at him, then turned back to Berman.

"His computer is missing," he said. "I searched the house and couldn't find it."

She shrugged but didn't say anything.

Matt pointed at the computer on Brooks's workstation. "Is there any way I could take a look?"

Berman's eyes widened a little. "Not unless you get a pass from the Supreme Court, Detective."

Matt heard someone shout out his name and turned. His heart almost stopped as he saw them hustling onto the floor with their IDs raised in the air. Two of the FBI's finest were here for a visit. Matt watched them approach, knowing that his time in the building was over.

"What are you doing here, Jones?" Fresno said in a loud voice as he turned to Berman. "And who are you?"

Berman stood her ground. "I beg your pardon," she said. "Who are you?"

"The FBI, ma'am, and you shouldn't be talking to this guy. He has nothing to do with this investigation. If he claimed he does, then he just broke the law. Is that what you did, Jones? Did you badge your way in and break the law?"

Matt grimaced. "Ms. Berman," he said, "these are agents Wayne Fresno and Benny Cook from the FBI's field office in Westwood."

"Am I supposed to be impressed?" Berman said.

Matt shook his head. "Not really."

Cook's face turned a bright red. "Beat it, Jones. We're on the clock right now. Get the hell out of here."

TWELVE

Matt drove south on North Sepulveda and made a right turn onto Manhattan Beach Boulevard. After another mile, he saw Brooks's house on the corner but continued down the hill until he reached a small, metered lot beside the bike path and beach. The five-mile trip from the *Times* building to Ocean Drive had taken less than fifteen minutes.

He climbed out of the car and glanced at the house still shrouded in the marine layer. When he noticed a street vendor working by the bike racks, he ordered a cup of coffee and a poppy seed bagel with lox and cream cheese. Then he set everything down on the hood of his car and looked back at Brooks's house buried in the mist.

He didn't see any trucks or vans from the crime lab in the driveway, which he found disturbing. And when he looked up and down the streets, he couldn't find a single patrol unit anywhere around. Even worse, the house should have been wrapped in yellow crime scene tape. The property should have been shut down and sealed off but wasn't.

Everything looked the way it probably had looked before the murders. Everything here at the beach appeared normal again. And nothing about it was righteous.

Matt grimaced when it suddenly occurred to him that this was probably all about local politics.

The neighbors wouldn't want to be reminded that a family had been murdered in their exclusive beach community. And they wouldn't want anyone else to know about it either. Leaving the crime scene tape up would have been bad for business. Seeing patrol units parked on the street would have hurt the value of their high-end homes. Matt couldn't help but conclude that Brooks and his wife and child were already on their way to being completely forgotten by everyone in the neighborhood. And that Lieutenant McKensie's call had been the right one. Cops around here were back to doing what they do best.

Writing parking tickets.

Matt let the idea settle in for a while. Then he held his hands out and noticed that his fingers were quivering.

He let it go, or at least he tried to.

He stared at the bagel in front of him but decided that he wasn't hungry anymore and would save it for later. Prying the lid off his coffee, he stirred a packet of sugar into the brew and took a first sip through the steam. It was strong and piping hot, which seemed to help bring him out of his foul mood. After another sip, he set the cup down and leaned his elbows on the hood.

It had taken this long to absorb what he had learned from Madina at the coroner's office this morning. But he thought he could now count on one detail as being fact.

At face value, what happened here went down the way everybody else thought it had: a brutal mass killing of a young family committed for no other reason than the psychotic thrill of murder. But for Matt, everything was different since he had spoken with the medical examiner. What stood out for the first time was that Ryan Brooks had been the primary target, not his wife or even his child. The monster had come out of the dark for a reason. And that reason had something to do with what Brooks himself had been up to. Brooks had endured thirty-seven stab wounds, his wife twenty-three.

The more Matt tossed it over, the more convinced he became that this had to be about Ryan Brooks, and everything else was just background noise.

These innocent people were not slaughtered by a stranger without a motive.

Matt glanced back at the house. A white Audi had just pulled in front of the garage and parked. When a man got out of the car, Matt realized that he recognized him. It was the same man who had been listening to his conversation with Brooks's editor just a half hour ago on the fourth floor of the *Times* building.

Matt took another sip of coffee, tilting his head down slightly while keeping his eyes pinned to the man. He was snooping around Brooks's house, giving the windows a careful look as if searching for a way inside the place. Before stepping into the side yard, he stopped to check the street behind his back. Everything about the guy seemed odd and suspicious. But even worse, when he finally caught Matt watching him, he started down the hill toward the lot at a hurried pace.

Matt set the coffee cup down, measuring the man in big chunks as he got closer. Dark hair and eyes, early to middle thirties, built like he works out, probably Asian, but it would have been more than a generation back.

The man climbed the seawall and dropped down into the lot. When he stood up and regained his balance, he looked at Matt and flashed a faint smile as he approached.

"I'm Vince Sato," he said. "Me and Ryan were best friends."

"Are you following me?"

Sato shook his head, the faint smile gone. "No," he said. "I wanted to hear what those two guys from the FBI had to say. When they left, I needed to get some air and drove down to look at the house."

Matt met Sato's gaze. "So what did they end up saying after I left?"

"They think they know who murdered Ryan and his family. And they think you're covering for him."

Matt shrugged and reached for his cup of coffee. "What can I say," he said finally. "They know 'em when they see 'em, huh."

"I don't think so," Sato said. "And my editor doesn't either. She kicked them out."

Matt set the cup down. Seeing Fresno and Cook get the boot would have made his day.

"Listen, Jones. Even if I hadn't found you here, I would've called."

"Okay," Matt said. "Why?"

"The computer," Sato said. "I heard you tell Berman that Ryan's computer is missing. That's not possible. Ryan doesn't misplace things that important. If it's missing, then it was stolen."

"I'm way past that, Sato. The question is why. And what about all those books on his desk about water rights?"

"He could have been working on ten or twelve stories. They'd all be in different stages of completion. At the same time, Ryan never mentioned anything to me about water rights."

Sato stopped talking as a young woman walking a Yorkshire terrier stepped off the bike path and got into a nearby car. Once she pulled away, Sato turned back.

"Here's the thing," he said. "Ryan could have easily been working on something that Berman had no idea about. That's not unusual—it happens all the time. You're working on something, and you don't really want to talk about it until you know you've got a story."

"How long have you been a reporter, Sato?"

"Almost ten years."

"Are you any good?"

The man laughed. "I think so."

Matt thought it over. "Do you see things that most people don't see?"

"I hope I do, but wouldn't you say the same thing?"

"Okay," Matt said. "Okay. So tell me what was going on with your best friend over the past few weeks."

Sato's face lit up like something clicked. "He's been different," he said as he thought it over. "Edgy. Nervous. But not for two weeks. I'd say closer to six."

"You're a writer. What do you mean by 'edgy'?"

"Unusually secretive," the reporter said. "Easily startled."

Matt let it settle in. It felt like confirmation. Something was going on in Ryan Brooks's life, and it got him killed. He could feel it in his bones.

Matt gave Sato a long look, sizing him up again. "Tell me about his wife."

The reporter shrugged. "There's not much to say. Cindy was a really nice person. I always thought Ryan was lucky to meet her."

"What did she do for a living?"

"She was an architect."

Matt thought about the brooch she was wearing in the photograph he'd seen in Brooks's study. The replica of the Library Tower.

"Buildings?" he asked.

Sato shook his head. "No," he said. "Homes. Remodeling. It's big business right now. Lots of money, especially on the Westside. She took some time off after Emma was born, then went back to work. Ryan said she got hot."

Confirmation.

The point in a case when a detective sees direction and finds his way. The murders weren't about Cindy or their infant daughter.

Matt looked at Brooks's house glowing in the mist as a ray of sunlight cut through the clouds. He turned back to Sato.

"The computer on his workstation at the office. I need to see what's in it. How do we make that happen?"

Sato shot Matt a look and spoke without even hesitating. "You meet me in the visitor's lot at one a.m. I know Ryan's password. I'll get you in."

Sato and Brooks were friends, Matt thought. Best friends.

THIRTEEN

Matt pulled into the lot behind the Hollywood station and found a place to park. He had received a call from Lieutenant McKensie, who said they needed to talk. Although his supervisor wouldn't say why, he claimed that it was urgent and wanted to meet in his office. Matt sensed that something had happened by the rough sound of McKensie's voice, and he guessed that it wasn't good. When he entered the squad room and looked through the glass into McKensie's office, he saw Chief Logan sitting with his supervisor in front of the desk.

They were waiting for him. And neither one of them looked too happy about it.

Matt hustled past his workstation and down the stairs, then stopped in the doorway. The chief gave him a hard look, measuring him with those dark, piercing eyes of his.

"What took you so long, Detective?"

"I had to cross town, sir."

"Well, get in here and close the door."

The chief pointed to a chair. As Matt sat down, he noticed two copies of the *Los Angeles Times* folded and tossed on his supervisor's desk. When he turned, he found the chief still eyeballing him in silence.

"Detective Jones," the chief said finally. "Why are you bothering the

FBI?"

Matt glanced at McKensie, who shook his head ever so slightly in warning, then looked back at the chief. "But I'm not bothering the FBI."

The chief seemed disappointed. He stood up and leaned against the desk.

"According to Agents Fresno and Cook, you're interfering with their case."

"Then Agents Fresno and Cook must be mistaken."

"You're not really gonna do this, are you, Jones? We've been waiting here for more than an hour. This isn't a game."

"Agents Fresno and Cook are mistaken, sir. All I've done is talk to a few people who knew the victims."

"And that's not investigating a case?"

"No, sir," Matt said. "The writer called me the night he was murdered. I thought that the people who knew him might be able to help me understand why. Anyone would want to know why."

The chief gave him another long look. "Well, the bureau thinks you're interfering with the case, and they don't like it. I don't like it, and you wouldn't either. Agents Fresno and Cook say you badged your way into the *Times* and represented yourself as a detective to Ryan Brooks's editor."

Fresno and Cook had lied. Matt couldn't let it pass.

"Brooks's editor is a woman named Kate Berman," he said. "I told her the truth the moment we met. It was the first thing I said when I greeted her. I wasn't there in an official capacity. I told her straight out that it was personal, sir."

"You're saying that Agents Fresno and Cook lied to their supervisor? That they're trying to misrepresent the facts?"

Matt got to his feet. He couldn't take it anymore.

"Yes," he said. "It sure sounds like it, sir."

"Anything else you want to get off your chest, Detective?"

Matt turned to McKensie, who had taken a seat, then back to the chief sitting on the corner of the desk.

"There's something wrong with Agents Fresno and Cook," Matt said. "I don't know what it is. I just know something about them doesn't ring true.

It's like they're broken and not right. They don't want to know what really happened. They want it to be the way they think it happened, which is ludicrous, sir."

"I'll keep that in mind, Detective. But I want you to come up here and see something."

Matt joined McKensie and the chief at the desk. They were unfolding the newspapers and setting them side by side. Checking the dates below the *Times* masthead, he realized that the newspaper on the left was from yesterday and would have been published before anyone knew that Brooks and his family had been murdered. The second newspaper had come out today, with full coverage of the killings on the front page. As Matt eyed the papers, he suddenly noticed that his photograph was on both editions.

The chief cleared his throat. "Do you see anything that stands out about these newspapers, Detective?"

Matt nodded, skimming through the copy. "One covers the award ceremony at the academy," he said. "And this one is all about the writer and his family."

"Anything else?"

"These pictures of me," he said. "Is that what you mean?"

"Yes," the chief said. "These pictures of you. In yesterday's paper you and your partner are being honored by the governor and his wife. I see three pictures of the four of you together. I see another with you and the governor talking to each other like you're old pals."

The chief stepped around the desk and pointed at today's paper covering the murders.

"Do you see the difference, Detective?"

Matt shook his head, confused. "I'm not sure where you're going with this, sir."

"In today's paper, we don't see the governor. We see three murder victims. We see a horrific tragedy. And we see you in the back seat of a car being interviewed by the Feds as if you were guilty of something. Over here is a second photo box with pictures of you and Dr. George Baylor, the serial killer who escaped three months ago. Yesterday's paper was good news. Today's front page is story after story of bad news. What I'm trying to say,

Detective, is that I want to see more of this and less of that."

The chief picked up the newspaper covering the award ceremony and tossed it on top of today's edition devoted to the murders.

"You're good for the department right now, Jones. And after what happened last month, your brothers in blue need you. Do you understand?"

Matt didn't know how to respond and kept his eyes down.

"Stay away from the FBI," the chief went on. "If they mess up the case, let them do it on their own."

The room went quiet for a long time.

Matt sat back in the chair, knowing that he couldn't say anything more than he already had. He couldn't mention his meeting with Madina at the coroner's office. Nor could he say anything about running into Vince Sato or the plans they had made for tonight. Worse still, he couldn't obey his supervisor or the chief. He had made a commitment to Ryan Brooks and his family. And it was a personal commitment. It was all wrapped up in who he was and wanted to be and hoped to become. It was all about his word and the promise he had made to himself the moment he stepped into their bedroom and found their bodies on the floor. It was all about doing what he hoped someone would do for him if it ever came to that.

FOURTEEN

Matt peered through the windshield and spotted Vince Sato waving at him from the shadows. He got out of his car, checked the near-empty lot, then started toward the entrance. It was 1:00 a.m., and as Matt joined Sato and entered the lobby, the building felt like it had slipped into a deep sleep. He glanced at the two guards watching TV behind the reception desk. They looked up, but only long enough to catch Sato flashing his ID in the air. From the lazy look in their eyes, Matt guessed they were ready to doze off.

He followed Sato into the elevator. When they reached the fourth floor and started walking down the aisle, Matt heard the sound of a radio playing. Four men and women from housekeeping were working on the other side of the room dusting off desktops and fitting wastebaskets with fresh bags from their carts. But behind them Matt could see a woman sitting at her workstation typing something into her computer.

"Don't worry about it," Sato said. "She won't even notice that we're here. The cleaning staff owns the place between one and two. People will start drifting in around three to sync up with the East Coast."

They reached Ryan Brooks's workstation, and Sato sat before the computer terminal. Rolling another chair over, Matt looked down and saw a small set of file drawers with a key still in the lock. When he went through the two drawers, he understood why the key was still in the lock. All he found were stationary supplies.

"I'm in," Sato said.

Matt rolled his chair closer and studied the computer screen. Sato had just opened Ryan Brooks's word processor. Unfortunately, the folder marked "Recent" didn't include any documents. The screen was blank.

"How does the system work?" Matt asked in a low voice.

"Not like this," he said. "Give me a second."

Matt watched Sato click the word "Open" and then "Browse." In an instant they were one layer down and skimming through a list of subfolders Ryan Brooks would have created on his own. Each folder had a title that seemed to correspond to a project the writer had been working on.

Sato pointed to the folder on top. "This is his story about the Oscars," he said. "And this one is an interview he did with a downtown developer two weeks ago. The son of the man who developed the tower. He's shaking things up."

Sato clicked the icon, and the folder opened. But instead of revealing a list of documents, they hit another blank screen. He tried another folder, and then another. In each case, the files appeared to have been deleted.

Matt shook his head. "I don't understand," he said. "He's been cleaned out. Who could get in and do this?"

Sato gave him a worried look. "No one."

"How come you have his password?"

"Sometimes we wrote stories together. I needed access to his folders, and he needed access to mine."

Matt sat back in the chair, watching Sato open every folder on the list. In the end they were all empty. Every document under Ryan Brooks's name had been deleted. Matt checked on the woman sitting at her workstation on the other side of the floor, then leaned toward the monitor.

"I've got two questions," he said.

Sato gave him another worried look. "This is bad, Jones. This is really bad. If someone got—"

"Two questions," Matt said in a calm voice. "First, do you see any folder here that has anything to do with water rights?"

Sato scrolled down the list, then shook his head. "No," he said.

"There's nothing here about anything like that. What's your second question?"

"You said it yourself this morning. He was afraid of something. You used the word *secretive*—unusually secretive. You called him edgy, nervous, easily startled—not for the past two weeks, but the last six."

Sato shrugged and seemed upset. "What are you trying to say?"

"Maybe he deleted these files himself," Matt said.

"Himself? Why?"

"Maybe he had a reason. Maybe he's got a backup hidden somewhere."

Sato thought it over. "I guess it's possible. I mean, obviously something has happened. Something's wrong."

Matt nodded, wanting to keep going. "What about his access to the internet? Check his browsing history."

Matt leaned back again, settling in the seat and thinking it over. He was watching Sato start the web browser. When the reporter clicked open the history logs, they had been wiped clean as well.

"It's hopeless, Jones. Something's going on."

"Yeah, you're right—something's going on. Ryan Brooks is dead. But we might not be. Try the address window."

"The what?"

"The address window," Matt said in a steady voice. "Open it."

Matt held his breath as Sato moved the cursor up to the address line. It was only a hunch. But if Brooks was as paranoid as his best friend claimed, Matt could see the reporter deleting files and even his browsing history as some primitive way of covering his tracks. On the other hand, deleting his address window most likely would have never crossed his mind.

"Do it, Sato. Open it up."

Sato clicked the window, and in a split second, two pages of web addresses opened before their eyes. They traded quick looks, with Sato appearing mesmerized as he turned back to the screen and began scrolling through the list.

Matt focused on the web addresses, his guess paying off. They might not have Brooks's personal files, but at least now they had something of a map.

"Do you see any repetitions?" he said. "Any places he went more than once?"

Sato nodded, nervous again. "There's a woman's name," he said. "Tina Griffin. She's repeated all through the list."

"Can we switch seats?"

"Sure."

Matt sat before the computer terminal and scrolled down the list until he reached the bottom. According to the dates beside each entry, this would have been the first web address Brooks had visited. Matt clicked the link and watched a new window open on the screen.

It was an article from the *Times* written three years ago, and it had nothing to do with water rights.

It was a story about the murder of a young woman, Tina Griffin, and her three-year-old son, Max. Their bodies had been found in an empty lot in an industrial section of the city not too far from downtown. Worse still, both the young mother and her baby had been stabbed to death.

Matt's eyes rolled over the words *multiple stab wounds*, then moved on and stopped when he heard Sato whisper the word *mutilated*.

Tina Griffin and her baby son Max had been mutilated.

Several moments passed as the murders sank in and the air in the room seemed to deaden. Matt looked across the floor. The woman was staring at him from her workstation. He could see recognition showing on her face. Ignoring it, he turned back to the monitor and read the story all the way through.

The murders had occurred sometime during the night, the victims not discovered until daybreak. Matt couldn't be sure how much information the reporter had been given, but it sounded like the case went straight up the food chain to the elite Robbery-Homicide Division. And that could only mean one thing. Charles Manson, Dr. Baylor, helter-skelter—the crime scene had to have been a mess.

Matt read the last paragraph. Jack Temps had been the lead detective from RHD in charge of the case, but Matt had never heard of him.

"Is this the reason Ryan Brooks was murdered?" Sato whispered in a shaky voice.

Matt turned to him. The writer's eyes were wide open, and Matt could see his fingers trembling.

"What?" Matt said.

Sato swallowed, and seemed frightened. "Is this the reason Ryan and his family are dead?"

FIFTEEN

Water rights...
Matt could remember the odd feeling he'd had while leafing through the files on Brooks's desk at the beach house. That tinge in his gut when he realized that the writer's laptop had been stolen. The warning bell that rang loud and clear when Lieutenant McKensie asked him why a reporter would call a detective to get his take on a story about what?

Water rights?

Matt had spent the rest of the night tossing it over in bed, and by sunrise it seemed obvious. What he'd found on Brooks's desk had been a con. What he'd found and seen was what the killer wanted him to find and see. And now with the murders of Tina Griffin and her son resurfacing, one more detail could be chalked up as fact.

The monster really had come out of the dark for a reason.

A repeat performance.

And no one was safe. Not even the children.

Matt pulled into the lot behind the Hollywood station, parked, and ran into the building. It was 7:35 a.m., and he was hoping to grab the spare charging cable out of his desk without running into anyone. He breezed past the holding cells and crossed the squad room. But just as he reached his workstation and slid the top drawer open—just as he fished out the cable to his cell phone—he heard McKensie's voice booming from the hallway.

"In my office, Jones."

Matt froze. The big man with the rough face and the shock of white hair was standing on the top step glaring at him with those emerald-green eyes of his.

Matt took a deep breath and exhaled, pocketing the cable as he followed his supervisor down the hall and into his office. When McKensie turned from his desk, he shot him another hard look and spent some time sizing him up. Suspicion was in the air—deep, dark clouds of the stuff weighing everything down.

"You look like shit," the big man said finally. "Get another good night's sleep, Jones?"

Matt tried to read the man's face but couldn't tell where he was headed.

"I was up late," he said.

"I'll bet you were. What are you doing here? You're supposed to be on leave."

"I had to pick up some things, that's all."

"At seven thirty in the morning?"

Matt nodded without saying anything.

McKensie sat down on the corner of his desk. "The department's holding a fundraiser at the Biltmore tonight. You're going with the chief. He wants you to wear your uniform."

Matt cringed, horrified. "What?"

"You're going to the fundraiser," McKensie said. "You'll meet the chief at the hotel. Seven sharp. How difficult is that to grasp?"

"But I don't want to go," Matt said, still stunned. "I don't do things like that. You're right. I'm on medical leave. I need my rest."

McKensie laughed. "You're the chief's new shiny object. You can rest later."

"His what?"

"He told you himself yesterday. The department needs you right now. He wants to show you off. Besides, everybody's gonna be there."

Matt shook his head and let out a groan like he couldn't believe this was happening. "Everybody's gonna be there," he repeated. "Are you going?"

McKensie smiled, his eyes twinkling. "Nada," he said. "I was a bad boy last Friday night. I'm not allowed out for a while."

"Well, I'm not either."

McKensie got up, walked around his desk, and sat down in the chair. The big man still thought it was funny.

"You're going," McKensie said. "And you can't get out of it. Not even with a note from your shrink. It's for the department. Everybody's going."

"Who's everybody?"

"The mayor. The city council. Who's your congressman?"

"Some guy," Matt said. "Some TV actor. I don't know his name."

"Well, whoever the hell it is, he'll be there, too. Maybe you can get an autograph."

Matt started pacing. He didn't know what to say. He didn't like situations like this—and being called somebody's "shiny object" made him angry. The whole thing felt worse than the ghosts hovering over his bed the other night.

He turned and gave McKensie a long look, still mulling it over, still stewing.

"Who's Jack Temps?" he said.

Something happened.

It was almost like riding through an earthquake. Almost like counting off the seconds before the ground stopped shaking beneath his feet. McKensie didn't say anything for a long time. Those green eyes of his got shiny, then turned inward, and then opened completely dark. When he spoke, his voice was low and dangerous.

"What in the world are you up to?"

Matt didn't understand his supervisor's strange response. And he knew he couldn't answer his question.

"I heard someone mention his name," he said. "I was just wondering."

"You were just wondering? Wondering about Jack Temps? You're full of shit, Jones. What are you up to?"

"I don't get it. He's a detective, right? Is he dead?"

McKensie's face hardened. "Close the door," he said. "And take a goddamn seat."

SIXTEEN

Matt remembered who Temps was the moment he closed McKensie's office door.

In an instant, he knew that he had just made a huge mistake. The kind of mistake that seemed so careless, it triggered waves of self-doubt and memories of Dr. May warning him that he wouldn't be ready to work another murder case for a long time.

Worse still, mentioning Temps's name had pushed Matt out in the open, and he had been forced to give McKensie a picture of what he'd been up to for the past couple of days. Not a complete picture necessarily, but more than enough for his supervisor to connect the dots.

What Matt found so strange had been McKensie's calm demeanor as he considered his options aloud. McKensie told him straight out that if he gave Matt up to the chief, it would be a burden to him and a nightmare for everybody else. At the same time, Matt wasn't really interfering with the Feds anymore as much as he had begun to probe the killings of a young woman and her son that occurred three years ago and remained unsolved. There was a chance that the two investigations were unrelated. Although McKensie openly admitted that his logic was more than shaky and basically ate shit, the big man decided that it sounded good enough to roll with. He told Matt that at least for the time being, he would keep his mouth shut. But his advice had been more daunting when Matt got up to leave.

"You need some quality downtime, Jones. You know it in your gut that you do, so go easy on this. Stay away from Fresno and Cook. And be careful when it comes to Jack Temps. Any way you look at it, the man's a snake."

Matt pulled out of the back lot onto Wilcox Avenue, continued through the light until he reached Sunset one block up, and made a right. When he hit Argyle Avenue, he turned left heading for the Hollywood Freeway entrance on the other side of Franklin. Within a few minutes he was bringing the car up to speed with Hollywood fading away in his rearview mirror.

He switched on the radio, found KNX News for traffic updates, but lowered the volume. He couldn't keep his mind off Jack Temps and knew that he had to prepare for what might happen when they met.

While Temps's fall as a detective would have been the news of the day on any normal day, the story had been overshadowed by a political crisis in Washington that lasted for more than a year. TV ratings for a dirty cop couldn't match up, and the department had plenty of time to do their housekeeping without much notice. Now Temps was working in exile—a former RHD bull transferred to the Topanga station in Canoga Park, an LAPD outpost so far away from downtown that even with light freeway traffic, Matt knew that he was facing more than an hour's drive.

He eased the car into the left lane and punched up the speed to a cool 85 mph. As he settled into the seat, he took a sip of coffee from the travel mug that he'd filled at home and was more than pleased to find the brew still piping hot. After a second sip he let his mind drift.

Matt had met guys like Jack Temps before. Not just in the LAPD but as a soldier in Afghanistan as well. They were the kind of people who always seemed to know too much about other people's business. People who at a glance came off so shady Matt knew that he couldn't count on them. This was particularly tough in a war zone when trust in others and staying alive were two sides of the same coin.

Matt didn't know much about what Temps had done other than the thumbnail sketch McKensie had just given him.

Temps had been working a murder case in which a fifteen-year-old boy had been killed at school after baseball practice. The detective's investigation had been quick and decisive. Within days, two boys from the same class who claimed their innocence were charged and arrested. Because there had been some sort of sexual element to the killing that involved torture, both teens were tried as adults and found guilty.

But the deputy DA had always suspected Temps of withholding evidence that pointed to two other teens in the same class, both sons of a wealthy actor with a popular cable drama that had been streaming for six seasons. Worse still, the DDA suspected that Temps had been bought off by the actor, taking cash to look the other way. The truth came out when the two teens Temps had fingered were murdered in prison. A cellmate stepped forward with a story that proved out and provided new evidence. After DNA tests were performed on the actor's sons, both teens were arrested, tried, and sentenced to twenty years to life.

From what McKensie had said, Temps denied that he had suppressed evidence or accepted money from anyone. And while he couldn't fully explain himself, there hadn't been enough evidence to prove otherwise. That's when the Police Protective League stepped in and said they had Temps's back. The detective should have gotten the boot and lost his pension. Instead, he was demoted, transferred to the Topanga station, and received six months' worth of back pay.

As Matt thought it over, McKensie's advice seemed even more telling now than it had when he first offered it. The actor and Temps owned the deaths of the original murder victim and the two innocent teens who had been killed in prison. Both men were dirty. But Temps was the more dangerous of the two because of the badge he carried. Any way you looked at it, McKensie had said, the man's a snake.

SEVENTEEN

Matt entered the lobby with his badge out and ready. One of two patrol officers at the counter, a woman about his age and height with a friendly smile, glanced at his ID but didn't seem to need it.

"What are you doing way out here, Detective?" she said.

Matt shrugged. "Just wondering if Jack Temps is around. If he is, I'd like to talk to him."

"You drove this far without knowing if he'd be here?"

He gave her look. "I wanted it to be a surprise."

She pursed her lips and pointed across the lobby. Matt couldn't help noticing that she had nice hands.

"He's in the squad room through those doors."

"Homicide?"

"No," she said. "Auto. Just follow the signs."

"Thanks."

Matt started to walk off but turned back when he heard the woman speak up again. She still had that faint smile going, and he caught the irony in her voice.

"Temps doesn't get many visitors," she said. "So I'm gonna guess you'll be a surprise, Detective."

Matt nodded again and could feel her deep brown eyes on him as he crossed the lobby and entered the squad room.

He had never been to the Topanga station before and had to admit that nothing about the place met his expectations. It was a modern building that still had that "new" smell to it. With a vaulted roofline, high ceilings, and windows the size of entire walls, he had never seen a police station anything like it before. As he scanned the squad room, he noted the Major Crimes table beside a wall of glass with a view of the hills. The Robbery table was directly in front of him with the Auto table around the corner to his right. Each area was designated by a sign hanging from the ceiling. But what struck Matt most about the floor was the openness. The cubicles looked as new as the building and were grouped together with low partitions so people could see and talk to each other. The setup reminded him of Brooks's workstation at the *Times*, only this seemed better because it didn't have a sterile feel to it. He remembered Lieutenant McKensie saying that Jack Temps had been demoted and exiled. While it might be true that Temps had lost his status as a homicide detective and that Canoga Park was a long way from the lights of downtown LA, it didn't look like anyone working here had a problem with that.

He shrugged it off and walked around the counter toward the Auto table. As he cleared the corner, he saw Temps sitting at his desk. It wasn't difficult to pick him out among the four detectives working the table. Auto was where a detective began his or her career, not ended it. Temps was in his mid-fifties, thirty years older than anyone he worked with. And even at a glance, Matt could tell that the man was sleazy.

"Are you Jack Temps?"

The detective looked up, his pin-like eyes sitting above the frames of his smudged reading glasses.

"That depends on who's asking, Mister, and how much money you want."

He started laughing, and the other three detectives, two young men and a woman, joined in. Matt brought out his badge.

"Matt Jones," he said. "Hollywood Homicide."

The laughing stopped. All four detectives sat back in their chairs, eyeballing Matt with great care now. Temps tossed his glasses on the desk.

"What's Matt Jones from Hollywood Homicide doing way out here?"

"It's about a case you worked three years ago, Detective. A case that's still unsolved. The murders of Tina Griffin and her son, Max."

Temps's left eye twitched, and Matt could tell that he had struck a nerve. A moment passed as Temps tried to regain his composure by cleaning his reading glasses with tissue paper. Matt gave him a hard up and down: mid-fifties, overweight and sweaty with thin strands of gray hair combed over a bald head. As if that picture wasn't pretty enough, Matt could hear the man wheezing from what he guessed was a lifetime of smoking cigarettes and drinking too much booze.

"That was a tough case," Temps said in a low voice. "Real tough. When did it become your business?"

Matt kept his eyes on him. "Last night, Temps. And the first thing I want to know is when did Ryan Brooks come out here to see you?"

Temps glanced at the three detectives staring at him and laughed again. Matt wasn't buying the laugh.

"I don't know what you're talking about, Detective."

"Sure, you do, Temps. Ryan Brooks was a reporter with the *LA Times*. He was researching the murders of Tina Griffin and her three-year-old son. Now he and his entire family are dead. You were the lead detective in charge of the case. You would have been his first call."

Temps shook his head as if ignorant of the details and looked up. Matt wasn't buying that either.

"I've never heard of him," Temps said.

Matt grimaced. "You would have been his first call."

Temps turned away from Matt's hard gaze and looked at the three detectives staring at him from their desks. "Would you guys give us a minute?"

All three nodded and got up. One of them gave Matt a dirty look and said something about needing some fresh air under his breath. Once they were gone, Temps's face changed, and Matt realized that he was alone with the snake.

"I don't know what you're inferring, Detective. But I'm gonna guess you drove out here because you think I screwed up the case."

"All I want to know is what happened."

Temps sat back in his chair again, chewing it over. "Have you ever been to the south end of Pico Gardens, Detective?"

Matt nodded. Pico Gardens was just across the river from downtown LA. An industrial section of the city with no industry. Abandoned factories, vacant warehouses, all the graffiti a junked-up punk could ever dream of, with ripped down fences and miles of barbed wire.

"That's where the bodies were found," Temps said. "Across the street from the railroad tracks where South Mission runs into Jesse Street. There's a dirt lot in front of an empty warehouse. They were found lying in the dirt."

"Okay," Matt said. "Okay, so it's a rough neighborhood."

"A lot of drugs, Detective. And a lot of gangs."

"And Tina Griffin lived nearby?"

Temps nodded. "She was a prostitute with drug issues. She and her son were knifed up pretty good. It looked like the woman had been gang-banged."

"What makes you say that?"

"Her private parts."

"What about them?"

Temps thought it over, then slipped his reading glasses back on.

"What about her private parts, Temps?"

"They were all messed up," he said.

Matt thought it over as he watched Temps open a bottle of water and take a long swig. When he glanced through the window, he heard Temps set the bottle down and turned back.

Temps leaned forward and slipped off his glasses again. "You know what, Detective?" he said in a voice that wouldn't carry. "I like working here. I like it a lot. It's been a second chance for me, and I'm trying to make good on it. I don't even care that I got knocked down to Auto. Do you understand what I'm trying to say to you? I don't want to mess things up over the murder of some whore who got thrown out with the trash. We did the best we could for that girl, and we worked it hard. The place we found her and her boy was a hellhole and probably always will be. Nobody wanted to talk to us, and the handful of people who finally did said exactly what I'm telling you right now. The case never went anywhere, Detective. It went cold the minute that girl and her boy were killed."

That girl and her boy.

Matt was losing his patience. "Where's the murder book?"

Temps rolled his head around like he thought he had said enough.

Matt leaned over the desk. "Where's the murder book, Temps?"

"You ever get the feeling that you're sticking your nose where it doesn't belong, Detective?"

Matt slammed his fist on the desk. "What's that supposed to mean? What the hell did you do with the murder book?"

Temps took a deep breath and exhaled with those pin-like eyes glued on Matt's face. Then he opened his bottom desk drawer, fished out a blue three-ring binder, and tossed it on the desktop. Now Matt was stunned.

"You kept it? You didn't send it down to Cold Case?"

Temps took another swig from the water bottle. "I must've forgot I had it. Seeing you probably jogged my memory some."

Matt grabbed the murder book, aghast. He weighed it in his hands. It felt light. Way too light.

"There ain't much to it," Temps said.

EIGHTEEN

Jack Temps stepped up to the urinal and unzipped his fly as he held a cell phone to his ear and waited for "Mr. Fix-it" to pick up at the other end. After eight rings he was beginning to lose his patience, but at least he could see Jones through the window tossing the murder book into his car and driving out of the lot.

At least Jones was gone.

He started to pee. It wasn't actually a stream but more of a light trickle. The way it had almost always been since his fiftieth birthday. That's when his doctor gave him the good news. His dick was broken, and his prostate had become the size of a grapefruit.

Good news. The kind that lasts forever.

The phone clicked sometime after the sixteenth ring.

"What is it now, Temps?"

Temps continued to pee, pointing the dribble away from the water to make less sound.

"We need to meet," he said.

"Never gonna happen, Temps. My day's wall to wall."

"Your day just changed. I'm driving in. Where are you gonna be in two hours?"

Mr. Fix-it hesitated.

"Where are you gonna be in two hours?" Temps repeated.

"Glendale."

"Do you remember that deli on North Orange?"

"Billy's. There's a restaurant there now."

"That's right, and a small parking garage next door. I'll meet you on the second floor in two hours. Don't be late."

Temps switched off his phone and slipped it into his pocket. His pee had slowed down to a series of droplets. When they grudgingly came to a final stop, he zipped up his pants and walked over to the sink. Temps usually avoided mirrors, but today he gazed at himself for a long time as he rinsed his hands.

Fate.

He could sense it lurking close by.

That first domino in a long line of dominoes tumbling over and dragging him into the void.

He noticed that his fingers were trembling slightly, and it upset him. Holding a paper towel beneath the hot water, he pressed it against his face and imagined himself screaming at the top of his lungs. Once the shrieking stopped in his head, he tossed the towel in the trash and walked out.

He made the drive to Glendale with plenty of time to spare. The second floor of the parking garage was nearly empty, and he backed his SUV into a space with a decent view of the ramp. Digging through the glove compartment, he found a mini Jameson and poured the shot of Irish whiskey into his coffee. He took a quick sip, and then another, settling back in the seat. After ten minutes or so, a black Town Car sped up the ramp and screeched to a stop in the next space over.

Several moments passed before the tinted window on the driver's side rolled down to reveal the governor's personal attorney and fixer. Temps looked at Alan Fontaine's mean face. He wasn't sure if he'd grown used to the man's shitty attitude or just become immune to it by now.

"What is it, Temps?" Fontaine said as he glanced about the parking garage. "Why all this?"

"We've got a problem. Actually, Fontaine, you and the governor have the problem. I'm just chump change. Your boy's the big fish swimmin' in the dirty sea."

"What the hell are you talking about?"

"I want more money. That's what I'm talking about. A lot more money."

Fontaine grimaced. "Screw you, Temps. Is that why you dragged me out here? There's no more money, so stick it!"

Temps took a swig of the spiked coffee. He felt his stomach begin to glow. He liked it. He had always liked it.

"Well, you better find more," he said. "A detective just stopped by the station. Matt Jones from Hollywood Homicide. He wanted to know everything I had on the murders of Tina Griffin and her little boy, Max."

Fontaine didn't take the news well and appeared stunned. "How the hell did that come up?"

"It gets better. A lot better. Jones thinks Griffin's murder has something to do with the killings at the beach."

"Jesus Christ," Fontaine said, shaking his head in disbelief.

Temps laughed. "Even Jesus can't save you and the governor this time, Fontaine. First Brooks, and now Jones. And Jones is gonna be a lot more trouble than the reporter. He's a cop. He's not gonna stop. He's not gonna let go."

Temps watched Fontaine take two quick breaths. When the man turned back to him, Temps saw his eyes go dead.

"Be careful, Temps. Knowledge can be a dangerous thing. You know what we did, and we know what you did. But then there's the believability factor. Who's gonna take the word of a disgraced cop over a governor who might be running for president?"

Temps laughed again. "Just about everybody these days. Listen, Fontaine, you and your boy need to do some real hard thinkin'. And whatever you guys come up with better be road worthy. This is death penalty shit, man. You know as well as I do that your boy's got issues. He's sick in the head and belongs in a cage. Now you guys owe me. I want more money, and I don't give a flying F if you gotta steal it or even print it. Just get it, or you're flyin' the plane on your own."

"Take it easy, Temps," Fontaine said. "I know we owe you. I'm just trying to think. I'll talk to the governor this afternoon. Where do things stand with Jones?"

Temps shrugged. "He's got the murder book, or what's left of it. I'm guessing he's doing what any detective would do right now. He's probably driving to the crime scene to check things out."

"Well, you need to keep an eye on that shithead. Do you hear me? As soon as you find him, you call me. I'll talk to the governor and work things out."

Temps watched the driver's side window close, with Fontaine's gummed-up face vanishing behind the darkened glass. He knew that he had gotten to the little bastard. He also knew that the governor's fixer was out of miracles and probably scared shitless.

And that was always good news.

He took another sip of coffee, savoring the taste of the Irish whiskey, and then gunned it down the ramp. When he hit the cashier's booth, he badged his way out of the garage without paying and floored it up North Orange Street. The freeway entrance was just a few blocks ahead. With any luck, he'd have eyes on Jones within half an hour.

NINETEEN

Matt inched his car over the ripped-down chain-link fencing into the unpaved parking lot. Estimating where the bodies of Tina Griffin and her three-year-old boy had been found from the photographs he had seen in the murder book, he pulled to a stop about twenty-five feet away. After a quick glance up and down the streets, he checked the mag on his .45 and returned the semiautomatic to his belt holster. Then he grabbed the murder book and climbed out of the car.

The corner of South Mission and Jesse Street was a large open space of empty parking lots, abandoned low-rise buildings and warehouses wrapped in a twelve-foot-high ribbon of graffiti that ran from building to building as far as the eye could see. The place had the appearance of being a mile or two beyond the gates of what was once known as the civilized world. It was almost like an urban desert of ruin where bricks and concrete and barbed-wire fencing stood in place of rocks and sand that had been worn away by time. If Tina Griffin and her son, Max, had called out for help in a place like this, Matt guessed that no one would have heard them.

He let the thought go, tossing the murder book on the hood of his car and leafing through it quickly. He had stopped at a gas station along the way, anxious to get a first look at what was in the blue binder. Almost immediately he had realized that half the book was missing. The preliminary reports by the detectives who responded to the crime scene before the case went to Temps had been removed. The reports from the Forensic Science Division and the coroner's office had been pulled as well. All that remained were a handful of crime scene photos, a shot of the two victims before they were murdered, and an odd attempt by Temps to keep a Chronological Record—poorly written and way too brief to be much help.

Matt had no doubt that it was Temps who cleaned out the murder book, and he questioned how the detective had ever made it to the elite Robbery-Homicide Division in the first place. Like a complete fool, Temps didn't seem to realize that digital copies of the missing reports were a matter of record. On the drive back into LA, Matt had placed calls to both David Speeks at the crime lab and Art Madina in the coroner's office, requesting copies of both reports as soon as possible.

Lieutenant McKensie had called Temps a snake. Matt agreed—he knew a dirty cop when he met one. He also knew that he couldn't trust anything Temps had said about the case. But there was more. A lot more.

There had to be a reason why the files were removed from the murder book. With Temps's dark history in play, Matt would've bet the house that it had something do with money.

Temps had been bought by someone. And after meeting the detective, Matt couldn't help wondering how much it had cost.

Matt wiped his forehead, turning the page in the binder and examining a photograph of Tina Griffin lying on a blanket with her son in a park. From the tall buildings in the background, the park had to be somewhere downtown. According to the photocopy of her driver's license in the Chronological Record, Griffin was twenty-eight at the time of her death. But as Matt gazed at her picture, he couldn't help thinking that she looked younger than that. She had a natural feel about her. A vulnerability. Matt couldn't tell if it was the way she wore her brownish blonde hair down to her narrow shoulders or the reach he saw in her light brown eyes. Her son seemed to share the same expression on his face. Something that didn't point to pain or suffering or even fear that Matt would have imagined came with a life of drug abuse and hooking. Instead, reading their faces, the clear looks in their eyes, he saw the exact opposite.

There was something else wrong with the photograph, and Matt picked up on it quickly. The way the little boy was dressed didn't jibe with what Temps had been trying to sell. Max appeared clean and neat and well cared for.

Matt flipped the page over to the crime scene photos and took a moment to chill before examining the dead bodies. Though Griffin had been found lying flat on her back in the dirt, her son was facedown with his legs crunched under his belly and his head turned. It seemed awkward, even strange. As difficult as they were to look at, Matt focused on Griffin and the number of stab wounds visible on her chest. The pattern seemed erratic, even random, just the way Ryan Brooks's had appeared when Matt found his body on the floor of his bedroom.

But there was something else going on here. There was something wrong with the photographs that Matt couldn't put his finger on.

His mind jetted to the surface. He could hear footsteps behind his back and turned, then shook his head in disbelief.

It was Vince Sato from the *Times*.

"What are you doing here, Sato?"

"I followed you."

"You followed me? Why?"

"I don't know," the reporter said. "I wanted to do something. I thought I could help."

Matt met his gaze. "This isn't help, Sato. You're a reporter, and you know better than I do why you can't be here. But even worse, these are mass killings. You could be in danger."

Sato's face lit up. "So you really do think they're related. I've been reading up on it. I think so, too."

Matt closed the murder book. "That was off the record," he said. "And that's exactly the kind of thing I mean. You can't be here."

Sato looked around, then turned back. "Maybe I could wait over by my car. When you're finished, we could talk."

Matt nodded, but not with much enthusiasm. Though he remained more than grateful for Sato's help with Brooks's computer in the *Times* building, they weren't the Dynamic Duo, and this wasn't going to work out. He watched the reporter walk off the lot in the oppressive sunlight. He could see him stepping over the torn-down fencing—

And then something happened.

Something clicked.

Matt ripped opened the murder book and took a second look at the crime scene photos of Griffin and her little boy lying in the dirt.

He could see it now. The big easy.

He felt a chill run up his spine, and his body shivered.

The crime scene photograph had been taken *through* the fence. Not over it, but *through* it. And the entrance had been gated. When he noticed the lock, he stared at it, double-checked the rest of the photos, then let his mind go.

On the night of the murders three years ago, the chain-link fence had been up and the property secured. Tina and Max Griffin hadn't been killed here.

Their bodies had been tossed over the fence. The actual crime scene was in another location. This had all been staged. This was a body dump.

TWENTY

Trouble.

Or was it more than that?

Jack Temps leaned his elbows against the steering wheel and feathered the focus ring on his field glasses. He could see Jones staring at something in what was left of the murder book, then turning back to the unpaved lot and examining the ripped-down chain-link fence.

Why did he seem so animated? So alive?

Temps tossed it over as he took a sip of his spiked coffee that had gone cold somewhere between here and Glendale. Then he noticed a man leaning against the hood of a white Audi parked across the street. Temps raised his field glasses, studying the man carefully. When he spotted the media pass pinned to his jacket, he pulled out a camera with a long lens and knocked off five shots. After zooming in on the license plate, he snapped another picture, set the camera to "Preview," and lowered it onto the dash so he could see the screen.

Temps unfastened the seat belt, reaching over his belly and digging his cell phone out of his pocket. After taking a moment to catch his breath, he called Central Dispatch and identified himself to the woman who answered the phone. Then he gave her the license number, along with the make and model of the car. A few minutes later, the dispatcher came back on the line.

"Vince Sato," she said. "Asian American. Thirty-five years old. Five foot nine inches tall, one hundred and eighty-five pounds. Brown eyes. Black hair. It says that he's a journalist cleared for media access. He's a writer for the *Times*."

Temps almost gagged. It felt like fate had grabbed him by the ankles and was pulling him deeper into that hole. The dispatcher's voice died off. Ten or fifteen seconds got lost in the confusion.

Vince Sato was another journalist. Temps tried to pull himself together.

"What have you got on him?" he managed.

"Nothing," the dispatcher said. "He's clean. I can email you a copy of his driver's license if you like."

"Thanks."

Temps didn't need the reporter's picture, but things were starting to get complicated. Where Sato lived might prove to be useful down the road. He gave the dispatcher his email address and cell number and got off the line. When his phone beeped a few minutes later, he opened the message, gazed at Sato's license, and read his home address. Temps had been a cop long enough to know the street in Santa Monica and could almost picture the reporter's house.

He took another sip of coffee, the taste of the Irish whiskey gone now. Setting the cup down, he gazed through the windshield and could see Jones crossing the street to talk to the reporter.

Double trouble. No doubt about it.

Temps grabbed his phone, opened his recent caller list, and poked his finger at the second name from the top. This time Fontaine picked up after the first ring.

"You found him?"

Temps hesitated. The fear in Fontaine's voice had fermented. Maybe the governor's personal attorney and fixer could feel the Fates pulling him into his grave as well.

"I found him," he said, finally.

"At the—you know—the place?"

"If that's what you want to call it, Fontaine. Yeah. I found him at 'the place.'"

"Shit," Fontaine whispered. "I spoke with the governor."

Temps sat up in his seat and raised the field glasses. Jones and the reporter were talking like they already knew each other. They seemed friendly, and he didn't like what it inferred.

"Before you get going, Fontaine, there's something you and wacko boy need to know. The amount of money you came up with won't work anymore. Everything just doubled."

"Hey, we're in a situation here. What are you talking about?"

"Jones has a new buddy. That's what I'm talking about."

"Who?"

Fontaine sounded horrified.

"Who is it?" he repeated.

Temps took a swig of coffee, finishing it off. He could see Fontaine squirming in his mind. "Another reporter with the *Times*."

"He's there?"

Temps set the empty cup down and adjusted the focus on his field glasses. "They're trading notes right now."

Fontaine didn't say anything for a long time. Temps almost thought that the phone had gone dead but could hear Mr. Fix-it's rapid breathing. After what seemed like two or three minutes, Fontaine came back on.

"Here's what the governor wants you to know, Temps. Are you listening?"

"I'm listening."

Fontaine cleared his throat. "You need to know how much he wants this to go away. How grateful he would be to anyone who could make this problem disappear. How much he would appreciate the dedication of someone who offered their time and service and good will for his benefit. There would be a place for you in the future, Temps. A place at the top."

A moment passed as Fontaine's voice faded and the words settled in. Temps kept his eyes on Jones and the reporter through the field glasses.

"Do you understand what I'm saying?" Fontaine asked.

"Yeah," Temps said. "I think I do."

TWENTY-ONE

Matt parked in a lot on West Sixth Street and started down the sidewalk. The Millennium Biltmore Hotel was around the corner one block up on South Grand Avenue. It had been dark for a couple of hours, and Matt stared at the skyline as he cut his way through the heavy foot traffic that had become part of downtown lately. The night air was ice cold, his uniform made of a thin cotton suitable for spring, summer, and fall, and so he walked quickly.

As Matt cleared the corner, a black Town Car pulled up to the hotel's entrance, and he was surprised to see Governor Hayworth climb out of the back seat with his wife, Lisa, and his attorney and front man, Alan Fontaine. This was a fundraiser for the LAPD, and Matt guessed that their presence would make Chief Logan very happy. He also hoped that with a headliner like the governor, he could make a brief appearance and not be missed if he ducked out early.

Matt followed the governor's entourage through the entrance and across the lobby. When they started to pass through the doors to the main ballroom, Lisa Hayworth turned back and met his gaze with a warm smile. Matt nodded at her, genuinely pleased that he had an ally here. But then he felt himself being pulled away from the stream of people and pushed through a stainless-steel door into the kitchen.

He sensed that there were two of them as he was thrown against a wall.

When he turned, he saw Fresno and Cook out of breath and backing away. A sous-chef, a young man half their size, stormed over in anger.

"You can't stand here," the sous-chef said. "You're in the way. We'll be serving soon."

Cook grabbed the man by the shirt. "Screw you, pal. Go away, or you're gonna get hurt."

Cook released his grip, and the sous-chef ran off.

Matt noted the agent's crudity and narrowed his eyes. "Is that the way you talk to people, Cook? Like you're a tough guy?"

Cook pointed a finger in Matt's face. "Screw you, too, you dirty cop!"

Matt had lost his patience and started heading for the door. But Fresno grabbed him by the shoulders and yanked him back.

"You're not going anywhere, Jones," he said. "Nowhere, until we talk."

Matt gave Fresno a hard look but didn't say anything.

"We heard through the grapevine that you drove out to the Topanga station this morning, Jones. You picked up a murder book on a three-year-old cold case."

Matt shrugged. "What's a grapevine, Fresno?"

This wasn't going to go their way. Matt had decided that from the beginning. And by now he could see the venom showing on their faces. It seemed clear that both agents would have preferred a fistfight.

Fresno pointed a finger at him. "What's the murder case, Jones? What are you up to?"

"If you heard that I picked up a file, then why don't you know what it is?"

"What?" Fresno said, looking bewildered.

Matt shook his head in disbelief. "It doesn't matter. It's none of your business."

"We think it is our business," Fresno said. "We think you're messing with our case."

Cook wrinkled his brow. "How's your uncle doing, Jones? You got any idea what the good doctor's up to these days?"

Matt leaned closer, refusing to take the bait as he lowered his voice. "Really, Cook? Is that the way you still see it? What about you, Fresno?

Why are you guys following me? I said it two days ago. You're making a mistake. But maybe it's more than that. Maybe you're not lost. Maybe you're covering for somebody. Who's paying you guys to screw up this murder case?"

Cook lunged forward. Fresno pulled him out of the way and spoke through clenched teeth.

"You're up to something, Jones. Whatever it is, we'll find out. And then that's it for you. Story over for Matt Jones."

Fresno pushed Cook out the door in a huff. Matt watched them vanish, wondering if he hadn't just hit on something. Temps had been bought. That became obvious from what Matt found missing in the murder book. Someone with deep pockets had to be pulling the strings. So why hadn't Fresno and Cook listened to Art Madina in the coroner's office? Why were they still insisting that the killer was Matt's uncle, Dr. Baylor? Wasn't that proof enough that Fresno and Cook had been bought, too?

Matt found the idea more than disturbing.

He straightened his uniform, then stepped into the hallway and entered the ballroom. It was bigger than he had expected, and more crowded. People were wall to wall, milling about and shouting over each other. Without counting, Matt guessed that there were more than fifty tables set for what looked like a multicourse dinner that would burn through most of the night. At the head of the room, he could see the chief talking to the governor with Alan Fontaine and a handful of journalists standing by his side. Searching through all the faces, he finally spotted Lisa Hayworth. She was looking his way and pointing at the bar in the back of the room.

Matt made his way through the crowd, sensing recognition on people's faces but ignoring it. At one point he turned back to check on the chief and caught Fontaine staring at him. It seemed odd, almost as if the governor's personal attorney had been sizing him up before quickly turning away. But Matt let it go as he reached Lisa and she gazed into his eyes.

"Who were those rough-looking men?" she asked.

Matt flashed a faint smile. "It wasn't anything important."

"Buy me a drink?"

"A glass of wine?"

She shook her head. "I'm not good at these things. Better make it a Tito's vodka, on the rocks with a twist."

He laughed. "I'm not good at these things either. I'll have the same."

Matt ordered their drinks, watching Lisa step out of the way and move to the pub table set in the far corner. She was dressed in a black pantsuit with a white blouse pulled together by a colorful vest beneath her jacket. Her eyes were bright and alive, her smile warm and gracious. He could remember seeing her at the Police Academy and thinking how her appearance seemed so institutional. But not tonight. Tonight, she looked elegant.

He brought the drinks over. Clicking glasses, they took a first sip, and then she laughed.

"Why is it that the first sip usually tastes so disappointing when you're not at home?" she said.

Matt smiled again. "Because they don't freeze the bottle."

She nodded with a smile and seemed to agree.

"Who were those men?" she said. "Really, Matty, who were they?"

He noticed the concern showing on her face and leaned closer. "The Feds," he said finally.

"What did they want from you?"

Matt glanced through the crowd at the chief and caught Fontaine staring at him again. Then just as quickly the attorney turned away.

"They're working on those murders in Manhattan Beach. Ryan Brooks and his family."

"The journalist," she said. "In the papers. The story said you found them."

Matt gave her a look and sipped his drink. "Yeah."

"But you're not working. You're on leave. I saw those men pushing you around. Why would they act that way?"

"Because they're frustrated," he said. "Because they don't know what they're doing. They've made a mistake, and the pressure's on."

"What did you tell them?"

Matt shrugged. "Just what I'm saying to you. They're headed in the wrong direction. By the way, what's going on with your husband's attorney?"

Matt watched her turn and find Fontaine in the crowd at the other end of the room. The man had been looking at them but turned away again.

"I don't know," she said, still eyeing him. "To be honest, he frightens me."

"He frightens you?" Matt said.

She turned back to him and met his eyes, then spoke in a softer voice. "Let's just say that he makes me uncomfortable. I asked my husband to fire him, but he wouldn't listen to me. Ever since, Alan keeps his distance."

Matt thought it over as he turned for another look at the man standing beside the governor. It was almost as if Fontaine was trying not to look at Matt but couldn't help himself. Like the attorney was Lisa's chaperone and keeping tabs on them.

Matt sipped his drink. "When was all this, Lisa? When did you ask your husband to fire him?"

"A couple of years ago, I guess. Maybe longer. It doesn't matter really. Not anymore. Not as long as he stays away from me."

"Did something happen?"

She took a moment and seemed to toss it over. "Something changed," she said finally.

"But you feel safe, right?" Matt said.

She never had a chance to answer the question. A waiter announced that dinner was served, and people started heading for their tables. As Matt set down his glass, a photographer noticed him with the governor's wife, stepped up to the pub table, and hit them right in the eyes with a white-hot strobe light.

TWENTY-TWO

Matt didn't need to enter the address from the photocopy of Tina Griffin's driver's license into his navigation system. It looked like no more than a five-minute drive from where she and Max had been found. He crossed the Seventh Street Bridge over the Los Angeles River and made a left on South Santa Fe Avenue. When he spotted the three-story apartment building on the corner, he pulled over.

He took a moment to collect his thoughts.

He'd had trouble sleeping last night. He hadn't been able to stop worrying about Lisa. It seemed clear that something was going on with Alan Fontaine. During the entire dinner, the attorney's odd behavior never stopped. He kept turning and sneaking peeks at Matt like he couldn't control himself. But it was the governor's conduct that bothered Matt most. At the Police Academy, Governor Hayworth had been all smiles, taking a picture with him and his partner and laughing at the media as they swarmed in. Last night the governor had completely ignored Matt and even turned away to avoid greeting him. Matt had been snubbed before and imagined that he would be snubbed again. But somehow this time felt different.

Or was it just politics?

Matt let it go and checked the street with great care.

The five-minute drive hadn't been long enough to cut through the devastated landscape and reach the other side. It was a bright, sunny morning.

Yet he didn't see a single person on the sidewalk or even a passing car in the street. The neighborhood seemed as quiet and still as a ghost town. He slung his laptop case over his shoulder, got out from behind the wheel, and walked up the steps to the entrance. To the right of the door, he found apartment 2C on the intercom and read the name below the buzzer.

S. Monroe.

Unable to tell if this was a man or a woman, he pressed the buzzer and waited. After several minutes without a response, he pressed the buzzer again and held it down for ten seconds. When no one answered, he tried the lobby door and found it locked.

He took a step back, eyeing the apartment building as he weighed his options. The graffiti wrapping around the first floor was just like every other building on the street. Leaving a note wouldn't work out here. And then, just as he started down the steps to his car, he heard someone speak over the intercom.

"What do you want?"

It was a man's voice. An older man who sounded impatient. An African American with an accent from the Deep South.

"Mr. Monroe?" Matt said.

"Who wants to know?"

"Detective Matt Jones, LAPD."

The man remained silent. Matt thought that Monroe had signed off.

"Mr. Monroe, are you still there?"

"What do you want with me?" he said.

"I'm working a case that has nothing to do with you. I was hoping we could just talk."

"Do I gotta do it?"

"You'd be doing me a favor," Matt said. "I'd owe you one."

More silence. More thinking it over.

"Walk into the street and hold up your ID," the old man said finally. "I wanna look at ya."

Matt did as he was asked, stepping into the street and holding his badge up in the air. He could see the man peering at him from a second-floor window to the left of the front entrance. He had a thin face, dark skin, and wiry hair that had turned a light gray. He gave the impression of being on the tall side and, from what Matt could see, was dressed in jeans with a T-shirt and button-down sweater. But none of that really compared to the man's eyes. They had a certain reach, and even through the glass, Matt could see the worry in them. After a few moments, the man vanished from the window. When Matt heard the buzzer unlock the front door, he hustled up the steps and entered the building.

The door snapped shut behind him. Adjusting the strap on his shoulder, he glanced about the small lobby. The building had to be nearly a century old—a three-story walk-up without an elevator. He could hear the sound of a television bleeding through a door on the first floor. Someone was watching a rerun from a comedy show with a heavy laugh track. An infant was crying from an apartment farther down the hall. When a man began shouting, Matt guessed that it was from the same unit.

He started up the staircase, listening to the old wooden boards creak. Stepping up to the landing, he saw the door to apartment 2C open slowly, then stop when the safety chain tightened. There was an eeriness about the place. A feeling of entering something strange. When he reached the door, he found Monroe waiting for him.

"What do you want, Detective? Why are you bothering me?"

Matt looked at the old man's heavily lined face through the gap in the door. The fear in his eyes was still there. Still hot.

"A woman lived in this apartment three years ago, Mr. Monroe. I was just wondering if you knew her."

"What woman is that?"

"A mother with a three-year-old boy. Tina Griffin and her son, Max."

Monroe shook his head. "Never heard of 'em."

The old man started to close the door. Matt blocked it with his foot, then pulled the photograph of Griffin with her son at the park out of his pocket.

"Maybe this would help jog your memory," he said.

Monroe glanced at Matt's foot, then leaned closer and stared at the picture. Matt caught the recognition beginning to bloom across the old man's face.

"You knew them, didn't you. You've seen them before."

Monroe shook his head and gave him a long look. "Not in real life, Detective."

"What are you saying?"

"A man came by here around six weeks ago. He showed me a handful of pictures with these same people in them. He said the mother and her boy were dead. He told me that they had been murdered. Up the street on the other side of the river."

"What did the man look like?"

Monroe shrugged. "My memory's no good these days. But he left a card. Wait here and I'll get it."

Matt watched the old man step away from the door, wishing the safety chain had been longer so he could get a better look at the apartment. He heard a drawer open and close. Within a few seconds, Monroe returned and passed a business card through the gap in the door.

It wasn't Jack Temps or whoever his partner might have been. The card had been left by Ryan Brooks.

The journalist had been here. Matt had confirmation now that Ryan Brooks had been actively working the case before his death. He took a deep breath and exhaled.

"So you're saying this reporter was here around six weeks ago?"

Monroe shrugged. "Somethin' like that. Maybe it was a couple of months. I'm not too sure. But you know what, I've been meaning to call him for a while. I forgot to give him something."

"Forgot to give him what?"

"Somethin' I found in a drawer. Let me get the lock so you don't have to wait in the hall."

The old man shut the door, removed the clasp from the lock, and opened up. As he crossed the room and began searching for something on the floor of a closet, Matt stepped in and looked around. It was an efficiency apartment with a dated kitchen and bathroom, a sleeping area, and a small space for a living room. Monroe kept the place clean and neat. But that's not what stood out.

"Is this your stuff, Mr. Monroe?" Matt asked.

The old man glanced back at him. "The place came furnished."

"When did you move in?"

"About three years ago, give or take."

"Do you happen to remember the date?"

Monroe shook his head and smiled as if baffled. He crossed the room and handed Matt a small knapsack.

"I found it in the bottom drawer of the chest when I moved in. I thought it was empty. Turns out it wasn't. They're in that front pocket."

Matt unzipped the pocket and fished out a stack of snapshots. He went through them quickly. They were pictures of Tina Griffin and her son cuddling on a couch. When Matt noticed the furniture that they were sitting on, he immediately understood that he had just made an important leap forward. The furniture was the same furniture he saw in Monroe's apartment, but the view outside the windows didn't match here or anywhere near this part of town. He could see palm trees. He could see the hills. In two snapshots the Hollywood Sign stood in the background big as life.

Jack Temps's summary of the murder case had been a complete fabrication. A deliberate attempt to deceive him. It took Matt's breath away.

The crime scene had been staged. And now he knew that Tina Griffin's home had been staged as well.

TWENTY-THREE

Matt stood in a small examination area in the property room staring at the cardboard box that contained Tina Griffin and her son's possessions. Their names were printed on the side, along with the LAPD case number. Below the number was the date the murders occurred and the location where their bodies had been found.

Matt couldn't help thinking that the box seemed small.

He picked up the clipboard, adding his name, section, and today's date to the list. Before signing the document, he skimmed through the people who had gone through the victims' possessions before him. He saw a number of names that he recognized from the Forensic Science Division, including David Speeks. Someone from the coroner's office had been here on behalf of the medical examiner, Art Madina. When he saw Jack Temps listed twice, he became concerned about the integrity of the contents. And then finally, a detective, Chris Webb, had been here from the Hollenbeck station just a couple of months ago. The Hollenbeck station's jurisdiction included Pico Gardens. It was more than possible that Webb would have been the first detective at the crime scene before the case got bumped up to Temps.

Matt jotted Webb's name down in his notepad, deciding to give him a call as soon as he finished up here. But before he could get started, his cell phone began vibrating in his pocket. He pulled it out and glanced at the face. David Speeks was calling from the crime lab.

"I just sent you an email, Jones. Tina Griffin and her little boy, Max. Everything from our end that you thought might be missing from the murder book is in the file."

"What about pictures?"

"Everything."

Matt pulled a chair away from the table and sat down. Checking the property room counter, he saw a female clerk looking something up on the computer for a man and woman dressed in plain clothes whom he assumed were detectives. He dug the pictures Monroe had given him out of his pocket and began thumbing through the stack. Snapshots of a vibrant young woman with her son.

"This was a body dump," he said in a voice that wouldn't carry. "What were you guys doing, Speeks?"

"I can't argue the point," the criminalist said. "It came up more than once at the crime scene. The place was clean. Way too clean. But you should talk to Madina and find out how the autopsies went."

Matt grimaced. Speeks and his team from the crime lab had screwed up.

He turned over the snapshot and looked at the next one—Tina Griffin feeding her boy spaghetti with his face encrusted in tomato sauce. But what mattered was the kitchen. It didn't appear dated. The refrigerator and stove looked brand new.

"Did you guys go to her apartment on Santa Fe?"

"Yeah," Speeks said. "We didn't find much."

"Did it ever occur to you that something might be out of place?"

"Like what?"

Matt turned to the next snapshot—Griffin reading a story to her son in bed.

"Come on, Speeks. If you were there, then you had to have seen that something was out of place."

"I don't get where you're going with this, Jones. What could have been out of place?"

Matt glanced at the three people at the counter again, then looked back at the snapshots and tried to keep his voice down.

"Her, Speeks. Griffin and the boy. That's what's out of place. They don't fit the neighborhood."

"Whoa, Jones. What are you trying to say?"

"Everything about this murder case stinks. That's what I'm saying. You blew it."

"Aren't you supposed to be on medical leave?"

"Ha!" Matt said as he jumped to his feet. "The crime scene is bogus, and so is her apartment. How did this get by everybody?"

Matt knew that Speeks had twenty-five years' worth of experience as a criminalist. That he was one of the best in the business, took pride in his work, and had a conscience. When he heard the tone of Speeks's voice, the determination, he knew that he had a willing partner.

"I'll go through everything myself," Speeks said. "You know I will, Jones. But while I'm doing that, look at what I sent you, talk to Madina, and then call me back."

The phone clicked.

Matt turned off his own phone and laid it down on the table. Then the clerk stepped out from behind the counter with a concerned look on her face.

"Is everything okay, Detective?"

Matt nodded. "Thanks. Sorry if I raised my voice."

She gazed back at him, then shrugged with a faint smile. "It happens."

He watched her return to the counter thinking she came off a lot like a librarian he knew in high school who always seemed to add something good to his reading list. Once she and the two detectives started talking and got back to work on the computer, he slipped a pair of gloves on and opened the box.

The inventory sheet only listed a handful of items, all of which were sealed in plastic evidence bags. Even at a glance he could see the edges of bloodstains that remained after the lab had taken their samples, the clothing ripped and slashed by the killer with what had to be a large knife. Matt picked up the boy's shirt and pants and a pair of Nikes so small, he stopped for a few moments and just stared at them in the palm of his hand. Pulling himself together, he opened the bag and took a closer look at Max's shirt. A name tag with just his first name had been sewn into the collar. Holding the shirt up to the light, he counted ten stab wounds—three in the front and seven in the back.

Matt knew that he couldn't let his mind wander. He couldn't let his imagination step into the room. And tonight, if he slept at all, it would be with the lights on.

He tried to clear his mind, then moved on.

The dress that the boy's mother had worn on the night she was murdered seemed skimpy, even racy, and didn't fit with anything he had seen her wearing in any photograph. He found her bra and panties and examined them through the plastic. When he came to her small purse, he slid it out of the bag and emptied its contents on the table. There wasn't much here. Twenty-two dollars in bills and a driver's license. But what struck Matt most was that he didn't find a credit card or even a bank card.

He picked up the inventory sheet but didn't see them on the list. Pulling the chair closer, he sat down at the table again and flipped the driver's license over so that he could see the front. He stared at it for a long time. And then he stared at it some more.

The quality of the photograph. The printing. The state of California's official seal.

It was just like the crime scene. Just like the apartment on Santa Fe.

Everything about it was fake.

TWENTY-FOUR

Matt veered into an empty parking spot on Twelfth Street and fed the meter. He was about a block and a half away from Vic Lopez's Taproom, a dive bar that was owned by Lopez, an ex-con he knew and occasionally went to for advice. But Lopez offered more than advice. The coffee was good and the food even better. Matt knew that if he could get past the tacos, the french dip roast beef with Mexican spices was one of the best sandwiches he had ever tasted. But even though his stomach had started growling twenty minutes ago, he wanted to wander through the Santee Alley and give himself a chance to think things over.

The Santee Alley was a flea market several blocks long with vendors selling the usual street fare: clothing, handbags, sunglasses, cell phone cases, jewelry, hot dogs, and anything else that might come to mind. This afternoon the place was packed with people as varied in their roots as the merchandise on the racks.

And Matt loved it.

He crossed the street and began working his way through the crowd. It had occurred to him as he left the property room that on every level possible, mistakes had been made in the investigation of Tina Griffin and her son's murder. He imagined that with Fresno and Cook on the job, or on someone's payroll, the murders of Ryan Brooks and his wife and daughter were lost in deep space as well.

He wondered if the picture Temps had painted of Tina Griffin as a drug addict and prostitute, the clothing she had been dressed in, the neighborhood her dead body had been found in—he wondered if all this had anything to do with why everyone, including Speeks in the crime lab, had dropped the ball. But even worse, after all this time, why hadn't anyone picked the ball back up again? Why hadn't there been any follow-through?

He thought about Max's shirt and the number of stab wounds he had counted just an hour ago. A three-year-old boy. A complete innocent. He remembered asking Madina how many times Brooks's daughter, Emma, had been stabbed. He could remember the ME's answer like they were still in the same room.

She was just two, Jones, and small for her age. She weighed less than twenty pounds. The only wound that mattered was the first one.

Matt stepped around a family crossing the narrow alley to a booth on the other side. He needed to stay focused. But still the questions kept coming.

These killings were in a world all their own. Who was he looking for? Who was pulling the strings?

After a few minutes he found himself back on Twelfth Street, saw the dive bar, and walked in. It looked like a thin after-lunch group, with very little conversation. Walking to the end of the bar, he sat down and pushed a menu aside. Once his eyes adjusted to the darkness, he looked around for Lopez but didn't see him here or in the dining room. The bartender, a man in his fifties with a hardened face, pockmarked skin, and two full arms worth of tattoos, stepped over.

"Is Vic around?" Matt said.

The bartender sized him up and nodded. "In the kitchen," he said in a gruff voice. "What can I get you?"

"A cup of coffee and a french dip with fries."

The bartender smiled, not bothering to write the order down. "You've been here before," he said.

"A couple of times."

"I remember you now. You're Vic's cop friend. You're name's Jones."

Matt nodded. The bartender kept the slight smile going and walked down to the computer at the other end of the bar to ring up Matt's lunch. While he waited, Matt pulled out his cell phone and skimmed through the

LAPD directory until he found the number for the Hollenbeck station's Major Crimes Unit. He hit "Enter," checking his notepad while listening to the phone ring.

A woman picked up. "Major Crimes."

Matt leaned his elbows against the bar and spoke in a low voice. "This is Detective Matt Jones out of Hollywood. Who am I speaking with?"

"Detective Larson," she said.

"I'm trying to reach another detective who works out of your station. I'm hoping that he can help me with a three-year-old case that went cold. The murders of Tina Griffin and her son. It happened on your turf, Pico Gardens, and a detective's name came up. Chris Webb. He may have been at the crime scene after the first responders called it in."

Larson cupped her phone and said something to someone else too muffled for Matt to understand. After a moment, she came back on.

"Who did you say you were looking for?"

"A detective," he said. "Chris Webb."

"I've never heard of a Chris Webb," Larson said.

Matt felt his skin flush. It was happening again. The man pulling the strings.

"Maybe he was transferred to another station?" Matt said, trying not to sound grim.

"I've been here for ten years, Detective. If Chris Webb ever worked here, I'd know him."

Matt closed his eyes as the words sank in. The bartender set down his coffee.

"You okay, Jones?" he said.

Matt opened his eyes, gazed across the bar at the man, and nodded. But he was sweating now. In the weeds and dying inside.

"Could you do me a favor, Detective Larson?"

"What do you need?"

"Just go up to the LAPD's personnel page. Type 'Chris Webb' into the search window and hit 'Enter.'"

"No problem at all, Detective. I was already halfway there."

Matt sighed, pushed his coffee out of the way, and listened to Larson typing on her keyboard. He knew from the spike in sound the moment she hit "Enter." And then the waiting began, the seconds ticking by like minutes, the dead air blistering his ears over the phone, the feeling of being a fortune-teller lost in the void.

When Larson came back on finally, her voice had changed. It was softer, more soothing. A real tell.

"I'm sorry," she said. "There's no Chris Webb anywhere in the department's system."

"Thank you, Detective," Matt said. "Thank you very much."

He switched off his phone, stunned. When he felt someone slap him on the shoulder, he turned and saw Vic Lopez grinning at him. And then the grin went dark.

"What's wrong?" Lopez said. "What just happened? Did somebody die?"

"You could say that."

Matt tossed Tina Griffin's driver's license on the bar and watched Lopez give it a long look. Lopez had been arrested, found guilty, and served time for forgery and printing counterfeit money. The paper he used had been pitch perfect. After bleaching the ink off one-dollar bills, he reprinted them as twenties. His operation brought in more than three-quarters of a million dollars before it was shut down. And Lopez's explanation made headlines. He had borrowed the idea, he'd said, after reading a crime novel by a British writer he liked. Matt could still remember Lopez's quote to a reporter from the *Times*.

I'm not sure how they found me. I did everything by the book!

Lopez pushed the driver's license back to Matt. "It's counterfeit."

"I guessed that much," Matt said. "But what's your take."

Lopez shrugged. "It's sloppy work. The picture looks like it was cut out of a snapshot. Look at the state seal. And the color of the ink is three shades too light. There's too much green in it. This was either done by an idiot or someone who needed to get it out the door in a hurry."

In a hurry, Matt thought. Before tossing Griffin's corpse over a fence and dumping her in the dirt with her little boy.

TWENTY-FIVE

He spotted it the moment he walked out of Vic Lopez's Taproom and stepped into the late-afternoon sunlight on Twelfth Street. He could see its reflection in a storefront window. A black SUV—an unmarked Police Interceptor with its engine running—halfway down the block.

Temps.

Matt took the shock without any hesitation in motion. Instead, he turned the other way and started walking toward his car. He took his time, stopping on several occasions and pretending to check his cell phone. But he had his eyes locked on Temps the whole way. With each and every window he passed, he could see the big man in the SUV following his progress down the sidewalk.

In an odd way, Matt felt sorry for Temps right now. He had stepped into Matt's world on the wrong day. The worst of days. And from the jolt of adrenaline coursing through his veins—the anger and rage he was feeling right now—Matt guessed that Temps's afternoon wouldn't turn out so well.

He reached his car, tossed his laptop case on the passenger seat, and climbed in. Pulling into the street, he glanced at his rearview mirror and saw Temps begin to follow. Matt lowered his visor to block the sun's glare, then looked at the clock on the dash. Dusk wasn't more than a half hour off.

Magic hour.

He cruised around the block, then turned away from the Fashion District, skipped across Skid Row, and rolled through Produce Alley to burn up more time. He could see men and women loading trucks with crates of fresh fruit and vegetables that he guessed had come off the field earlier in the day. Every time he checked the rearview mirror, Temps was six or seven car lengths back.

After another half hour or so, the sun began to set in the distance. Matt made a left turn onto South Central Avenue and started to pick up speed. When he hit Seventh Street, he barreled over the bridge, made another left, and rolled over the chain-link fence where Tina Griffin and her son had been found. But Matt had no intension of stopping where the bodies had been dumped. Instead, he crossed the dirt lot and pulled directly in front of the abandoned warehouse.

The huge bay doors were long gone. Switching on his headlights, he inched the car forward until the interior of the dilapidated building filled with light. The place had been gutted by looters and was completely empty. For a moment he wondered why he didn't find homeless people camped out here. But then his eyes swept over the graffiti and he remembered the neighborhood he was in. No one was safe here, not even the people with empty pockets. All he saw were pigeons roosting on the ceiling beams and staring back at him as if they sensed trouble ahead.

He killed the headlights. Pocketing a flashlight from the glove compartment, he checked his .45 and got out of the car.

Even without looking he knew that Temps was watching from somewhere behind him in the gloom. Now it was just a question of what it would take for Temps to make the mistake of getting out of his SUV.

Matt stepped into the warehouse, crossing from the illumination of the streetlights outside into the darkness. When he sensed that he was invisible, he moved behind a column and turned around for a look. He could see the black Interceptor parked beside a building across the street. Although he couldn't make out Temps's face in the shadows, the bead from the head of a lit cigarette was more than visible.

He was still in his SUV. Still weighing the odds.

Matt kept a basic evidence collection kit in the trunk of his car.

Thinking that it might give Temps a push, he switched on his flashlight and walked back outside. He pulled the murder book out from his case and popped open the trunk. Grabbing the kit, he walked toward the warehouse as if on the trail of discovering new evidence. Once he was inside, he lowered the blue binder and the evidence kit to the ground and opened the case. Then he laid his flashlight beside them and stepped back into the darkness.

He wondered if it would be enough. He took a deep breath, let his mind settle, and peeked around the column.

It worked.

He could see Temps crossing the street. When the detective started walking over the chain-link fence on the ground, Matt spotted the semiautomatic in his right hand.

It suddenly occurred to him that Temps might not be motivated by curiosity. He might have another reason for making a move this risky. Another reason why that gun was in his hand. After all, how could he possibly explain himself? How could he explain why he was even here?

Matt turned back and peered around the column, checking on Temps's progress. The detective looked like he had picked up his pace and was walking with purpose now. And he seemed keenly aware of his surroundings—looking to his left and right and behind his back to make sure they were alone.

Matt pulled out his .45 and chambered a round. He glanced at the bait on the floor—the flashlight set beside the evidence kit and the murder book. And then he turned back, eyeing Temps and waiting. The detective was thirty feet away from the building, then twenty feet, then only ten.

When he stepped into the warehouse, his shadow from the streetlights behind his back stretched across the entire length of the floor. Matt watched him spend a few moments looking around the large empty space with his pistol up and ready. Then the big man's eyes keyed in on the evidence kit.

He walked over to it. He knelt down and gazed inside the case.

And that's when Matt touched the back of his neck with the muzzle of his .45.

"Drop your gun," Matt said. "Drop it, or I'll blow your head off."

Temps froze. "But I'm a cop."

"Then you'll be a dead cop, Temps. I don't give a shit who you are. Drop the goddamn gun!"

Temps let go of his pistol. Matt watched it skid a few feet away, then gave Temps a hard kick between his shoulder blades, knocking the big man down. Matt thought that he looked panic-stricken and let him squirm onto his back before raising the .45 and pointing it at his face.

"Why are you following me, Temps?"

"I'm not."

"Really?" Matt said. "Do you have friends around here?"

Matt could see the concern growing in Temps's eyes. He was watching Matt get into a pair of gloves, then holster his own gun and pick up Temps's semiautomatic.

"Why the gloves?" Temps said in a low voice riddled with fear and suspicion. "What are you doing with my gun?"

Matt gave the pistol a quick look—a 9mm Smith & Wesson 17+1. After checking the large mag, he stepped closer and pointed the gun at Temps's face.

"You're gonna commit suicide tonight, Temps. You're a disgraced cop. You couldn't take it anymore. Being a piece of shit finally got to you. Tonight you decided to do yourself in."

"You're gonna kill me, Jones?"

Matt shook his head. "No," he said. "You are."

"Jesus Christ."

Temps started trembling. From the odd expression on his sweaty face, it seemed clear that he couldn't believe this was happening.

"Before you do it, Temps, before you knock yourself off, I'm gonna need to ask you a few questions."

Temps's eyes got big. "What questions?"

Matt knelt down and looked him in the eye, still pointing the gun at his face. "Who were they?"

Temps shrugged nervously, his eyes dancing between the gun and Matt's eyes. "This is crazy," he said. "Who were who?"

"The victims, Temps. The two people you dumped over the fence right out there. Tina Griffin and her son, Max. Somebody came up with their names. It's either you or whoever's paying you."

"What do you want from me?"

"I want their real names," Matt said. "Now who were they?"

Temps wiped a tear off his cheek. Sweat was percolating all over his forehead.

"Tina Griffin and her son, Max," he said finally.

Matt grimaced, jamming the muzzle of the Smith & Wesson into Temps's mouth and driving the big man's head into the floor. "Do you wanna eat your gun now, Temps? Do you wanna take it deep? What are their names? Think hard, Temps. Think smart."

Matt pulled the muzzle out and struck Temps over the head with the barrel. He watched Temps cringe as he took the blow, then struggle to find his balance and sit up. When Matt began to smell urine, he looked down and saw that the detective was wetting his pants.

A moment passed. Temps's voice changed after that. He became quieter, almost as if he understood that fate had stepped in.

"Would you mind if I had a smoke, Jones?"

"Go ahead."

"The pack's in my shirt pocket. My lighter's there, too."

"Go ahead."

Matt watched the big man reach into his pocket slowly and with great care, then light up and cross his legs. The blood dripping down his forehead didn't seem to bother him, but his eyes remained teary and he kept wiping his meaty cheeks.

"The crime scene out there was a fake, Temps. The girl's home address and apartment on Santa Fe were fake. And her driver's license is so bogus, she couldn't have walked into a bar and bought a drink. Now tell me who she was. I want her real name."

Temps took a long pull on the smoke, his body still trembling from head to toe. "You don't know who you're dealing with," he whispered.

"What?"

Temps met his hard gaze. "You don't know who you're dealing with, Jones. Believe me. The girl and her boy have been dead for three years. In another three years, they'll still be dead. For your own goddamn good, you need to walk away from this one. Take a vacation. Get healthy. Be safe and let it go."

"It's never gonna happen, Temps."

Temps chuckled in irony. "That's what I told them you'd say."

"Who?"

"I'm sure you'll find out someday."

"You're in over your head, Temps. And let's face it, you're no genius. You pulled files out of the murder book and deliberately tried to mislead two murder investigations. When I accused you of dumping the bodies over there, you should have denied it, but you didn't. Are Fresno and Cook in on it, too?"

Temps thought it over as he took another drag on his smoke. "I guess they could be," he said finally. "But to be honest about it, I don't really know. I only know what I'm supposed to know. If I stick my nose in any deeper, they'd kill me."

A moment passed as Matt's wheels turned. He glanced outside at the ruined landscape. Beyond the urban desert of barbed wire and wrecked buildings he could see the skyscrapers towering above downtown LA, so stunning, so close, but so untouchable from here.

"You're not worth killing, you piece of shit," he said finally.

He stood up, weighing the pistol in his hands as he turned back to Temps.

"Does that mean I'm not committing suicide tonight?" Temps whispered in desperation.

Matt ejected the mag, tossing the bullets into the darkness. Then he threw the pistol against the rear wall.

"Not tonight," he said. "Nobody deserves to die in a place like this. Not even you."

TWENTY-SIX

He had spent most of the night tossing it over. He could have killed Temps for a lot of reasons. But by sunrise, he'd come to the conclusion that the detective was worth more alive than dead. And even now as he headed for Manhattan Beach, checking his rearview mirror, he still thought that he'd made the right decision.

Matt had learned something important at that warehouse last night.

Temps's role in the murders went beyond anything he would have expected. The big man hadn't just ripped pages out of a murder book and taken money to look the other way. He had been an active participant in the killings of Tina Griffin and her son. He'd been paid to clean up the crime scene and get rid of the bodies.

A young mother and her three-year-old boy dumped over a fence by an LAPD detective from the elite Robbery-Homicide Division.

Matt doubted that Temps had the intelligence to create new identities for the victims, nor did he think the detective had the talent to make a driver's license with Tina Griffin's name and picture on it—no matter how poor the result turned out to be.

But Temps's had a dark résumé. And it was a safe bet that he knew someone who could have done all those things.

Every one of those things.

Matt let it slide as he made a right onto Manhattan Beach Boulevard and gunned it through the intersection. Despite the risks, he wanted another look at Ryan Brooks's house on the beach before he made contact with Madina in the coroner's office. He needed to walk through the house and refresh his memory of the crime scene. He needed to walk through the murders, one by one, and weigh them beside the murders of Griffin and her son.

It was a cold, breezy morning. As he started down the hill, he could see a rough sketch of the pier lost in the murky fog. It didn't look like a beach day. And when he reached Ocean Drive and slipped into the five-hour lot, he wasn't surprised to find more than half the parking spaces empty.

He glanced at his watch, wanting to make this quick. Grabbing his things, he fed the meter and legged it down the sidewalk. The marine layer was so thick that he could barely see Brooks's house just a half block ahead. After passing the garage, he stopped and checked the street for any evidence that the property might be under surveillance. It didn't seem like a good day for that either. All he could see was a wall of swirling mist.

He turned back to the house, thinking that the place appeared to be lost in a deep sleep. Stepping up to the front door, he glanced at the flowers in the pot—still in full bloom—and shivered.

He took a moment, and then another, before he rang the doorbell and moved over to the window. Cupping his hands around his eyes, he peered through the glass into the foyer and waited for a response that never came. The feeling of stillness seemed so pervasive, the silence so overwhelming, that he guessed things were safe.

He dug the key that he'd taken from Cindy Brooks's key ring out of his pocket and opened the door. Then he stepped inside, locked up as quietly as he had entered, and walked into the kitchen.

The cat's water bowl had been removed, and he could see fingerprint powder on the countertops and drawer handles. The house smelled musty with the faint odor of rotting blood in the air. After a few moments, he became aware of a noise coming from the second floor. It sounded like it might be the tassels from a curtain or blind tapping against a window frame. As he followed the sound up the stairs, the smell of decay became more harsh. And as he reached the landing and stepped into the master bedroom, the odor was wretched.

Matt ignored it as best he could, letting his eyes sweep over the bloodstains on the white carpet until they reached the slider and a small private deck. Someone had left the door cracked open, probably to air out the place.

He looked at the tassels tapping against the door frame and listened to the waves crashing on the beach. And then his eyes drifted over to the dresser against the far wall.

The top drawer was open and filled with jewelry. Necklaces and bracelets were laid out on the dresser's surface side by side beneath a lamp that someone had switched on.

Matt felt his heart begin pounding in his chest as he realized that he wasn't alone. He glanced back at the open slider, then turned toward the bathroom door and quieted his breathing. He could see the shadow of a man on the wall beside the shower. Slowly, and without making any sound whatsoever, he lifted his .45 semiautomatic out of its holster and stepped around the bloodstained carpet where Cindy Brooks had been stabbed to death.

"I know you're in there," Matt said, still eyeballing the man's shadow. "Your best bet is to show yourself with your hands up in the air."

The man didn't respond. A heavy silence took over the room.

"If you need time to think it over," Matt said, "then you're making a big mistake, Mister. Show yourself now, or I'm coming in."

Matt took another step closer, ready to enter and fire his weapon. With the muzzle of his .45 leading the way, he crossed the threshold and began turning toward the intruder.

"It's me, Jones! It's me! Please don't shoot! Don't do it!"

The man stopped shouting. Matt recognized his voice and lowered the pistol.

Vince Sato, the reporter from the *Times*, moved in front of the mirror with his hands raised. His body was shaking, and he looked terrified.

Matt exhaled, miffed. "You could've been killed, Sato. What the hell are you doing here?"

"A favor for Cindy's sister."

"What kind of a favor?" he said. "Come on. Lower your hands and get out of there."

Sato avoided the dried blood and walked through the doorway into the bedroom, his hands still trembling. He wiped the sweat from his cheeks and mouth, glanced at the open dresser drawer filled with jewelry, then tried to meet Matt's gaze but couldn't.

"I'm looking for something," he said.

"What?"

"A piece of jewelry that their father made. He teaches at an art college back east. It had a lot of meaning. Her sister doesn't want it to get lost."

Matt watched Sato find a clean spot on the bed and sit down, then noticed that Ryan Brooks's closet had been left open. Inside he could see racks filled with his shirts and slacks, even a couple of sports jackets. Stepping around the dried pools of blood for a closer look, he glanced over his shoulder at Sato, then started going through the writer's clothing.

"What's the piece of jewelry?"

Sato took a deep breath and tried to calm down. "A brooch," he said. "She wore it all the time."

"She liked it."

"Yeah," Sato said. "It's a replica of the Library Tower downtown. She was an architect—I already told you that. Her dad made it for her. I can't find it anywhere."

Matt shrugged, then spotted something shiny in the breast pocket of a leather sports jacket. He pulled it out and examined it carefully, his imagination suddenly on fire. It was an LAPD badge—something Fresno and Cook or anyone on Speeks's team shouldn't have missed when they processed the house.

"Let me ask you something about your friend, Sato."

"What?"

Matt held the badge in his hand, still staring at it with his back to the reporter. The badge appeared to be so well made that he couldn't tell if was real or not.

"Ryan Brooks," he said. "What kind of a guy was he?"

"A good guy. Why?"

Matt narrowed his eyes, still chewing it over. "Would you say that he had balls?"

"What are you talking about, Jones?"

Matt turned and shot the reporter a look. "Would you say that Ryan Brooks had the brass to impersonate a police officer?"

Sato didn't respond and began shifting his weight on the bed like he might be afraid to answer the question. Matt turned back and went through the leather sports jacket. He found what he was looking for in the left side pocket. It was a leather ID wallet exactly like the one Matt carried. He opened it and read the name.

LAPD Detective Chris Webb, Hollenbeck Station, Major Crimes Unit.

A long moment passed as the revelation settled in.

It had been Brooks who signed in at the property room for a look at Tina Griffin and her son's possessions.

Ryan Brooks.

It took Matt's breath away. It was an illegal act. An outrageous act. And Matt couldn't help but admire him for it.

"What do I do about the brooch?" Sato said.

"The what?"

Sato pointed at the jewelry in the open dresser drawer. Matt's mind surfaced, but only halfway.

"I'm afraid you're out of luck, Sato. Her sister will have to wait."

"Why?"

"If Brooks's wife wore it all the time, then she probably had it on when she was killed. It's evidence now. Just hope that the undertaker doesn't pin it to her chest when he puts her in the box."

Matt pocketed the badge and ID wallet. Then he dug his cell phone out, found Art Madina's number at the coroner's office, and hit "Enter." As he listened to the phone ring, he hustled downstairs, opened the slider, and stepped out into the fog on the main deck. Seven rings went by before Madina finally picked up.

"I need to see you," Matt said. "It's important."

"Tina Griffin and her little boy."

"How did you know?"

"Speeks gave me a heads-up. Two murder cases three years apart, but that's no excuse, Jones. I still can't believe that we missed it."

Matt thought it over as he watched the fog being pushed across the deck by the breeze. It seemed so hypnotic. Two murder cases three years apart.

"I'm on the other side of town," he said. "I'll see you in an hour."

TWENTY-SEVEN

Matt watched Madina pull up a file filled with thumbnail images of the woman known as Tina Griffin and her son, Max. Despite the small size, Matt could see that photographs from the crime scene were included with pictures taken during the two autopsies. Then the medical examiner split the large screen and opened several high-definition shots of Cindy Brooks's neck and upper chest taken at her home and during the autopsy.

Matt rolled a chair over and sat down. Madina turned and gave him a long look.

"How did Tina Griffin come up on your radar, Jones?"

"Her name isn't Tina Griffin," Matt said. "The ID was bogus on both her and the boy."

Madina let go of his keyboard. "Bogus?"

"We don't know who they are, Art. The crime scene, her home address—all of it was made up."

"Everything?"

Matt nodded. "Everything."

The ME suddenly appeared more worried than usual and got up to close the door. When he was interrupted by a colleague in the hall, Matt glanced at the images on the monitor and let his mind wander.

Someone had gone to a lot of trouble to pull these murders off. And

Matt couldn't help thinking how close Brooks must have gotten to spotting the loose ends and tying them up. It seemed obvious that he had been a journalist with courage and focus and, like Matt, would have seen through Temps the moment he first laid eyes on him. Matt had been thinking about it ever since he found Brooks's fake LAPD badge and ID. After meeting Temps, Brooks's next move would have been to hunt down the crime beat reporter at the *Times* who witnessed Speeks and his crew processing the crime scene. As Matt chewed it over, it seemed more than likely that the reporter could have overheard the crime scene techs expressing exactly what Speeks had said yesterday over the phone. The reporter would have told Brooks that many on the crew seemed suspicious from the beginning and thought that Tina Griffin and her son had been murdered somewhere else.

Matt wondered how Brooks came up with the victim's home address but guessed that the crime beat reporter could have given him that information as well. He thought about Monroe, the man who had moved into the apartment on Santa Fe Avenue around the time of the killings. Brooks would have looked at the furnishings in that place and sensed that something was wrong just as Matt had. Maybe that's what pushed him into taking the risk of impersonating a detective and examining Tina Griffin's possessions in the property room.

As Matt played through the events one after the next, he realized that this had to be the pivotal moment.

Once Brooks got a close-up look at the victim's counterfeit driver's license, all of his suspicions would have been confirmed.

The identities of the victims were being covered up. Someone was pulling a lot of weight behind the scenes.

Matt checked on Madina. The ME was still speaking to his colleague in the hallway. By the sound of their voices, Matt assumed that there was a problem of some kind and turned back to the images of the victims on the monitor.

How close did Brooks get?

Did he connect the dots?

Did he figure it out?

Did he identify the killer and make it to the finish line?

Is that why he called and wanted to meet? How did he put it that night on the phone?

From what I've heard, you're still on medical leave, Jones. I was hoping that you might have some free time. The story I'm working on is straightforward enough, but it needs a pair of eyes like yours. A detective's eyes. Someone with your instincts and gift. Someone who can tell me if I'm on the right track or just making things up along the way.

Someone who can tell me if I'm on the right track or just making things up along the way.

It suddenly dawned on Matt that Brooks had to have reached the finish line. He had to have identified the killer. It was the only reason why he would have called Matt for advice that made any sense. Brooks called because the knowledge he had gained must have been frightening. There had to be some outrageous aspect to who murdered the young mother and her son.

But far worse for Brooks and his family, by all appearances he must have tipped his hand. As the writer began connecting the dots, the murderer must have figured out that he'd just been tagged by Brooks. That he needed to protect his secret, come out of the darkness, and strike the journalist with a mortal blow.

The thought had an eerie aftertaste to it that lingered for a while. Then Matt heard the door close and watched Madina slide his stool in front of the oversized monitor on the wall.

"I'm sorry, Jones. Murder's big business again. We're backed up downstairs and trying to sort out schedules."

"I understand."

"Okay," Madina said. "So Tina Griffin is a Jane Doe. For the sake of this meeting, I'm gonna continue to call her Tina Griffin. Is that okay with you?"

Matt nodded. He knew that it would be easier for him as well.

"The reason I asked you how Griffin came up when you first walked into my office is simple enough. Whoever killed Griffin and her son murdered Ryan Brooks and his family."

"I've been there for a while," Matt said. "What matters to me right now is evidence. Two sets of murders, three years apart, one killer. Can you prove it in court?"

Madina picked up a pen, increased the monitor's brightness, and pointed at Tina Griffin's shoulder. Matt rolled his chair closer, stunned. The killer had bitten her. Just like Cindy Brooks, the bite marks began on her shoulder and ran across her upper chest.

"Bite marks," he said as he tried to collect himself.

"They're as good as fingerprints, Jones."

"I don't know what to say."

"They're a perfect match."

Matt let in settle in for a moment. "The original detective, Jack Temps, claims that Griffin was gangbanged. That the damage to her genitals was visible. That she was known in the neighborhood as a drug addict and a prostitute."

Madina opened the file beside his keyboard and turned to the second page. "We did find semen in her body and on her upper thighs, but only from one man. This is from three years back. Speeks made a DNA run against the database of known felons but never got a hit."

"What about the damage to her genitals?" Matt said.

Madina shook his head. "Nothing that you wouldn't find consistent with just having had intercourse. I don't know what he's talking about. The killer ejaculated, and then he murdered her. The damage is to her entire body, and it was caused by a knife. A large knife."

"How many stab wounds, Art?"

"More than Brooks."

"How many more?"

Madina checked his notes again. "The killer stabbed her forty-seven times."

Matt looked away from the monitor as images of what Tina Griffin's last few minutes might have been like began playing in his head. When he pulled himself together, he spoke, but in a lower voice.

"What about drug addiction?" he asked.

Madina frowned as he leafed through the file. "Who's this detective?"

"Jack Temps."

"Well, whoever he is, he must have had really bad information all the way around. No needle marks were found anywhere on her body. Her nasal passages were clean, and she was healthy and in good shape. Her blood was perfect. She had the liver and kidneys, the lungs and heart of a teenage girl. This young woman took care of herself. You just told me that her home address turned out to be bogus. I think we could prove that, too, just by the lack of toxins in her blood. There's no way that she came from the neighborhood where she was found."

Matt sat back in the chair, still eyeing the monitor. Everything Temps had said, every detail, every nuance—all of it had been a lie. He wasn't sure why it surprised him this late in the case. Maybe it was more about the scope of the detective's corruption. The purity of the man's darkness.

"You've got a problem, Jones."

Matt's mind surfaced. Madina was staring at him.

"I know I've got a problem," he said quietly.

"No," Madina said. "I mean you've got a big problem. We counted thirty-seven stab wounds on Ryan Brooks and twenty-three on his wife. On Tina Griffin the killer stabbed her forty-seven times with a knife the size of a bayonet. And what about the infant girl and the little boy? I wish I could say that these are brutal killings because they are. But they're so much more than that. These people were mangled, Jones. Butchered. And this guy's still out there. He's still walking the streets."

Madina's words settled into the room like a radioactive cloud.

Matt could see it happening. He could see it in his head again. Clearer this time, with more detail, just like a wide-screen movie. The woman known as Tina Griffin being stabbed over and over again. He thought that he might be sick. He needed to make it stop and get out of the building. He needed to take a drive and get some fresh air.

TWENTY-EIGHT

Matt squinted as he gazed at the sun just above the western horizon. It was 4:00 p.m. In another hour it would be dark.

He pulled out of the lot onto North Mission Road heading south for a drive that he thought probably included another look at where Griffin and her son had been found. Madina had given him digital copies of the autopsy reports, the same information that Temps had ripped out of the murder book. Matt wanted to park somewhere and spend some time reviewing them from beginning to end. Letting the rush-hour traffic thin out, making a return trip to ground zero, sounded just about right.

The view at this end of the city was horrendous. Despite the wrecked landscape, the two-story piles of who-knows-what dumped on acre after acre of empty lots, he found the ride soothing and tried to focus on what he'd just learned.

He knew that the veil was beginning to come undone. He could feel it in his gut. They had managed to peel away enough layers to begin to understand what had happened. As he mulled it over, he thought about Temps and checked the rearview mirror.

The headlights from the nearest car were at least two blocks behind him. If Temps was out there, if he'd licked his wounds and begun following him again, Matt imagined that he would keep his distance for another day or two. Unless it wasn't about following him, but something else like—

Matt let it go.

The drive to Pico Gardens took another twenty minutes. Passing the warehouse and dirt lot, he swung the car out of the glare from the streetlights and parked in the shadows beside a building across the way. Then he killed the engine and let his eyes skim through the neighborhood. Almost immediately he noticed four people beneath a tent pitched against a wall on Jesse Street. It looked like some sort of makeshift taco stand in the middle of nowhere. Lanterns were hanging from ropes stretched between the tent poles. Remarkably, a tractor trailer had just stopped in the middle of the street, the driver hopping out of his cab to buy food.

Matt slung his laptop case across his shoulder and walked over.

The tent was larger than it first appeared, with enough room for a small propane grill, a three-foot-long counter for assembling food, and a table with its own lantern and six folding chairs. Matt guessed that the middle-aged woman working the grill ran the place with her teenage daughter and that the two men sitting on coolers and wearing Dodger caps were her husband and father. He also guessed that if he unzipped the duffel bag on the ground behind the husband's feet, he would be staring down the barrel of a 12-gauge shotgun.

But what struck Matt most about the place was the food. It looked fresh and smelled good. After the two women sent the truck driver off with his dinner, Matt felt his stomach begin to growl and ordered two chicken tacos with black beans, guacamole, and a cup of coffee. As they built his tacos, he caught the woman's smile and her husband's nod and took a seat at the empty table. By the time his food was plated, he had Madina's autopsy report on Tina Griffin up on his laptop and had already started reading.

What soon became clear was that Madina had more evidence than he had mentioned in his office. The bite marks on Griffin could connect the murders of her and her son to the killings of Ryan Brooks and his family. Based on Griffin's overall good health, the medical examiner could back up the photographs Monroe had given Matt that showed she wasn't from the neighborhood or living anywhere near it. But as Matt paged deeper into Madina's final summary, it looked like the medical examiner could prove that it had been a body dump as well.

Matt finished the first taco, took a sip of coffee while looking around, then returned to the autopsy report.

Griffin's boy had a broken left knee that occurred after his heart had stopped beating. Both knees were marred with deep cuts and dirt stains. His hands and forehead were in the same condition. When compared to the soil in the lot, the lab indicated a perfect match. The boy's mother was in even worse condition after being tossed over the fence. She had been found lying on her back. X-rays taken during the autopsy revealed that her spine was riddled with hairline fractures.

Matt sensed something was wrong and looked up quickly. A black SUV had just blown through the intersection and pulled to an abrupt stop pinning Matt's car to the building across the street.

An Interceptor.

Temps.

But probably not "the follower" this time.

Matt felt the sudden rush of adrenaline. He glanced at the family working the taco stand, the worry showing on their faces clear and overwhelming. As he turned back to the Interceptor, he lowered his right hand below the table and reached underneath his jacket until he felt his pistol.

And then he waited. There would be no mercy tonight.

Several minutes passed. Matt couldn't see what Temps was doing behind the darkened glass. Tightening his grip on the gun, he knew that he would have to make his move the moment the Interceptor's door opened. But when both front doors opened at the same time, he paused long enough to identify two men's faces in the darkness.

Temps must have taken the night off.

Round two belonged to agents Wayne Fresno and Benny Cook from the FBI, staring at him while they waited for another tractor trailer to pass by. The truck lumbered around the corner, and Matt watched them cross the street. He couldn't get over how mean they looked. How obvious it seemed that they wanted to make trouble. Still, he let his hand fall away from his gun, reached for his cup of coffee, and took a sip.

Fresno grabbed a chair and flipped it around, then sat down backward in Matt's face. Cook remained on his feet, trying to intimidate Matt by moving out of his line of vision and standing in the gloom.

The conversation wasn't starting very well.

As Matt steadied his breathing, he watched the man he thought might be married to the woman working the grill get up from his seat on the cooler and move in beside her.

Then Fresno slapped Matt across the face.

Matt took the blow, eyeballing the FBI agent with caution.

"What's with you, punk?" Fresno said. "You afraid of us now?"

Matt remained motionless. Silent. He dropped his right hand below the table and onto his lap.

"What were you doing talking to Madina?" Fresno said in a gruff voice.

"You guys don't have anything better to do than follow me around?"

Fresno leaned closer. "What were you guys talking about?"

Matt kept his mouth shut, trying to get a read on things. He sensed danger but thought that it might be more than that. Everything about them was out of line.

"Two friends catching up," he said finally.

Fresno shot his partner a look, then turned back, tough as nails.

"Two friends catching up," he said. "Did you hear that bullshit, Benny?"

Cook laughed. "Sure did, Wayne. I heard it real good."

Fresno took a moment and appeared to be sizing Matt up. When his dark eyes dropped to the table, he opened his jacket in a deliberate manner, revealing the semiautomatic strapped around his shoulder. Amateur hour. The man was a fool.

"What's your hand doing underneath the table, Jones?"

"I've got no idea what you're talking about."

"Bring it up," he said. "And bring it up slow."

Matt watched the FBI agent's eyes follow the motion of his hand as he raised it off his lap and lowered it to the table.

"Good enough?"

"Better, Jones. Now tell me what you were doing in the property room."

"Who said I was in the property room, Fresno?"

"A little birdie told me," he said. "What are you up to? Why are you working a cold case while you're supposed to be out on leave?"

Matt shrugged and shook his head. "I'm not working anything."

Fresno pointed his index finger at him. "What's the Tina Griffin murder gotta do with the Ryan Brooks killing?"

Matt remained silent. He didn't trust either one of these guys. He didn't know who they were working for. He didn't know how much they were being paid. And like Temps had said last night in the warehouse, everyone involved in the murders had their own role. None of them knew each other, so none of them could testify against one another if it ever came to that. Worse still, everything about right now felt like a fishing expedition. The more Matt knew, the more jeopardy he would be in.

Fresno snapped his fingers. "You didn't hear me, Jones? Then I'll give you another chance. What's the Griffin murder gotta do with what happened in Manhattan Beach?"

Matt grimaced again. "Who says it does?"

Fresno's brutal face flushed with anger. "Maybe we say it does, you little punk. Two kids stabbed to death. Are you saying there's no connection?"

Matt rocked his head back and forth, still eyeballing the man hard. "I'm not saying anything, Fresno."

Matt's cell phone let out a single pulse indicating that he had just received a text message marked "important."

"I've gotta take a look at my phone," he said.

Fresno stood up. "I don't give a shit what you look at, Jones. Come on, Benny. This place stinks. Let's get out of here."

Matt watched Fresno knock the chair down, then join Cook and cross the street. When they drove off, he pulled his phone out and read the text message on the screen.

911. Call me. Sato.

He powered down his laptop and slid it into its case. As he opened his wallet for a twenty-dollar bill, the man standing behind the grill left the woman's side and walked over. He gave Matt a long look.

"Bad men," he said finally in a quiet voice.

Matt met his gaze and nodded. "Very bad men," he said.

TWENTY-NINE

Matt pulled through the intersection and gunned it, heading north on Mission Road for the freeway entrance. As he began using the street's shoulder and even crossed the double yellow line to pass cars, he brought Sato's number up on the dashboard media screen and hit the "Enter" button on his steering wheel. Sato picked up on the first ring and sounded nervous.

"What is it?" Matt said.

"You need to see something," the reporter said in a harried voice.

"What is it, Sato?"

"You need to see it."

Matt passed a Subaru lowrider, the teenage driver making room for him and tapping his horn twice with a wave. Fifty yards ahead Matt could see the freeway entrance closing on him fast.

"Where are you?" he said.

"Brooks's place. I never left."

"It's rush hour. We'll see how it goes."

Sato paused a moment, then spoke in a lower voice. "You need to be careful coming in, Jones. The marine layer's thin tonight. I think someone's out there."

Matt grimaced. "Cops?"

"I don't know," the reporter said. "It's dark, but I'm hearing noises."

Sato was losing it. Matt could tell by the reporter's voice that he was terrified.

"Be cool and sit tight," Matt said. "I'll be there as soon as I can."

Matt ended the call, then hit the freeway entrance, accelerating up the ramp and into heavy traffic. The left lane was reserved for carpoolers. Reaching under the seat, he pulled out an LED light bar, set it on the dash, and plugged it into an outlet below the audio system. Once the lights started flashing, he swerved to the left and barreled up the carpool lane pushing slower-moving cars out of the way. Within thirty-five minutes he had reached Manhattan Beach Boulevard, switched off the light bar, and slowed down to a cruising speed that wouldn't attract attention.

Sato had been right. The fog remained but had thinned some. As he started coasting down the hill, he looked at Brooks's house, noted that the windows were dark, and began to feel even more uneasy about things. Trying to keep his imagination reined in, he checked the parking lots but didn't see anything out of the ordinary or anyone who stood out. Still, he turned down Ocean Drive, passing the house slowly and cruising around the block for a second look. When he circled back to Manhattan Beach Boulevard, he drove straight down the hill to the metered lot by the bike path on the sand.

Half the spaces were empty. Matt killed the engine, spending several minutes looking things over. With the lights out, and through the dark mist, Brooks's house had that spooky feel to it again. Matt pulled out his cell phone, found Sato's number on his call list, and hit "Enter." Just as before, the reporter picked up on the first ring and sounded panic-stricken.

"You're still alive," Matt said in a low voice.

"That's not funny, Jones."

"It wasn't meant to be, but you're sitting in the dark."

"I've got a flashlight."

"What about those noises you said you were hearing?"

"They come and go."

"What about now?"

"Everything's quiet."

"Good," Matt said. "Where are you in the house?"

"Brooks's study by the front door."

"I'm on my way in."

Matt ended the call as he ripped open the glove compartment and grabbed his flashlight. Sliding his laptop case beneath the passenger seat, he fished the key to Brooks's house out of his pocket and locked up the car.

He took a moment to scan the property, then used the walkway and started up the hill beside the house. Hopping over the fence, he hustled through the garden, pushed open the gate in the privacy wall, and found himself standing before the front door. Once he was inside, he gazed through the doorway into Brooks's study and saw a male figure sitting on the couch.

"Is that you, Sato?"

A flashlight switched on. "It's me," the reporter said in a subdued voice.

Matt entered the room, turning on his own flashlight and pointing it in the reporter's face.

"You're scaring the shit out of me, man. What is all this? What's so important that you couldn't tell me about it on the phone?"

Sato got up and crossed the room to Brooks's desk. "Because you have to see it with your own eyes."

"See what?"

Sato handed Matt a file folder. "The reason why Brooks and his wife and child were murdered."

It hung there in the darkness. In the dead air scented with the dead family's spoiled blood.

Matt sat down at the desk and opened the file. Within a heartbeat he realized that Sato had found Brooks's working file on the murders of Tina Griffin and her son. Notes were included that covered the reporter's first impression of Temps after meeting him at a diner. For reasons Brooks didn't understand at the time, the detective had refused to meet him at the Topanga station, citing the need for privacy.

Matt didn't find any of what he'd just read surprising.

But then he flipped the page over to reveal a series of eight-by-ten color photographs. He panned his flashlight over the images and studied them carefully.

They were photographs of the governor of California, James D.

Hayworth, with his staff at an outdoor event. It looked like they were on the field at a park and had brought in a professional pitmaster to slow-roast an entire pig. The gathering appeared informal, and Matt guessed that it had been something put together for an advertising campaign or a fundraiser.

Brooks had used a yellow marker to circle two people of interest, and as Matt's eyes zeroed in on their faces, the shock almost knocked him down.

They were photographs of the woman known as Tina Griffin, holding her infant son Max, and standing by the governor's side as he greeted supporters and waved them toward the picnic tables.

Matt gasped and turned to Sato, whom he found standing beside him in the darkness training his flashlight on the photos and mesmerized by them.

"Where did you find the file?"

"Hidden under a set of towels in the linen closet upstairs," the reporter said. "You need to keep going."

Matt pushed the photographs aside to reveal two more. The first was a close-up shot of the governor's face. The second was a shot of Griffin's son, a blowup of his face that had been time stamped.

Matt could feel his body beginning to tighten up, the hairs on the back of his neck standing on end.

The snapshot of the boy had to have been taken shortly before his murder. He would have been three years old at the time and no longer an infant. But Brooks had a good reason for magnifying the image. The boy's features were beginning to shine through. His eyes. His nose and chin. Even his cheekbones and the plain of his face.

"He was a love child," Matt whispered.

Sato nodded. "He had to be," he said. "With all of his father's features. Look at their eyes. They're identical."

"So who's the woman?"

"There's a copy of the birth certificate deeper in the file. Her real name was Emily Kosinski."

"And her boy?"

Sato gave him a long look. "David."

Matt leaned back in the chair and let it settle in. David was the governor's middle name.

After a while, he glanced at the file and saw Brooks's handwritten notes on the victim's background. But instead of trying to decipher the reporter's scrawl in the bad light, he turned back to Sato.

"Tell me about Emily Kosinski. Who was she?"

"According to Brooks, she was a smart twenty-eight-year-old woman with a three-year-old love baby. She had a master's degree in poly sci from Michigan University."

Matt gave Sato a look. "You've got a shitty poker face, Sato. You're holding back something. I can see it clear as day."

Sato nodded again, his hands trembling. When he spoke, he could barely get it out.

"Emily Kosinski and Governor Hayworth spent a lot of time together, Jones. She was his intern."

Matt took a deep breath and shook his head. Then he got up and walked out of the room. He needed air. Fresh air.

He crossed through the great room, opened the slider, and stepped out onto the deck. Obviously, Emily Kosinski wasn't a doper or a whore or any other thing that had come out of Temps's dirty mind. She had been a woman with brains who was on her way to places. But even more, she was a young woman having an affair with a powerful man who had serious psychological issues.

A vicious killer.

A man who had stabbed her with a knife the size of a bayonet over and over again. A man who, as Madina put it, couldn't stop.

A memory surfaced. A series of moments when he saw the governor at the LAPD fundraiser. The odd way that Alan Fontaine had kept looking at Matt as he spoke with Lisa Hayworth, the governor's wife, at the bar. That strange moment when the governor sensed Matt's presence and had turned his back to avoid greeting him.

Obviously, Temps had reported back to them that Matt showed up at the Topanga station last week and wanted to know about the murders. That he had taken what was left of the murder book.

As Matt considered Brooks's investigation, it all rang true. There had to be some outrageous aspect to the identity of the killer and there was. On the night of the fundraiser, the governor and his fixer knew that Matt had reopened the case and their secret was in jeopardy of being exposed.

It suddenly occurred to Matt that the governor's wife might be in trouble. She had mentioned something about being afraid of Fontaine. That something had happened a few years back that changed things. She couldn't be sure of the exact date or even the timing. All she knew was that something had happened in their lives and it frightened her. Matt could remember asking her if she felt safe, but they had been interrupted. Lisa never answered the question.

Now he knew what had happened in their lives. Now he knew why things had changed. A double murder had occurred, and Lisa was living with the killer.

THIRTY

Temps lowered his head below the dashboard as they walked out of Brooks's place. He was parked behind a row of trash cans on the other side of Manhattan Beach Boulevard, invisible in the shadows and lost in the dark mist. But his view was crystal clear, and the file folder he saw Jones carrying out of the house looked like trouble.

They'd found something.

He could see it in their smug faces as they made their way down the hill to the lot on the beach.

Temps dug into the grocery bag on the passenger seat and fished out one of the six mini Jamesons he'd bought at the market that afternoon. Twisting off the cap, he poured the shot of Irish whiskey into his thermos filled with lukewarm coffee and took a long swig.

He could feel his stomach begin to glow. But then the coughing started, and all the wheezing, and he tried to force himself to relax. All of a sudden it looked like he might have a lot to do tonight—a lot on the line—and he needed to pace himself. Like the governor, he needed this to go away.

Jones was the first to pull out of the lot. Once he crossed Ocean Drive and vanished into the traffic on the boulevard, Temps sat up in the seat and turned to watch the journalist in his white Audi exit the lot and start up the hill.

Temps checked the time and let ten seconds roll off before he pulled his black Interceptor out of the gloom and brought the SUV up to speed. Spotting Sato's Audi a block ahead, he backed off the gas and let several cars pull in between them. He could afford to lie low because he knew that in all probability, Sato was heading for only one of two places. The *Times* building by LAX was one choice. But it was after seven, and Temps guessed that the reporter's home in Santa Monica would be the more likely destination. And that made everything a lot easier. Central Dispatch had sent Temps a copy of Sato's driver's license two days ago. He had the man's home address and knew the neighborhood like the back of his hand.

He pushed through the next intersection, took another long swig of his spiked coffee, and looked for a tell. It came as the Audi passed the airport and continued north on Lincoln Boulevard.

Sato was on his way home—no doubt about it—and Temps glided into the right lane and slowed the Interceptor down. It was the smart move. Temps knew that his SUV had a way of standing out, and there was no upside to being noticed tonight. But even more, he wanted the reporter to get home and begin to relax. He wanted Sato to drop his guard.

He watched the Audi pick up speed and begin weaving through the congestion. It looked like Sato was anxious to close out his day. After a few more blocks Temps lost sight of the car and switched on the radio to a country station.

It took three songs by older artists he had never heard of and fifteen commercials for products he would never buy to reach Santa Monica. He didn't mind really and, to some degree, found the sound soothing. As he made the turn off Fourth Street, he spotted Sato's car in the circular driveway and found a place to park three doors down. Knocking back a last gulp of coffee, he slipped on a pair of gloves and grabbed the gym bag off the passenger-side floor.

It was a cold and breezy night, the marine layer just thickening enough to provide cover. Temps could remember the street from his days wearing a uniform when he often worked in tandem with the Santa Monica police. But as he started down the sidewalk, something was different about the neighborhood tonight. Even through the mist, it seemed like it had been painted and polished and received some sort of upgrade.

Sato's house was on the other side of the street just ahead, and he stopped to give it a steady up and down. It was a single-story Mediterranean with stucco walls, a clay tiled roof, and a two-car garage. From the bluish light flickering through the palm trees above, Temps realized that there was a pool behind the house. Like most homes in Los Angeles, everything inside the place would be oriented toward the backyard, not the front.

And while that might stand in his favor tonight, there was a lot more to it than that. There was a bad vibe here. And he'd sensed it almost immediately.

He looked at the entrance. Sato appeared to be airing out the place. While the screen door was closed and most likely locked, the front door stood wide open. He checked his back, then crossed the street and walked up the driveway. Once he reached the front steps, that bad feeling hit him in the gut again.

Every window was lit, every curtain drawn, and it seemed so unnatural to him. From where he was standing it was virtually impossible to pin down where Sato might be in the house.

He crept up the steps to the screen door and peered inside. The front rooms to the left and right were clear. At the other end of the foyer he could see the kitchen. The overhead lights were on, and the faint sound of a TV filled in the background. Still, there was no sign of Sato. No presence or feel to the place. Though the reporter might be in the back by the pool, the air seemed too chilly, and Temps didn't think he could count on it.

He flicked a credit card down the seam between the lock and doorjamb, opened the screen door, and stepped inside. Digging into his gym bag, he drew out a 9mm Beretta already fixed with a sound suppressor and hoped that he wouldn't have to use it right away.

He needed answers tonight. Some idea of what these guys—

The gym bag slipped out of his hand and hit the floor.

Temps cringed at the sound, then slung the bag over his shoulder and tried to focus. Underneath the sound of the TV he could hear the refrigerator and an ice maker. Below that, he picked up the low rumble from a small motor that he couldn't identify. But he didn't hear footsteps. He couldn't hear a human being moving around. Sato hadn't reacted to the sound his gym bag made when it fell onto the floor.

He kept reminding himself that this was a death penalty case. If he screwed things up, he'd burn. He kept playing the words in his head.

He moved down the foyer in silence and stopped in the doorway, eyeballing the kitchen. The TV was mounted on a wall by the dining area, with a laptop computer set on the table and in the process of starting up. On the counter by the sink he saw a sandwich on a plate beside a glass and bottle of beer. But then he became aware of that sound again. It was louder here. Scanning the room one more time, his eyes stopped on the bright light beneath a doorway. He shook his head when he figured it out. Sato was in the bathroom with the exhaust fan running.

Maybe the bad vibe had passed. Maybe he was in the clear.

Temps lowered his gym bag onto the table, stepped over to the bathroom, and listened. After giving himself a few moments to chill, he wrapped his hand around the door handle and started to turn—

"Can I help you?" Sato said.

Temps froze. The reporter's voice wasn't coming from the other side of the closed door. It had been a scam. Sato was standing in the hallway behind his back. Somehow, the reporter had known that he was in the house.

"I'm armed," Sato continued. "Before you turn around, before you try anything crazy, you might want to get rid of the gun you're holding."

Temps chewed it over for a while, then lowered his piece to the floor and turned around. Sato was pointing a 9mm Glock at him. Still, Temps thought that he might have the upper hand. The reporter had no idea that Temps's service pistol was strapped to his shoulder beneath his jacket. All he needed was a little time.

Temps glanced at the Glock, then sized up his opponent in quick chunks. Sato was smaller than him. Easily a hundred pounds lighter. Though it looked like he worked out, he appeared too heady to be street tough. Too wordy to come through during a physical crisis. He glanced back at the gun, then Sato's face.

"Are you sure you know how to use that thing, pal?"

"You're not my pal," Sato said. "And with any luck, I won't have to."

Temps watched the reporter enter the room and reach for a telephone on the counter. When he turned the phone over and his eyes moved to the keypad, Temps made his move, lowering his shoulder and charging forward like a bull. He saw the phone drop away as they tumbled onto the floor. He could even see Sato pointing the Glock at him and repeatedly trying to fire the weapon. Unfortunately for the reporter, in the heat of the moment his finger appeared to have slipped off the trigger and he kept pressing the guard.

Temps yanked the gun out of his hand and tossed it on the other side of the room. Then he grabbed Sato's head and banged it into the floor. The reporter was no more match than a young teen now. Without the gun, he appeared terrified—and they were eye to eye.

"How much do you guys know?" Temps growled through his teeth.

"Nothing," Sato managed. "Nothing at all."

Temps banged his head into the floor again, harder this time. "How much do you guys know?"

"Nothing. I swear. We're stumped, Temps. We can't get anywhere."

"You're lying to me, Sato. And I'm not buying it. It's not gonna work. What was in the file Jones carried out of the house tonight?"

Sato shook his head, feigning complete ignorance. His face had turned red, his eyes glassy, and he kept trying to squirm away. Temps grabbed his shoulders and drove his back into the floor.

"What was in the file, you piece of shit?"

"I don't know," he said. "Please don't do this. Please don't hurt me."

Temps reached beneath his jacket for his Smith & Wesson service pistol and jammed the muzzle into Sato's mouth. Now the reporter was weeping and yelping. Temps pushed the gun in deeper until Sato started choking on it.

"You're still bullshitting me, Sato. And all you're doing is making me angry. It's up to you. Talk, and I'll go away. Keep your mouth shut, and I'll pull the trigger eighteen times. Nobody will be able to fix you after that. They'll clean up the mess with a mop and a bucket of Mr. Clean. Party over."

Sato's hands wrapped around the semiautomatic as he strained to pull it out of his mouth. "Okay," he was trying to say. "Okay."

Temps eased up on the gun, still overtop the man.

"Talk," he said. "Now."

Sato was hyperventilating and still weeping. Mucus dripped out of his nose and mouth as his eyes lost their focus and crashed onto the floor.

"We know everything," he said finally. "Governor Hayworth had an affair with his intern, Emily Kosinski. She got pregnant and had the child. When the boy began to look like his father, when people started to notice, the governor freaked out and killed them."

Sato's eyes met Temps's fierce gaze, but only for a second before dropping back onto the floor.

"That's it, Temps," he said. "That's everything. That's all we know."

Temps inched his face closer. "That's not it. That's not everything. Now give it up, or you're done."

Sato looked at the gun in Temps's hand, then glanced at the man's face. The detective's eyes had gone dead.

"You helped the governor cover it up," he said finally. "You got rid of the bodies, Temps. Because of you, the case disappeared."

"What about Ryan Brooks? Who else knows?"

Sato didn't answer the question but turned to Temps and grimaced like he might just be thinking, *What a prick!*

Temps clenched his teeth and poked him in the cheek with the gun. "Who else knows, Sato? Who else knows?"

The reporter shrugged and turned away, and Temps couldn't take it anymore. Holstering his service pistol, he plunged his right fist into Sato's jaw. It was a harsh blow. So raw that Sato's body jerked upward and went limp on impact.

Temps slapped him across the face just to make sure that he was really unconscious. When the reporter didn't respond, Temps crossed the room and ripped open his gym bag. He pulled out a full-body hazmat suit. He had bought a dozen of them on the internet for $14.95 each during a Christmas sale last month. It was made of a thin plastic and meant to be tossed out after a single use. As he got into the suit and tied the hood over his head, he checked on Sato and thought about his next move. Temps knew that he hadn't touched anything and that even if he had, he'd been wearing gloves since he got out of the Interceptor. Still, he might have left something of himself behind during the struggle.

He grabbed Sato by the feet, dragged his limp body to the other side of the room, and dumped it. Then he opened the cabinet below the sink and found a bottle of kitchen cleaner and a roll of paper towels. With great care he sprayed the floor and wiped it down, tossing the handful of paper towels he'd used in the toilet and flushing them away.

The bathroom light and fan were still on, and he switched them off. When he noticed the overhead lights in the kitchen, he turned those off as well and crossed the room to the dining area. Sato's laptop had completed its boot sequence. After shutting the computer down, he stuffed it into his gym bag along with Sato's gun, then leaned over and picked the 9mm Beretta up off the floor. As if a matter of habit, he checked the fit of the sound suppressor and knew that he was finally ready.

He took deep breath and crossed himself with a grim expression on his face. Pointing the weapon at its mark, Temps started walking toward Sato just as the reporter began to stir. Just as he opened his eyes and raised his hands in the air.

Temps pulled the trigger six times as he crossed the room.

He felt the blood spatter strike the hazmat suit and looked at the spray pattern all over the cabinets and walls. Chaos in motion.

Temps stopped at Sato's feet and gazed down at the reporter's dead body. His eyes were still open. It looked like he was staring at a ceiling a hundred miles away. Maybe even the stars in the sky through the roof. Blood had already begun pooling on the floor.

Temps collected the shell casings, dumping them into a plastic sandwich bag and sealing the top. As he grabbed his gym bag and left the house, he couldn't help thinking that he wished Sato hadn't opened his eyes. But by the time he got out of the hazmat suit and reached the 405 Freeway heading for the Valley, the thought vanished and was replaced by a new one.

He could remember switching off the lights and locking the front door. But he thought maybe he'd forgotten to turn off the TV.

THIRTY-ONE

Matt couldn't place the tremor rolling through his body. It had come on suddenly. A deep wave of emptiness enveloping his core. A darkness as true and pure and palpable as a midnight sky without any stars. He wasn't sure where it had come from. And after several minutes, it vanished, and he couldn't be sure where it had gone.

If Dr. May had asked him to describe the moment, he might have said that it felt like a premonition. Like something horrible had just happened, or was about to happen, somewhere in the world.

It felt like dread.

He was sitting in his car on a narrow street in the hills off Beachwood Drive—above the market and café, but lower than the Hollywood Sign built just below the peak of the mountain.

He checked the street in the gloom and eyed the houses.

He had run Emily Kosinski's name and found her former home in Hollywood Hills. While he didn't see much purpose in entering the place, at least for the time being, he had matched the property with both the address on her real driver's license and the pictures Monroe had given him. The house and views out the windows were identical. There could no longer be any doubt. The governor's intern had lived here in the canyon and not in a rundown apartment on South Santa Fe Avenue in Pico Gardens.

Matt pulled the charging cable out of his cell phone and found

Governor Hayworth's field office in LA on the state's website. It was a few minutes after eight. Despite the hour, he knew that the underlings in government offices worked into the night and that most likely he wouldn't have any trouble reaching someone. He also knew that for a call like this one, the lower they were in the food chain, the better off he would be.

All he wanted was the "official line." The story that the governor had come up with to explain his intern's disappearance.

Matt paused a moment to go over what he might say. To play it safe, he thought that he should probably pretend to be someone else. After a while he decided to use the name Ryan Brooks had invented when he impersonated an LAPD detective. Once he was ready, he pressed the link on the governor's website and brought the phone to his ear. Three rings went by before a woman with a middle-aged voice took the call.

"Governor Hayworth's office," she said. "Los Angeles."

Matt looked out the window at Emily Kosinski's former home, thinking about her and her little boy, David.

"Hello," Matt said. "This is Chris Webb. I'm a friend of Emily's. We studied political science at Michigan together. I'm trying to reach her. I called her home number, but it must have been changed. I was hoping she was still at work."

The woman didn't respond. Matt thought that the call might have been dropped.

"Hello," he said. "Are you there?"

"Yes, of course," the woman said finally. "Your name again?"

"Chris Webb. Me and Emily go way back."

She cleared her throat. When she spoke, Matt could hear the emotion in her voice. A certain degree of gentleness mixed with sadness.

"When was the last time you spoke to Emily, Chris?"

"It's been a long time," Matt said. "Three years maybe. I've been overseas."

"You're a soldier?"

"I was in Afghanistan."

It sounded like the woman was closing her door. "She doesn't work here anymore, Chris."

"That's okay," Matt said. "Did she leave a phone number, or even better, a new email address?"

"I'm afraid not."

Matt could tell that the woman was becoming distressed now. It occurred to him that this call was more important than he had first imagined. It was part of the crime. A picture of the murder from a different angle.

"Do you remember when she left?" he said.

The woman cleared her throat again. "About three years ago. I remember it being quite sudden."

"What happened?"

"Her mother passed away. She needed to help her father."

"Do you know where?"

"No," the woman said. "She never came back to the office. She never wrote or called to let anyone know."

"If she didn't call or write, who told you that she left?"

"The governor's attorney," she said. "Mr. Fontaine. He emptied her desk, packed up her things, and sent them to her."

THIRTY-TWO

Dots were connecting. Confirmations being made.

Matt sat in the waiting room outside Dr. Julie May's office. It was 10:00 a.m., and the male receptionist, an obvious cop who had drawn desk duty, had just told him that the psychiatrist was running late with her first patient today.

Matt found a seat in the empty room and eyed the magazines on the table with no interest. When he looked up at the walls, he began to feel like they were pressing in on him. Despite the receptionist's odd glances his way, he got up and started pacing. Still, he couldn't shake the feeling of being closed in and wondered if he shouldn't just call off the appointment and reschedule it for next week.

Not that a delay would have really mattered.

He had spent the night reading Brooks's file from beginning to end. It seemed clear to Matt that Brooks knew exactly what he had and that what he really wanted from Matt was some sort of backup before he told the world that the governor of California, a man who most people believed was destined to become the next president of the United States, had an affair and love child with his intern, then snapped and brutally stabbed them to death. Brooks would've needed hard evidence before he broke a story like that. Something irrefutable to box the governor in and beat back the tidal wave that would come from the cable news channels and social media outlets that supported him.

Knowledge could be frightening, and Matt imagined that Brooks was in a very dark and lonely place when he called and asked to meet. A dark and lonely place the night that turned out to be the last night of his life.

But that wasn't what had been preying on Matt's mind all morning.

As he read through Brooks's notes last night, he had tried to reach Vince Sato, and the reporter never returned his call.

Reporters always returned their calls. It was who they were. It was an inherent part of their being.

When Matt tried again this morning and Sato didn't pick up or call back, that uneasy feeling in his gut evolved into full-blown fear. It had happened to him before. It had happened less than a month ago during the Love Killings in Philadelphia, and the outcome hadn't turned out very well.

He knew that he couldn't do anything about it for several hours. That he would have to control himself. Still, he needed to get out of this room. He needed to get out of the building.

He walked over to the reception desk. But before he could say anything, the man hung up the phone and said, "The doctor will see you now."

Matt turned just as he heard a door opening and saw Dr. May giving him a long look. After hesitating a moment—after realizing that he had been snared—he entered her office and listened to the door close behind his back.

"I don't have time for this," he said. "Not now. Not today, Doctor."

He turned and found her still appraising him.

"We should reschedule," he continued. "Anytime next week is good for me. You name it, and I'll be here."

She lowered her brow, still measuring him. "You name it, and I'll be here?" she repeated in a sarcastic voice.

There was a door on the far wall that opened into the hallway so patients could avoid exiting through the waiting room. Matt ignored the doctor's attitude and started heading for the door. But before he could even get going, Dr. May stepped in his way and hit him with those eyes of hers. Matt found it difficult to look away from her and watched as she took his hands and began examining them.

"You're a wreck," she said. "You've got dark circles under your eyes, and your fingers are trembling."

His eyes danced over her face. He had thoughts and feelings about her that he knew he shouldn't have, but he couldn't help it today. He tried to ignore them and step away, but she moved even closer, turned his hands over, and tightened her grip.

"I've got a lot going on right now," he said.

She shook her head and met his gaze. "You need to end this right now, Matthew. Let the FBI do their job. Let them handle it."

"I can't," he said. "It's too late. It's bigger than that now."

"Tell me."

"I wish I could, but you wouldn't be safe."

She frowned with uncertainty, like she didn't believe him. Like maybe Matt was circling the drain and making all this up in his head. She didn't say the words, but Matt could see them on the tip of her tongue.

Post-traumatic stress disorder.

A textbook case.

"It's not what you're thinking," he said.

"Then come sit with me on the lounge and tell me what I'm thinking."

He looked at the lounge beside her desk. "I can't," he said.

"Yes, you can. For a little while you can."

She led him across the room. Matt lay back on the lounge, watching Dr. May roll over her chair and sit down beside him.

"Tell me," she said in a softer voice.

"I can't. I won't. It's not safe."

She spent a moment mulling it over. "You're not ready for this, Matthew."

"You might be right about that."

She shook her head, still eyeing him carefully. "This was supposed to be our time together. Talk time. Healing time. Once a week."

He looked at her, wrestling with all the heat that suddenly seemed to be invading the room.

"Are you talking to me as a doctor or as a woman—Doctor?"

She smiled as if taken by surprise, then leaned back slightly. "A little of both, Matthew. But mainly as your friend. I'm worried about you. If you don't take care of yourself, who will?"

THIRTY-THREE

As he started down the hall to Speeks's office in the Forensic Science Center, he gave Sato one more try. The phone rang twice before being directed to the *Times*'s voice messaging system. When the computer indicated that Sato's mailbox was full, it gave Matt chills.

Something had happened. Something hideous and grim.

He tried to let it go but realized that the worry had become so real and deep, it might as well have been his own shadow.

He looked down the hall, saw Speeks wave from his desk, and hustled the rest of the way. He had called ahead for the meeting the moment he had left Dr. May. Although Speeks sensed the urgency in his voice and wanted to know more, Matt had refused to tell the criminalist anything over the phone.

Matt entered Speeks's office and closed the glass door. After a quick look around, he sat down in the chair.

"Is it safe in here?" he said.

Speeks gave him an odd look. "Safe?"

"Yeah," Matt said. "Do you think we're safe? Do you think anyone can hear us?"

Speeks's odd look deepened. "What's this about, Jones?"

"That murder case three years ago. Tina Griffin and her little boy, Max."

"What about it?"

"Their identities were made up. Everything about them. Their names, their backgrounds, even where they lived—it was all part of a cover-up."

Speeks leaned his elbows on the desk. "A cover-up?"

"Has Madina said anything to you?"

"Not yet."

"Well, I'll explain everything later. What I need right now is a favor."

"What's going on, Jones?"

Matt glanced through the glass door as a man and a woman dressed in scrubs walked down the hall. When they were gone finally, he turned back to the criminalist.

"For now, the less you know, the better," he said. "If you trust me, that's all that matters."

Speeks appeared confused, maybe even suspicious. But when he spoke, he did it quietly.

"What do you want me to do?"

Matt slid his chair closer to the desk. "You ran your DNA samples against known criminals. Felons."

Speeks narrowed his eyes. "That's right. We had his semen. We went nationwide but never got a hit. The killer's not in the system."

"I want you to make another run, Speeks. But this time I want you to do side by sides using samples from Griffin, her son, and the killer."

"Against the same list?" he said. "Felons?"

Matt shook his head back and forth. "No, Speeks. This time you're gonna make the run against all known state employees. Everyone from the bottom to the top."

It hung there—far too ominous to settle in.

This was exactly what Ryan Brooks would have needed to knock down a heavyweight like the governor. Not circumstances. Not guesses or theories, no matter what they might have been based on. In a murder case this egregious, the only thing with enough juice to move the bar would be facts. Science. Evidence that was ironclad and inarguable.

"State employees?" Speeks said in an even quieter voice.

Matt nodded. "And if you get a hit, it's gonna be heavy. You gotta do this yourself, Speeks. You can't use a tech. No one else can be involved on any level. No one else can know what you're doing."

"You're freaking me out, Jones."

Matt knew that he had spooked the man but ignored it and pushed on. "If you get a hit, you need to bury the report somewhere in the system. Then find a place where you can't be overheard or even seen. Call me, but not on a landline. Use your cell and call me on mine."

Speeks stared at him for a while. "You know who it is, don't you."

Matt didn't say anything and got up from the chair.

Speeks kept his eyes on him. "You already know that I'm gonna get a hit, Jones. You know who killed these people."

Matt started for the door, then turned back. "Just be careful, Speeks. And make the run as soon as you can."

THIRTY-FOUR

Temps peered into the lab through the plate-glass window. It looked like Speeks was sorting through blood samples at the counter. Speeks was a criminalist, not a lab technician, and would have no reason to be working with samples of any kind. Worse still, while the man's face was hidden behind a protective mask and plexiglass shield, his eyes said everything Temps needed to know.

Something important was underway. Something secret and bound in urgency. And it started the moment Jones had walked out of Speeks's office and exited the building.

Temps had been at it all morning—bleary-eyed, but on the job. His first stop of the day had been to a government building just west of Chinatown. He had watched Jones pull into the underground garage and park, holding a cell phone to his ear and totally preoccupied by the call. But even better, Temps had made it into the lobby just in time to see the detective ride an elevator that stopped on the sixth floor. According to the building directory, the LAPD's Behavioral Science Services had opened a new suite of offices on the sixth floor.

Jones was seeing a therapist.

Temps could remember feeling uncertain about this. He could remember walking outside and finding a place to sit under the trees by a water display and staring at the fish. After waiting until he thought Jones's therapy session might have started, he found the number on the LAPD website and called the reception desk. When he asked to speak with the detective, he received the answer he had been dreading.

Detective Jones couldn't be reached right now. Detective Jones was meeting with—Dr. May.

Dr. Julie May.

Jones really was seeing a therapist. A psychiatrist, no less. A doctor. A confidant. One of the few people in the world Jones might trust enough to talk about his private matters. His personal issues.

His secrets.

Temps's body shuddered, his mind breaking back to the present. Speeks was moving the samples to a temperature-controlled rack in one of the refrigerated cases mounted on the wall above the counter. Closing the glass doors, the criminalist started to get out of his protective gear.

Temps stepped away from the window and into an empty office across the hallway. Standing in the darkness, he watched Speeks hang up his smock and peek out the door. When two lab techs passed by and turned the corner, the criminalist lowered the lights in the lab and rushed down the hallway like he had just robbed a bank.

Everything about Speeks's behavior, everything that Temps had just witnessed, looked more than suspicious.

Temps crept back across the hall and entered the lab. He could feel his heart pounding as he lifted the tray out of the refrigerated racks and began reading the labels in the light feeding into the room through the window and door.

Sato had been telling the truth last night. Jones had figured it out. And now he was hoping that Speeks could give him the proof he needed.

DNA evidence. The stuff juries eat up like candy.

Speeks was preparing to make another run with blood samples taken from the governor's former intern and her son—both listed under the false names they had been given, Tina and Max Griffin. Beside these were a third set of samples—the semen left behind by the killer—which Temps knew would point to the man who fathered the boy: the governor himself.

Temps started wheezing. Everyone involved in the murders would get the needle. Every one of them would die.

He stared at the samples as the horror of his own death began to settle in. The inner certainty he had that when he got to Heaven's Gate, he would be rejected and thrown down the rathole to hell. The idea of spending eternity with every asshole he had ever beaten up, shot dead, or arrested. His gaze began to lose its focus, then sharpened again as he thought about Matt Jones.

This was all his fault. All his doing.

A cop on medical leave sticking his nose where it didn't belong. And what about his big mouth? My God, how much of this had he told his stupid shrink?

Temps pulled out his cell phone and entered the first number on his "Recent Calls" list. When the receptionist picked up, he turned and kept his eyes on the hallway outside the lab. His fingers were quivering, and he tried to calm down.

"This is Detective Jack Temps from the Topanga station," he said. "I'd like to make an appointment with Dr. May."

The receptionist cleared his throat. "You'd have to talk to her first."

"It's important," he said. "Is she available?"

"She's between appointments but let me check."

Temps winced, then began eyeing the trays of samples from other cases in the refrigerated racks. He pulled one out and examined it closely. They were blood and semen samples sorted by gender and type. When he found two that might work, he put them aside and returned to the blood sample Speeks had listed under Max Griffin's name. Using his thumbnail, he peeled off the fresh label just as the phone clicked.

"This is Dr. May," the psychiatrist said. "What seems to be the problem, Detective?"

Temps curled his lips in the gloom. He had taken a chance by using his real name because he knew that he had to, and it had paid off. He could tell by the sound of the psychiatrist's voice that Jones had never mentioned him by name before.

"I'm sad, Doctor. Really depressed."

"We all go through that from time to time," she said in a gentle voice.

"Especially when the days get shorter during the winter months."

Temps looked back at the two samples he had pulled from an unknown case and covered the first label with the one he'd just removed from Max Griffin's blood sample.

"Working for the department isn't fun anymore," he said in a low voice that rattled. "I don't feel appreciated by the people I work with, Doctor. I want to get on my feet again."

"I understand," Dr. May said. "It almost feels like you're stuck in reverse."

Temps noticed a benchtop magnifier on the counter. Switching on the light, he peeled off the label from the semen sample he knew would point to the governor and used it to cover the label from the second unknown sample he'd selected.

"Exactly," Temps said as he smoothed down the label and inspected his work. "Like I'm stuck in reverse. I want to feel good about myself when I get up in the morning. I need your help, Doctor. I need it bad. I want to come in before I do something stupid. Before I hurt myself."

"What are your hours, Detective?" Dr. May said.

"I'm working undercover right now. It's a pretty big case. It would have to be after hours."

"I can do that," she said. "What about tonight?"

Temps returned the blood and semen samples to both trays, placed them back in the refrigerated racks, and switched off the light on the magnifier.

"That would be great," he said.

"How's seven sound?"

Temps moved out of the darkness to the door, checked the hallway, and stepped out of the lab.

"It sounds like I'm on the road to recovery," he said. "See you tonight."

THIRTY-FIVE

Matt measured Sato's house as he drove by and knew in his gut that the reporter was dead.

It was almost noon. Every curtain and blind in every window had been drawn or closed. Even at a glance, the place had the look and feel of a mausoleum in a graveyard. Worse still, Sato's car was parked in the driveway, and this morning's newspaper had been tossed into the garden by the front steps and never picked up.

Everything about the one-story house appeared dark. Everything grim.

Matt idled past the next two houses, turned the car around, and pulled over. It seemed like a quiet neighborhood. The only people he saw were a crew of landscapers cutting a lawn in the middle of the block.

He took a deep breath as he eyed Sato's house and considered his options. Like Manhattan Beach, Santa Monica had its own police department with limited resources. Calling 911 would be the right thing to do. But he guessed that if Sato really had been murdered, the case would be seen as part of the Ryan Brooks killings. The FBI would take over the investigation, and Agents Fresno and Cook, with all their talent and due diligence, would never let Matt in to see the crime scene.

It dawned on him that the only way to justify entering the house on his own would be to claim ignorance. While there was no real indication that a crime had been committed—no physical reason to think Sato might be dead—the fact remained that the reporter hadn't returned his calls for the last twelve hours. For all Matt knew, Sato could have fallen, was unable to reach a phone, and in need of immediate medical attention.

Matt got out of the car. As he started down the sidewalk, he could see his supervisor, Lieutenant McKensie, laughing in his face. No one would ever buy it. Even Matt didn't buy it.

But what did it matter now?

He jogged across the street and stepped up to the front door. After ringing the bell several times and listening to the sound echo through the house, he tried the door handle. The door was secured with a dead bolt and wouldn't budge.

Matt knew that he could pick the lock if he had to. But after a quick check of the neighboring houses lining the street behind his back, this door wouldn't be his first choice. He moved away from the entrance and noticed a gate in the privacy fence by the garage. Hustling across the driveway, he flipped the latch and entered the backyard.

Vince Sato lived well—no question about it. There was a large pool here that included a spa, an expansive terrace with a gas fire ring, and an area off to the side for his grill. Palm trees lined the entire rear of the property, and Matt could hear them rustling in the cool winter breeze.

He stepped over to the house, tried the back door, and found it locked. It was made of glass and reflecting the sunlight shining through the palm trees. Squinting through the glare, Matt leaned closer, cupped his hands around his eyes, and peered inside.

At first the images didn't register—everything still too hard to see. The sun kept moving in and out of the clouds, the world going dark, then bright, then dark again. Matt pressed his face against the glass and tried to focus. He could hear a TV through the door, that lawnmower half a block—

He flinched.

He saw the body.

Sato was on the floor with his head resting again a kitchen cabinet. His eyes were pinned open and blank and reaching for something far away. His face looked as if it had been punched in by a heavyweight boxer. Bullet holes, four or five of them, peppered his chest and belly, with another catching him in the neck.

Matt slammed his fist against the door, then backed away and sat down on a chair by the pool. His chest had tightened, and he felt like he couldn't breathe. Like a piece of his being just got tossed out of a car and thrown down a rocky cliff.

That tremor came back, twisting its way through his core.

He realized that he had been worried about Sato ever since the day he'd met him. That he had admired him and liked him. That he hadn't wanted him to get hurt. That he understood why he and Brooks had been best friends.

He took a moment, trying to picture the faces of all the victims that began three years ago with the brutal killings of Emily Kosinski and her little boy. He didn't know why it seemed like an important thing to do until he doubled back and reached the death of Vince Sato.

From what he could tell so far, Sato's murder was unlike all the rest. He hadn't been stabbed to death with a knife. Instead, the reporter had been beaten, probably while being pressured to talk, then gunned down execution-style.

Temps.

It had to be Temps.

Matt walked over to the door and gave the dead bolt a sober look. Digging a small leather case out of his pocket, he flipped past his set of auto jigglers and went straight for the lock picks. He guessed that the dead bolt turned toward the door hinges and slid a tension wrench into the lock. After applying only the slightest pressure, he began working the pins with a short hook. One after the next tumbler clicked into place, and within forty-five seconds he had hit the last pin and the tension wrench began turning.

The door swung open.

Matt checked for an alarm, saw that it hadn't been armed, then got into a pair of gloves and stepped inside. The smell venting from the corpse appeared so foul that he grabbed a towel hanging from the oven door handle and covered his nose. Switching off the TV, he moved to the other side of the kitchen, avoiding the blood spatter that seemed to be almost everywhere.

He noticed an uneaten sandwich on the counter set beside a glass and bottle of beer. He could hear the heater shut down, then the ice maker dropping a set of cubes into a freezer tray. As the house settled into an eerie silence, he checked the floor for shell casings but didn't see any.

It had to be Temps.

Matt turned back to Sato. The reporter's face appeared more than bruised—his nose and a front tooth were broken. But it was the way his body had been laid out on the floor that bothered Matt most. There was something wrong with his posture—his legs—almost as if he had been dragged across the room and dumped. Like he had been unconscious at the time. Matt knelt down and glanced at the reporter's eyes before spotting another bullet wound. It was in the palm of his hand. He wondered if Sato had regained consciousness just as the killer began shooting. He wondered if Sato had tried to block the shot.

A long chunk of time passed, the images in Matt's mind hideous and nasty. He was sure of it now because he could see it happening. Sato opening his eyes and raising his hand in the air.

Sato had been awake when he died. Terror-stricken, and helpless.

Matt stood up and walked over to the dining area wondering why his imagination always wanted a say in the things he experienced as a detective. The darkest things. As he took in the blood spatter, he glanced at the table and noticed a power cable and a pointing device. They were here, but the computer that went with them wasn't.

He thought about Ryan Brooks's house at the beach. The only thing missing had been his computer.

Matt checked the counters by the sink and stove. Walking out of the kitchen, he searched through each room until he reached the front of the house.

The killer had taken Sato's computer with him. Like Brooks, Sato had been murdered for what he knew.

As Matt tried to guess what information Sato might have had that he didn't, he gradually became aware of the sound of two men talking outside the front door. And he recognized their voices. It was Fresno and Cook.

The doorbell rang, the harsh sound reverberating through every room in the death house.

Matt hustled over to the window and parted the slats in the blind. The two FBI agents were standing at the door and had their game faces on.

They rang the bell again, then started banging on the door with their fists. After Fresno spit in the garden, he began shouting.

"We know you're in there, Sato. And we know you're helping Jones. You either tell us what's going on, or you're spending the night in jail. What the hell, let's make it a week! Do you hear me? No free pass, pal! Now open up!"

The banging stopped, and Matt saw them press their ears against the door to listen. After a few seconds, they glanced at each other and backed away from the house. Matt moved to the other window and peered through the slats. It looked like Fresno and Cook had just spotted the gate by the garage. They were crossing the drive. They were vanishing into the backyard.

Matt knew that he couldn't be seen here. He couldn't be found here. Not at a crime scene weighted down by cause where they could do anything they wanted to him and get away with it.

He legged it down the foyer, hid behind a set of French doors, and peeked around the corner. Fresno and Cook were checking out the pool and spa and shaking their heads with frowns on their faces. After a few moments, they started toward the house.

Matt could feel the rush of adrenaline tumbling through his body as they stepped closer and closer. When they reached the back door and leaned toward the glass for a look inside, he ran back down the foyer to the front door. Unlocking the dead bolt, he eased the door open and slipped outside.

He could hear them in the backyard now. It sounded like they had just spotted Sato's corpse and realized that he had been shot. Murdered.

Closing the front door behind him, Matt rushed across the street and jumped into his car. As he reached Fourth Street, he blew through the stop sign and made a hard left turn.

THIRTY-SIX

Matt gunned it down Fourth Street, heading south for the entrance to the Pacific Coast Highway and the 10 Freeway beyond. As he used the controls on the steering wheel to page through phone numbers, he spotted a Police Interceptor heading north at high speed. The black SUV whizzed by, but not fast enough for Matt to miss who was behind the wheel.

Temps.

Matt looked into the rearview mirror and watched the detective slam on the brakes and begin to turn around. Blowing through another stop sign, Matt made a right and floored it down the street. He checked the rearview mirror again, didn't see Temps, and turned back to the media screen on the dash. When he found McKensie's cell number, he jabbed the "Enter" button on the steering wheel with his thumb.

McKensie picked up just as Temps made the turn a half block back.

"I'm in trouble," Matt said.

"I know you are."

"I need help, Lieutenant."

"We'll see about that, but I'm gonna have to put you on hold, Jones. Is that okay?"

"Whatever you've gotta do, but please do it quickly."

The phone clicked and a weird, outdated version of elevator Muzak began playing over the car's audio system. For a split second, Matt couldn't believe this was happening. Temps had picked up speed and was closing in. Matt imagined that he could end all this in less than ten seconds. He could slam on the brakes right now, wheel out his .45, and put six rounds through Temps's windshield. No one in the world would miss the piece of crap. No one would complain about him shooting a dirty cop. But this was a residential neighborhood. More than a handful of teens were skateboarding off the curb and into the street. Matt had to weave through them to get by. But even more, the kids seemed to know that they were watching a car chase and that the Interceptor, although unmarked, was being driven by the police. As Matt glanced into the rearview mirror, he could see them giving Temps the finger and shouting obscenities at him.

Matt looked up just as a large delivery truck began backing into the street from a driveway. It seemed obvious that the driver didn't see them racing toward him. Matt measured the truck's progress and watched as the road before him began to narrow. Deciding to risk it, he jammed his foot to the floor and felt the car rocket forward. He pounded his horn, checked the mirror, and pounded the horn again. He was only thirty-five yards away now. Then twenty-five yards—the delivery truck still inching back. Then ten yards away. Then whoosh—

Matt blew through the narrow space between the truck and a row of parked cars with his eyes darting back to the rearview mirror. The truck had backed all the way up and was blocking the street. For some reason, the driver was getting out of the cab and appeared angry. As Matt slowed down and made a left onto Ocean Avenue, he wondered if Temps hadn't hit the truck with his Interceptor.

The Muzak stopped, and the phone clicked over the speaker system.

"You still there?" McKensie asked in a raspy voice.

"I'm here, Lieutenant."

"We need to talk."

"At the station?"

"No," McKensie said. "Not here."

Matt looked back at the road, listening to his supervisor give him an address on North Grand Avenue in Pasadena.

"That's a residential neighborhood," Matt said.

"Yes, it is," McKensie said. "As far away from the station as possible. The Feds have it in for you, Jones. These guys don't like you."

"And I thought we were in love."

McKensie didn't say anything.

Matt tightened his grip on the wheel as he tried to picture the street in Pasadena.

"Whose house is it?" he said finally.

McKensie cleared his throat. "The chief's."

The phone went dead.

Matt watched the media screen on the dashboard go blank and tossed it over. He had this feeling—this uneasy feeling. He reached for his laptop case, grabbed his medication bag, and popped open a bottle of Tylenol. Swallowing two caplets with a swig of bottled water didn't make him feel any better. He glanced in the rearview mirror and didn't see Temps. But even that didn't seem to help.

THIRTY-SEVEN

His effort to avoid confronting Temps had cost him time and forced him to take the long way across town. Still, he made the trip to Pasadena in less than ninety minutes, exiting off the 134 Freeway onto Orange Grove Boulevard. Within a few more minutes he made a right off Holly Street and started idling down North Grand Avenue.

It was a neighborhood of large homes shaded beneath a canopy of oak trees that had to be over a hundred years old. The chief's house appeared to be halfway down the block on the right. The one with the limo parked at the curb. But as Matt got closer, he noticed the black Suburban and two motorcycles parked ahead of the limo and realized that it was Governor Hayworth's entourage.

His pulse started pounding in his ears.

He slowed the car down to a crawl, trying to buy time and get a better look at the chief's place. It was the only Victorian on the street. Checking the porches on the front and side of the house, he didn't see anyone. Not even the governor's security team.

He pulled over and grabbed his laptop case. As he got out of the car, that feeling of uneasiness came back, but with more definition, and he wondered if he might not be walking into a trap.

He tried to shake it off, eyeing the limo and starting down the sidewalk. He could see the driver behind the wheel, but it looked like someone had stayed behind and was sitting in the back seat.

And then the limo's back door snapped open.

Matt turned—spooked—and gazed inside. It was the governor's wife, Lisa, flashing a warm smile at him.

"I've been watching you in your car," she said. "What took you so long?"

Matt stared at her without saying anything.

She paused a moment, measuring him as her smile faded. "You don't look so good, Matty."

"I've been busy," he said in low voice. "How about you? How are you doing?"

Her eyes moved to the chief's house, then flicked back to the driver on the other side of the privacy window. Waving Matt closer, she scooted across the seat.

"I think they're up to something," she whispered.

It hung there. Matt checked his back and took another step closer.

"Your husband and his attorney?"

She nodded, opened her purse, and pulled out a business card. "They're acting very strangely. It's been bad for a week. Real bad."

She was in danger. Matt could feel it in his bones.

"Do you think this has anything to do with what happened two or three years ago?" he said.

She met his eyes. "I don't know," she said. "That was just a feeling that something had happened. This is different. They're holding private meetings in the study. Just the two of them. They're whispering to someone on the telephone."

"Do you know who?"

She shook her head. "No," she whispered. "But my husband's nervous about something. And he's angry, and he won't talk about it. He can't sleep at night. All of a sudden, he finds it hard to even look at me."

She glanced at the business card in her hand, then passed it to Matt.

"Now, I'm nervous, too," she went on. "At least I'll be home for a little while. He's scheduled ten days of fundraisers here in LA. We won't be going back to Sacramento until the middle of the month."

CITY OF STONES

"Where's home in LA?"

"The Palisades."

Matt pulled his ID wallet out of his pocket. Just as he handed Lisa one of his own cards, the chief's front door opened and Governor Hayworth stepped outside with his attorney, Alan Fontaine. Their eyes went straight to Matt and stayed there. Then their faces turned to stone.

Matt looked back at Lisa as she slipped his business card into her purse. "If you need me," he said under his breath, "or even if you just think maybe you need me, be sure to call."

Matt backed away as the governor and his fixer approached the car. They looked awkward and stiff and no one said anything. Still, it seemed clear to Matt that Fontaine had been branded with a vicious sneer. Maybe even born with it.

He watched them get into the limo and close the door. Then the rear doors on the black Suburban opened. Two motorcycle cops stepped out and climbed onto their bikes. Twenty seconds later, the governor and his entourage pulled away from the curb in formation. Matt moved to the sidewalk. He could see Lisa looking at him through the rear window. He could see the fear in her eyes until the limo turned at the corner and vanished.

In the silence that remained he was struck by an odd sensation. A feeling coming from somewhere deep inside himself.

This case wasn't going to end well.

THIRTY-EIGHT

As Matt entered the kitchen behind his supervisor, he turned and saw the chief at the table brooding over what appeared to be a glass of ice water. The chief was dressed casually in plain clothes. Matt had never seen him out of uniform before and couldn't explain why it seemed so strange.

The chief pushed his glass away. "You're circling the drain, Jones. And if you keep it up, you're gonna drag all of us down with you. It could take two decades to bring the department back. An entire generation. But I won't be here to see it, and you won't either, because everybody in this room will be working as night watchmen at a goddamn Walmart!"

The chief pounded the table with his fist and sprung to his feet. Matt tried to say something, but the chief cut him off.

"Keep your mouth shut, Detective. And sit down. You, too, McKensie."

Matt glanced at his supervisor, then pulled a chair away from the table. After he sat down, the chief grimaced and moved to the counter by the sink.

"I just got a call from the FBI," the chief said. "They want to know what you were doing at Vince Sato's house. They want to know why you ran away."

"They never saw me," Matt said.

"I told you to keep your mouth shut, son, and I meant it. They saw your car parked across the street. They know you were there. They think you had something to do with Sato's murder."

Matt took it in and remained silent as he sat there. He took it in as the idea of Fresno and Cook's corrupt existence ripped through his gut and began to eat its way through his soul.

The chief leaned over his shoulder, seething. "It gets better, Jones. It gets sweeter. The Feds think you murdered Sato to suppress evidence, and they've warned the governor about you while they build their case. The governor was just here. You were seen with him at the awards ceremony. Pictures were taken of the two of you together. Pictures that made the newspapers and every cable outlet in the country. The kind of pictures I told you I wanted to see more of. But that's all crap now. That's all over. The governor wants you to stay away from his wife. He thinks that you belong in a cell. He's worried about his reputation. And why shouldn't he be? He could be the next president of the United States."

The chief's voice had evolved from a distinct level of restrained anger to something far more unbridled. And then, finally, he just stopped shouting. He stepped over to the window and seemed to be deep in thought and brooding again.

Matt weighed the silence in the room, then glanced at McKensie before turning back to the chief.

"The governor's never gonna be president."

"What?" the chief said, aghast.

"He's never gonna make it, sir."

The chief appeared horrified. Speechless. Matt could feel the man's steely eyes drilling him in the back as he opened his laptop case and tossed Ryan Brooks's file on the table.

McKensie cringed. "What the hell is that, Jones?"

"This is the research Ryan Brooks was doing that got him, his wife, and his daughter killed."

"What research?" the chief said.

Matt stood up and moved to the other side of the room. "The governor was having an affair with his intern, Emily Kosinski. They had a son. Unfortunately, the infant became a boy, and at the age of three, people began to think that they could see who the father was. I'm guessing that the governor had a good idea of what it would cost him if anyone found out the truth. Based on what I've learned from Madina in the coroner's office, he had some sort of psychological meltdown. He flaked out and stabbed them to death. With help from his attorney and an LAPD detective who's been disgraced, the bodies were given new identities and dumped in an abandoned lot in Pico Gardens. The whole thing has been covered up ever since. But then Brooks started asking questions and pieced the truth together. When the reporter got too close, he and his family ended up dead."

It didn't take long to settle in—the air white-hot like the house had suddenly been incinerated. Matt turned and leaned against the counter. Both McKensie and the chief appeared to be in shock with their wheels turning. In shock, and playing the same story in their heads.

"Who's the disgraced detective?" the chief said finally.

McKensie slapped the table. "Jack Temps," he said. "That's why you were asking me about him, right?"

Matt nodded. "And I'm sure he's the one who murdered Vince Sato last night. It was a beating followed by an execution. I'd bet everything I have that Temps is the one."

"Everything?" the chief said. "It looks to me like you've already done that, Detective. What about the Feds?"

"Dirty," Matt said. "Involved in some way, but I'm not sure how."

The back door opened, and the chief's wife walked in carrying two bags of groceries. She glanced at Matt and McKensie, then lowered her eyes like she was embarrassed.

"I'm sorry for interrupting," she said to her husband. "I didn't know you were here."

The chief shrugged like it was okay and helped her with the groceries. "Where are the kids?"

"Soccer practice," she said. "I'll deal with the groceries later. No harm."

Matt watched the chief interact with his wife, surprised by how his hard demeanor seemed to melt away so quickly. His wife had to be somewhere in her late forties, a pleasant-looking woman with brown eyes and light brown hair. But it was the way she handled herself that seemed to stand out so much. Her presence was unusually expressive and gentle, and Matt imagined that she could brighten the mood in any room she entered, just as she had today.

"You know Howard, Maggie," the chief said to her. "And this is Detective Matt Jones."

She turned and looked Matt over, her lips curling into a faint smile. "I know who you are," she said. "Welcome to our home, Detective."

Matt nodded, then watched her glance at the chief and open the door to leave. Her smile came back.

"I'm meeting Sharon for a walk around the Rose Bowl. I'll see you later. Sorry."

The chief smiled back. "Don't worry about it," he said. "Say hi to Sharon for me, and have a good time."

The door closed, the outrage of the past half hour, the raw emotions, somehow changed. The chief opened the file on the table and began leafing through Brooks's notes. As he skimmed through the details, he shook his head several times, rubbed his chin, and groaned.

"What are you doing to back up these claims, Jones? That's all they are, right? Claims? Theories? The way it may have been?"

McKensie leaned over the file with his reading glasses on. "Obviously, Brooks needed something more than this, and that's why he called you, Jones."

Matt returned to the table and sat down. "Madina says that Kosinski had sex before she was murdered. The killer left his semen behind. We're running a sample against all known state employees. We're also doing side by sides of her and her boy against the semen sample. But we already have one piece locked. Madina told me that the bite marks on the governor's intern match the bite marks found on Brooks's wife. He thinks they're as good as fingerprints and said they'd hold up in court."

The chief let out a nervous gasp. "Jesus Christ," he said in a quieter voice. "The man could be the next president of the United States."

"Like I said before, Chief, I don't think that's gonna happen. Not if we can get him with the science."

CITY OF STONES

"You were supposed to be on medical leave."

"I'm sorry," Matt said. "I'm sorry it turned out this way."

The doorbell rang. No one moved, but all three looked at each other. When the bell rang a second time, Matt leaned back and peered down the foyer with the chief. In typical Victorian style, the front door was made of glass and oak and covered with a curtain sheer enough to see the two men standing on the front porch.

"It's them," Matt said.

The chief gave him a look. "The Feds?"

Matt nodded. "The governor must have called and told them I was here."

The chief took a deep breath and exhaled, then exited the room. "Sit tight," he said on his way out.

Matt listened to the chief march down the foyer, unlock the door, and swing it open. When he heard Fresno's voice, he traded a knowing glance with McKensie and nodded again.

"Chief Logan," the agent said. "We're with the FBI. We're looking for one of your detectives. He works out of the Hollywood station. Matt Jones."

"I haven't seen him," the chief said. "He's on medical leave."

A moment passed. Matt could only imagine the look on Fresno's face.

"You're not really gonna play it this way, are you, Chief?"

"Which way's that, son?"

"We have information that Jones was seen here in the last hour. It comes from a good source."

"Well, your source isn't as good as you thought. Your information's wrong."

"But that's his car right over there, Chief."

The chief glanced at Matt's car for a moment before clearing his throat. "Let me see your IDs again. Hand them over."

Matt shot McKensie a look, then got up from the table without making any sound. Peeking through the dining room and living room, he could see the two FBI agents staring at the chief with suspicion and attitude.

"Agents Fresno and Cook," the chief said as he inspected their IDs. "I'm saying it aloud so I can match your faces to your names and won't forget if I'm ever asked. Agents Fresno and Cook. Let me give you some professional advice. When the chief of the Los Angeles Police Department tells you that someone isn't here, they're not here. Do you understand what I'm saying?"

Fresno and Cook just stood there, the silence staggering.

The chief handed their IDs back. "Do you see that SUV with the tinted glass across the street, Agent Fresno? What about you, Agent Cook? Do you see it?"

"We see it," Fresno said.

"Well, you'll find two more just like it stationed at both ends of the block. That's my security team. Now get off my property and out of my neighborhood, or I'm calling them in."

"What?" Fresno said.

"You heard me the first time, Agent Fresno. Get out."

Fresno stared back at the chief in shock and appeared confused, even dumbfounded.

Matt had always heard that the chief had brass but couldn't believe what he'd just witnessed.

Still, the best part was in the offing. The best part came when the chief closed the door on the two agents, quietly and casually, then hit the dead bolt.

THIRTY-NINE

Matt moved in beside the chief and McKensie and gazed out the living room window.

It took Fresno and Cook time for the chief's message to sink in. But after fifteen minutes of sitting in their car, barking and whining at someone on their cell phone, pounding the dashboard and smashing the steering wheel—they eventually drove off. According to the chief's security team, when the agents reached the corner, they kept moving and were seen driving down the entrance ramp to the 134 Freeway. Matt assumed that they were heading back to Sato's house to oversee or gum up the works as the technical crew processed the crime scene.

But what really mattered was the wake the two agents left behind.

Matt walked out of the house understanding that the chief had taken an enormous risk on his behalf and that the results from the DNA runs were never more vital. But far worse, if Matt had made a mistake in judgment, if they didn't get a decisive hit, the governor had the means and the power to rewrite his own reputation and destroy everyone involved in the investigation. If they didn't get a clean hit that pointed to the governor, the doom-and-gloom scenario the chief had warned about would take down the entire department.

Matt found the idea unnerving and shivered.

He checked the clock on the dash as he pulled into the street, deciding to circle the neighborhood and exit on the quieter end of the block. It was half past four and already dark. Rush hour would be in full bloom, the drive to his house on the Westside brutal. He hadn't passed more than a few houses when he saw something out of the corner of his eye.

A Police Interceptor had just pulled into a driveway across the street and was backing up to turn around.

Matt eased his car over to the curb and killed the headlights.

He could see Temps behind the wheel. The detective must have spotted the chief's security team on the corner and wanted to avoid them by sneaking out of the neighborhood the way he had come in.

Matt gave Temps a head start, then switched on his headlights and pulled back into the street. As he picked up speed, he could see the detective passing the freeway entrance and making a right turn onto Colorado Boulevard. Temps didn't appear to be in a hurry. Still, as he drove by the Original Tommy's Hamburgers in Eagle Rock and continued through Glendale, it became clear that he was using surface streets and on his way back to the Westside.

Matt was sorry that they had driven by Tommy's. He couldn't remember the last time he'd eaten, and the sight of the place felt like it deepened the hole in his stomach by a foot or two. Worse still, his coffee mug had gone dry. He tried to shake it off, grabbing a bottle of water as he followed the SUV through another intersection, but the hole in his belly only felt worse.

Curiously, Temps left Colorado Boulevard behind, passing Forest Lawn and Universal Studios. As he cruised out of the Valley and down the hill into Hollywood, Matt started to become suspicious. He no longer believed that the detective was heading for Sato's house to see what might be going on. And this wouldn't have been the way for a return trip to Ryan Brooks's place in Manhattan Beach.

Matt turned up the heater, then watched Temps reach Sunset Boulevard and begin to accelerate through traffic. More curious than ever, he tightened his grip on the wheel and closed the gap. They blew through Westwood, then Brentwood, the road coiling through the hills like a rattlesnake. Speeding out of a hard curve, Matt reached into his pocket for the business card the governor's wife had given him and held it under the light from the dash.

It dawned on him that Temps could be on his way to the governor's house in the Palisades. A few minutes later, he saw Temps make a left off Sunset and knew that his hunch had just been confirmed.

He slowed the car down and let the SUV disappear around the corner. Then he glanced at the address on Lisa's card again. It had never occurred to him that they lived in the same neighborhood. That his own house was less than a mile away. He thought about all the narrow roads etched into the hills and pictured the governor's address in his memory. After a few moments, he could see the house in his mind and realized that the best way in would be from the other side.

Matt barreled down the street into the darkness, racing by a thick wall of bamboo that lined a property for nearly fifty yards. After rolling through a series of sharp curves, he made a quick left and spotted the governor's compound on the right.

He hit the brakes hard, veering into the curb and killing the engine. The house stood behind a five-foot-high wall, the front entrance around the corner. As Matt got out of the car, he noticed a pair of headlights sweeping through the trees. He closed the door and knelt down.

It was the Interceptor, inching to a stop on the other side of the street. Matt had a clean view of Temps behind the wheel and watched the detective shut down the SUV. But then something strange happened. Temps spent almost ten minutes sitting in the dark. He wasn't talking to anyone on his cell phone. Nor was he eating or drinking anything.

Temps was staring at the back of the governor's house.

Studying it the way a burglar might if he was looking for a way in.

FORTY

Temps flopped over the wall and hit the ground with a thud. After a moment or two, the detective reappeared behind a tree, eyeing the back of the governor's house. Matt could hear him wheezing from the climb and thought that he might be taking a time-out to pull himself together and catch his breath.

When Temps moved deeper into the backyard, Matt crossed the street to the wall and peered through the branches. He could see Temps hiding behind a different tree now.

Why was he doing this?

Matt turned to take in the house. It was a two-story eclectic mix of contemporary and traditional, with huge windows and French doors that opened to decks wrapping around both floors. The second floor was completely dark, but that hardly mattered. Temps's concern would have been with the lighted windows and doors on the first floor.

The governor was home.

He and Fontaine were standing by a desk in the study with the door closed, pouring cocktails and clicking glasses. The governor's wife was there as well, but sitting by herself in the great room talking to someone on her cell phone. The TV had been turned on to a cable news station, but Lisa didn't seem to be paying much attention to it.

Matt turned back to Temps. When he didn't see him behind the tree, he scanned the yard quickly and spotted the hulking figure creeping through the shadows toward the other end of the house.

Matt let his eyes skip forward.

He could see it now. The way Temps had planned to break in.

The roof to what had to be the back of the garage was only ten or twelve feet off the ground, the wall adjoining a raised deck that ran the length of the house. Temps had made it up the steps and was climbing onto the rail. Just above the roof and within reach was the deck on the second floor.

Matt went over the wall, dropped into the gloom, and found Temps already on the roof of the garage. Despite the detective's ruined body, he was lifting himself over the rail and onto the second-floor deck as if the climb had been easy. When he tried the first set of French doors, they opened without making any sound.

Temps entered the dark room and closed the door. But then he did something Matt found incredibly odd.

Temps switched on the lights.

Why was he doing this? It seemed so out of place. So outrageous.

Matt cantered through the shadows and onto the deck. Stepping onto the rail, he hoisted himself up to the roof and climbed to the top for a look over the other side. The governor's security entourage was parked on the street out front. The two motorcycles were here, along with the black Chevy Suburban that Matt remembered seeing at the chief's house. Although the SUV's windows were tinted, the interior light must have been on. Matt counted the silhouettes from four people sitting in the front and back seats. When he checked the street, he spotted a sheriff's cruiser idling behind a hedgerow on the corner. The deputy sheriff sitting behind the wheel looked like he was taking a nap.

Matt shook his head, sliding down the roof and stepping over the rail onto the second-floor deck. The first set of French doors opened to the master bedroom, and he could see Temps standing in the doorway to the hall, apparently listening to what was going on downstairs. As Matt kept an eye on him, he reached into the outdoor light fixture and twisted the bulb until the deck went dark. Then he moved closer to the door and peered through the glass.

Temps must have been satisfied with what he had heard and turned back to the bedroom. His eyes were big and wild as he scanned the entire space. Stepping into the bathroom, he gave it an unusually long look. Matt wondered why he seemed so preoccupied with the tub and floor. After several minutes, the detective snapped out of it, crossed the bedroom to one of the two chests, and started going through the drawers.

Curiously, Temps skipped over Lisa's jewelry and handbag and even a billfold filled with cash. He was working quickly. When he finished with the first chest, he moved over to the second.

And that's when Matt could no longer ignore the questions surfacing in his head all at once.

Temps was obviously searching for something. Something specific. And it was important enough to put himself at risk doing it.

But that only seemed like the beginning.

How did Temps know that this was the master bedroom? He never walked down the deck. He never checked any of the other windows or doors. Matt had seen it with his own eyes. Temps climbed over the rail and picked this set of doors as if on automatic pilot. How could he have known that this was the governor's bedroom unless he had been here before?

But even more, why had he been so preoccupied with the tub and floor in the bathroom? Why did he spend so much time in there? Why was it the first thing he did once he had confirmed his own safety? And why did it seem so peculiar—the expression on his face like he'd been overcome with thoughts and his wheels were turning?

Why was the whole thing giving Matt chills?

It suddenly dawned on Matt that there could only be one answer that made any sense. After a week of beating the streets, Matt had just found the crime scene. These had to be the rooms where Emily Kosinski and her three-year-old boy were murdered.

The longer Matt wrestled with the idea—the more details he gave it—the more likely it seemed.

While in office the governor and his wife lived in Sacramento, the state capital. That's where the legislators met. That's where the state's business was conducted. His home here in the Palisades would have been empty most of the time. It was secluded. As Matt gazed at the view from the deck tonight, he couldn't see the lights from a single house anywhere through the trees.

Emily Kosinski worked out of the field office in LA. Because LA was the biggest city in the state, because this was where most of the movers and the shakers lived, Matt imagined that the governor spent a lot of time here with his wife staying behind in Sacramento.

If the governor and his intern were having an affair, this would have been the perfect place to spend time together. Nights together. Nights that included so much privacy that they could wake up together in the morning and no one would have ever known.

If the governor had been having an affair, this was the place where no one would have ever guessed. And if the affair was over, if things needed to come to an end—albeit untimely and horrific—this would have been the place where—

Blood was shed.

Matt grit his teeth, knowing that he had to get inside for a look.

He shook it off and focused. Temps had just closed the bottom drawer in the second chest and could be seen rushing over to the doorway. The big man took a nervous step into the hall, listening to something coming from the first floor again. Though the fear showing on his face appeared overwhelming, his concerns seemed to fade soon enough, and he opened the closet door.

His search was quick, almost fleeting. The second closet turned out to be a walk-in, and Matt lost sight of him for two or three minutes. But when Temps walked out finally, he was empty handed.

Matt moved deeper into the shadows toward the deck rail, fearing that Temps might be on his way out. He could see him standing in the middle of the room giving it a hard last look all the way around. But then, as if struck by an idea, he pulled a small flashlight out of his pocket and rushed around the bed to a painting on the wall. He tilted the frame out, pointing the beam of light underneath and examining the back.

After checking behind a second piece of art, he moved to the other side of the bathroom door and tried a third. Matt could tell when Temps hit pay dirt, watching him lift the frame off the hook and toss the painting on the bed. A large manila envelope had been taped to the artwork's cardboard backing.

Temps opened the envelope and turned it over. As a stack of eight-by-ten photographs slid out, his eyes got big and wild again. Even worse, he actually flashed a grim smile and shook his head. Matt strained to get a look at the images, but Temps was already returning them to the envelope.

The detective had found what he'd come for and seemed pleased with himself. He hung the painting on the wall, even straightened it, then switched off the lights and turned to the French doors.

Matt scampered over the rail, slid down the roof, and leapt onto the deck. Glancing at the governor still in his study with Fontaine, he rushed into the darkness, stepped behind a tree, and peered through the leaves.

Lisa was still sitting before the TV talking to someone on her cell phone.

Matt turned back to the other end of the house, watching and waiting, his patience gone.

Temps was having a difficult time getting over the rail and onto the roof while holding the envelope. For several moments it looked like he might lose his balance and fall. But then he tossed the envelope onto the lawn below and made the awkward climb down. Matt could hear him wheezing and coughing as he staggered through the shadows and finally spilled over the wall.

After a few grunts and groans, the Interceptor's door opened and shut, and the engine lit up. Matt watched Temps drive off, then turned and gave the house a long look. Temps had found something, but Matt thought that he had found something here, too.

The crime scene.

The place where Emily Kosinski and her little boy, David, had been killed.

FORTY-ONE

Temps pulled down the ramp into the building's parking garage and found a space reserved for patients. As he knocked back a gulp of coffee spiked with Irish whiskey, he checked the time. It was ten minutes after seven, and he was late for his "after hours" appointment with Dr. May.

He took another swig from the cup, then pulled a napkin out of the bag and wiped the sweat off his forehead. Although he tried, he couldn't get rid of the dark thoughts in his head. He wasn't used to this kind of workload, nor did he like the pressure that came with it. Every step of the way felt like someone had been holding a gun to his head. Every step of the way came with images of being strapped to a gurney, wheeled onto a stage before an audience, and given the needle.

The last dose. His finale.

He could see the poison moving through the clear plastic tube to the catheter and needle in his arm. He could feel the drug shutting down his eyes and ears and inching its way toward his heart and brain.

And then what? His rejection at the Pearly Gates?

He wondered if the people sitting in the audience enjoyed watching a man die. He wondered if the audience would get to their feet while applauding, maybe even shout, *Encore! Encore! Let's kill him again!*

Temps had witnessed two executions in his earlier life as a respected homicide detective. He could remember that in each case the surviving family members had a certain glint in their eyes. They always seemed to be smiling. But it was never a happy smile, he recalled. It was more like the kind a child wears when he or she grinds a bug into the sidewalk with their foot.

Temps took a third swig, savoring the taste of the whiskey. As he set his drink down in the cup holder, he noticed that his hands were shaking and tried to pull himself together. He checked the new piece holstered to his shoulder. It was another 9mm Smith & Wesson 17+1 semiautomatic. He'd replaced the old one because he needed to stop the worry that came with it. He could remember shoving the muzzle into Sato's mouth and watching the reporter grab the pistol in a pathetic attempt to yank it out. The memory had begun to haunt him because he knew what a modern crime lab could do with fingerprints and saliva.

He dug a breath mint out of his pocket and popped it into his mouth. After a quick look in the mirror, he got out of the SUV and started walking down the aisle to the lobby doors. Security cameras seemed to be everywhere, and he deliberately lowered his gaze as he entered the building and stepped into the elevator. Whatever he ended up doing tonight needed to be done, simple as that. He had no choice in the matter.

That's what "the end" looked like, he told himself. That's where "the end" got its name.

Its start.

The elevator doors opened onto the sixth floor. As he followed the signs around the corner to the LAPD's new home for Behavioral Science Services, the number of cameras seemed to double. He reached the door, took a deep breath, and crossed himself. And then he walked in.

Dr. May was sitting at the reception desk reading something on the computer. She looked up with clear eyes and smiled. Temps nodded back as he glanced around and realized that the suite was empty, and they were alone.

"Nice to see you, Detective. My office is right through this door."

Temps watched her stand up and walk around the desk. She had looks, brains, even class—she had everything—and he took this as a sign of bad luck. He'd been hoping that the psychiatrist would look more like a punching bag. A woman no one spent too much time thinking about.

It made him nervous, and he could feel his hands shaking again. He stepped into the office and turned after he heard her close the door.

"You've been drinking," she said.

"Maybe a little."

She frowned. "Are you drunk?"

Temps shook his head and met her eyes. He wasn't going to make it. He'd had it. Already.

"Screw you," he said.

"What?"

"You heard me."

She started to back up toward the lobby door. Temps grabbed her arm and locked the door. Then he ran her across the room and tossed her onto the couch.

"I lost my reputation a long time ago, Doc. But I'll be damned if I'm gonna go down for murder."

"Murder?"

"Yeah, Doc, murder. Now I need to know everything Matt Jones said to you. And believe me, your life depends on you telling me the truth."

Her eyes widened. "He doesn't talk about business," she said quickly.

Temps shook his head. "Your life depends on it, Doc. Now tell me the truth."

"I am telling you the truth."

"But you're not convincing me. There's no gray tonight. Just black and white. Just you and me."

"You're scaring me," she said. "I want you to leave."

"That's not gonna happen, and you're making me angry. Where's his file?"

Temps pulled out the Smith & Wesson. Dr. May's eyes got glassy and she started trembling.

"He doesn't talk about his work," she said firmly. "He told me that if he did, I'd be in danger. I told him to leave it alone and let the FBI handle it."

"Give me his file."

"No," she managed. "Never."

"You don't get it!"

Temps looked at her on the couch and flipped. He became dizzy, and everything felt like it was moving in slow motion now. Stuffing the pistol into his holster, he picked the woman up by her armpits. She was trying to kick him. She was trying to push him off and bite his arm. When she started shrieking, Temps hit her in the face with his right fist. And then her head snapped back, and she stopped moving, her body dropping back onto the couch. It was a vicious blow. The kind that ends a boxing match. Blood was trickling out of her mouth and dripping down her chin onto her white blouse.

Temps shook his head, staring at her with a fierce expression on his face.

"I told you not to make me angry," he said.

FORTY-TWO

Matt popped the trunk, found his evidence collection kit behind his gym bag, and pulled it forward. While he would have preferred to have Speeks here tonight, along with the crew and technology that came with the crime lab's truck, without hard evidence and a warrant from a judge, none of that was possible.

All he had right now was that feeling in his gut. That knot that wouldn't go away. This was where Emily Kosinski and her little boy were killed. And he had to know if this was true.

Not later. Now.

He slipped on a pair of gloves and opened the kit. Searching through its contents, he transferred the things that he thought he might need into a small knapsack.

He had purchased the luminol powder for $16.95 on Amazon's website. Removing the sprayer, he filled the bottle with distilled water and shook it slightly. Once the powder mixed with the water, the label indicated that its shelf life was about twenty-four hours, well within the hour or two he would need tonight. He tightened the sprayer to the bottle and placed it into the knapsack. After checking his UV flashlight for power, he found his safety glasses, added them to the bag, and zipped it up.

The harsh glare from a car's headlights swept across his face and through the trees overhead. When the car turned the corner, Matt closed the trunk and watched it pass. It was another lowrider, packed with teens, laughing and listening to music without a care in the world. Clouds of smoke billowed out of the windows, the sweet peppery scent of weed perfuming the moist air.

Matt waited until they vanished up the hill before strapping the knapsack around his shoulders and crossing the street. He peered over the wall through the branches, appraising the house and listening to the neighborhood. He could hear a dog barking in the distance, a pair of coyotes farther up the ridge. Scanning the lighted windows on the first floor, he found the governor still behind his desk in the study. He was pouring another round of drinks for himself and Fontaine, and then, finally, he filled a third glass.

Matt went over the wall, rushing through the shadows toward the other end of the house. When he turned back to check, the governor and his personal attorney had joined Lisa in the great room. They were standing before the fireplace clicking glasses as if celebrating good news.

Matt moved up the steps onto the deck, then climbed the rail and hoisted himself onto the roof of the garage. Kneeing his way up to the deck on the second floor, he lifted himself over the rail and swung open the French doors.

He was in.

Eyeing the darkened room carefully. Listening to the conversation downstairs. Feeling his heart pounding in his chest because the voices sounded so close.

He let the knapsack drop off his shoulders, ripped it open, and grabbed the bottle of luminol. Then he walked into the bathroom, spraying the tub and floor and everything else he could remember Temps had been staring at. Returning to his bag, he slipped on his safety glasses and fished out the UV flashlight.

And then he stopped and listened. Something was going on downstairs. Some sort of disruption. He suddenly became aware of his breathing and wondered what his options might be if someone walked into the room. He hadn't planned for an encounter, nor had he thought about his fate or possible demise. When he heard the governor laugh, the conversation seemed to resume, and he moved back to the bathroom.

He could feel his breathing begin to even out, his mind settling down. But then he switched on the UV flashlight.

A long moment passed, and then another, as the horror of what stood before his eyes began to register.

It was blood. And it was everywhere.

It seemed clear that an effort had been made to clean things up. But so much of the room had been missed.

Matt sprayed the wall over the tub and watched the patterns of blood spatter fan all the way up to the ceiling. He sprayed the wall above the counter and two sinks, the walls on both sides of the door, the vanity by the window, the cabinets and a closet door, and then the molding that wrapped around the entire room.

The blood spatter was everywhere. Charles Manson. Dr. Baylor. Helter-skelter. He was staring at the work of a madman.

Matt heard someone coming up the stairs and recoiled in panic. He switched off the flashlight, then turned in horror as he spotted his knapsack on the carpet in the middle of bedroom. It was too late to fetch it. The footsteps were too close, and he was running out of—

The lights switched on.

His eyes rocked across the room to the French doors and the reflection in the glass.

It was Lisa, staring at his knapsack.

He brought a finger to his lips and eased out of the bathroom. She flinched and let out a gasp.

The governor, who had been talking to Fontaine, must have heard her and sensed something was wrong. "Are you okay, honey?"

Matt met her eyes and stepped closer. He could tell that she was nervous and trying to compose herself. When she spoke, her voice sounded awkward.

"I'll be down in a minute," she said.

The governor appeared to buy it and started talking to Fontaine again. Lisa moved even closer, lowering her voice to a whisper.

"What are you doing here?"

"Turn off the lights."

She gave him an incredulous look without moving.

"Turn them off," he repeated.

She walked over and hit the wall switch, the bedroom going dark but for the light feeding in from the hallway and stairs. When she returned, he led her over to the bathroom and turned on the flashlight.

After that, her face changed. It was the same face he remembered seeing when he was a boy living with his aunt in New Jersey. It was the look of curiosity and wonder, only now he could see her being overtaken by shock and worry.

"What is it?" she whispered.

"Blood."

"Blood?"

Matt nodded.

"Whose?"

"Your husband's intern," he said. "Hers and her son's."

Lisa lowered her head and began wiping the tears away from her eyes. "Oh my God," she managed. "Emily."

Matt could hear her weeping. Her fingers were trembling.

"Emily went away three years ago," she whispered in a shaky voice. "And she never came back. Is that what this is about? Is this the reason why they've been acting so strangely?"

Matt switched off the flashlight and slipped it into his pocket. Then he touched her hair and smoothed it back.

"You've gotta be strong, Lisa. You've gotta be tough."

"But I'm not tough."

Matt wiped a tear off her cheek with his thumb. "It won't be long. I promise you it won't."

She met his gaze, her eyes wet and glassy. "Matty," she whispered under her breath. "Oh, Matty."

Matt lowered his hands to her shoulders trying to comfort her. "What was behind this painting?"

Her eyes danced over his face in confusion. "What are you talking about?"

"I didn't find your house on my own, Lisa. I followed a detective here. A man named Jack Temps. He broke into this room tonight. He was looking for something. It turned out to be a stack of pictures in a manila envelope. The envelope was taped to the back of this painting. What were the pictures of? What did your husband have that needed to be hidden?"

She shook her head as if dazed. "I have no idea," she said. "But you're gonna need to get out of here."

"What's happening?"

"He's made up his mind. He's running for president. Tomorrow night he'll make it official. He's holding a press conference at the Biltmore."

"Okay."

"You don't understand," she said. "We're going out to dinner tonight. Sort of a celebration, if that's even possible now. Once we leave, the security system in the house will be armed. You won't be safe, Matty."

He followed her gaze to the ceiling and an alarm sensor in the corner.

"They're everywhere," she added.

"I need ten minutes," he said. "Can you stall them?"

Matt heard the governor clear his throat. "We're ready to go, honey. Glen's back with the car."

Lisa turned to the door. "I'll be right down."

Matt stepped in front of her. "Who's Glen?"

"Our driver."

"Just give me ten minutes."

"I'll try," she whispered. "But hurry, Matty."

She glanced at herself in the mirror and wiped her eyes again. Then she grabbed her purse off the dresser and slipped her earrings inside before vanishing down the stairs. Matt walked over to the door and listened as she joined the governor and Fontaine. She was saying something about how she couldn't find her earrings. After the governor suggested that she do without or pick another pair, it sounded like she dropped her purse and the contents spilled all over the floor.

Lisa had just given Matt his ten minutes.

He rushed into the bathroom, digging his phone and the UV flashlight out of his pockets. Setting the light on the counter, he opened the phone's camera and began documenting the blood spatter on the walls. But after a few minutes, the possibility occurred to him that the bathroom only told a small portion of the story.

Matt stepped into the bedroom, holding the light in one hand and the luminol bottle in the other. He walked over to the bed, spraying the backboard and walls and watching the blood spatter burst all over the room. When his eyes drifted down to the lower corner of the backboard, he froze and almost gasped.

It was the mark left behind by a hand once covered in blood. A small hand. A woman's hand.

The image shook every bone in his body. Matt could see the murder happening as if he had been in the room. He could see Emily Kosinski trying to defend herself. Trying to hold on. And he could see the governor's frenzied eyes as well. He could see the man raising a knife the size of a bayonet in the air and stabbing his intern over and over again. The woman who had given him a son. A governor getting rid of his problems. A psychopath giving in to his demented mind.

First one, and then the next. First the mother, and then her child. Everything over and done.

When Matt pulled himself together, he noticed that the first floor had become quiet. His eyes went straight to the alarm sensor on the ceiling and then to his watch.

Moving feverishly, he ripped off five shots with the camera before grabbing his things and bursting out onto the deck. Just as he closed the French doors, he saw a light on the alarm sensor begin blinking.

He turned and took a deep breath. Despite the cool night air, his clothing was soaked through with sweat.

He could hear the dog still barking in the distance and that pair of coyotes still up the ridge.

Matt climbed down to the ground and walked across the backyard. The windows on the first floor were dark now, but through the glass he could see Lisa getting into the limo with the governor and his attorney. He scaled the wall, tumbling over the other side. As he looked up and steadied himself, he couldn't believe what he was witnessing.

A man, dressed in black, looked as if he was trying to break into his car.

It seemed so outrageous and rude. The act. The timing.

Matt rushed forward, but the would-be thief had fresher legs and ran off into the night.

FORTY-THREE

Temps crossed the room to Dr. May, still sprawled out on the couch. After he checked her pulse, he listened to her shallow breathing. The blood trickling out of her mouth had stopped a few minutes ago, and she seemed to be drifting in and out of consciousness.

He didn't really remember punching her. It seemed more like a hallucination. Some sort of emotional breakdown. But at least the shrieking had stopped. At least the office was quiet now.

He got up and walked over to the bank of four lateral filing cabinets against the wall beside the door. He had spent an hour searching the first three for Jones's personal records and couldn't find them. The problem was with Dr. May. She was a shrink and, he guessed, the kind of egghead who was wrapped too tight. None of her labeling made any sense. Forget about alphabetical order. There wasn't a single file that had been labeled with a patient's name. Instead, they were all numbers. Some sort of demented code that would have taken a medical degree to break.

Temps had to pull each file, open the cover, and search out the patient's name, which for some inane reason was never listed at the top. It was taking too much time, and he found the doctor's idiosyncrasies completely unnerving.

She stirred. She looked like she was dreaming about something.

Temps shook his head, then turned back to the fourth cabinet and started sifting through the first of four drawers. Of the files he had already discarded, he had discovered three cops whom he knew and had worked with. He had read their files from start to finish, savoring their most personal thoughts and wondering how any of them ever passed the entrance exam. All three were total whack jobs. All three should have been locked up and put away a long time—

He heard something and lowered the file in his hand to the floor.

When he turned, he saw the light beneath the door to the lobby go dark. Someone was here, rattling the door handle and trying to get into the office. Worse still, Dr. May was awake and staring at him with a blank expression on her face.

Temps rushed over to the door and killed the lights. Unfortunately, it hardly mattered. So much ambient light was spilling through the windows, he could almost make out every piece of furniture in the room.

He stopped and listened. He could hear two voices whispering on the other side of the door. Male voices. Rough voices.

He gave the office a quick check and spotted a closet. Hurrying over to Dr. May, he met her eyes and hoped that she understood what he was about to say.

"What's your name?" he whispered.

She had to think it over. "Julie," she said finally.

"Julie what?"

"Julie May."

"You're a doctor, right?"

She nodded. "Yes. I think so."

"Good," he said. "Now you need to listen to me, Doc. That sound you're hearing. The men trying to open your office door. My guess is that you have visitors neither one of us would want to meet. You could keep your mouth shut, and maybe they will go away. Or you could scream, and I guarantee you, they'll be here to stay."

She stared back at him for a moment, probably trying to decide who was the greater threat. "What do you want me to do?"

"In the closet," he said. "On the floor. Hurry."

The sound of the intruders trying to get past the locked door filled

Temps's mind with worry. Following Dr. May into the closet, he kept the door cracked open and sat down beside her.

The men in the lobby now were throwing their shoulders into the door. Temps remembered how cheap the lock had looked and assumed that it was only a matter of time now. He glanced at the shrink, and then, as he watched the door burst open and two men enter the room, he pulled out his 9mm Smith & Wesson and crossed himself.

He could see their faces in the gloom. He knew them. Fresno and Cook from the FBI. And it didn't take much to guess why they were here. They wanted the same thing he did. They needed to know what Jones knew.

The two agents had flashlights. Once they checked out the office, they gave the bank of four lateral filing cabinets a long look. It would have seemed obvious to them that someone had been through the first three. Temps had never been able to clean up after himself and had left stacks of discarded files on the floor.

They moved over to the fourth cabinet and slid open the first drawer. Shaking their heads at Dr. May's labeling system, they pulled out files ten at a time and glanced at the cover pages. Once a file was rejected, they tossed it on the floor and moved on to the next.

But then they came to the third drawer. Temps watched them open a file and walk it over to the desk. He could see the beams from their flashlights piercing the darkness. The grim smiles on their faces. Their nods and grunts.

They'd found it. They had Jones's personal file.

Temps turned to Dr. May. She was staring at him. She was nervous, her entire body trembling.

"You stay here, and you won't get hurt," he whispered under his breath.

She didn't respond, and as he rose to his feet, he didn't much care. Tightening his grip on the gun, he opened the closet door just enough to step out into the gloom, then closed it behind him.

"That file belongs to me," he said in a steady voice.

Fresno and Cook flinched, then pointed their flashlights in Temps's face. Temps ignored the glare and stepped forward with his piece raised.

"Is that you, Temps?" Fresno said.

The detective nodded. "It's me."

"What's with the gun?"

Temps didn't answer, watching Cook back off to the side out of the corner of his eye. Maybe Cook thought that his play would work. Maybe the FBI agent thought that he could get away with it because everybody in the whole wide world knew that Jack Temps had hit the skids and lived in disgrace. Jack Temps was a nobody.

Temps gave Fresno a tough look. "The file you're holding in your hand comes with me. Now pass it over."

Cook drew his gun. "Bullshit, Temps. FBI business. Get the hell out of here."

Temps turned to Cook and, without hesitating, pulled the trigger. The muzzle flashed in the darkness five times, and Cook's worn-out body snapped back against the wall and tumbled onto the ground before the agent could fire a single shot. The sound from the blasts was horrendous, bouncing off the walls of the small office for what seemed like a good piece of forever.

Temps took two quick steps forward and peered through the smoke. He could see Fresno switching off his flashlight and making a nervous run for the door with the file. Temps grit his teeth and put two rounds in the agent's right shoulder. When Fresno turned back with his own gun flashing, Temps hit him with six rounds in the chest. Fresno started to fall like a tree struck by lightning, firing three shots into the wall before he finally collapsed onto the carpet with a thud.

Temps's ears were ringing. Still, he could hear the muffled screams coming from inside the closet.

He ripped the door open, watching Dr. May wave her arms and hands at him in panic.

"Shut up!" he said. "Do you hear me, Doc? Shut the hell up!"

He slammed the door on her, shaking in rage. Clouds of smoke from the spent rounds had filled the entire room, and Temps started coughing and wheezing. Somehow he made his way back to the desk, turning Cook's body over for a quick look. There was no point in checking the man's vital signs. Cook had already made the one-way trip to Hates and, no doubt about it, already earned his horns.

Temps tried to wave the smoke away from his face, still coughing and straining to catch his breath as he checked on Fresno. He could see the agent staring at the ceiling with that odd look in his eyes. The look he had seen when he gunned down Vince Sato, the look he had seen with so many others that always brought on the chills. Reaching for the file in Fresno's clenched fist, he gave it a yank, but it wouldn't budge.

He took this as a bad omen. A bad sign on a bad night.

Feeling his chest tighten, he knelt down and pried Fresno's dead fingers open. Then he grabbed the file and ran out.

There was nothing he could do about the security cameras. They were mounted in the hallway, the emergency staircase he used instead of the elevator, and in the parking garage where he hustled down the aisle. He got the Interceptor's door open, tossed the file onto the passenger seat, and climbed in.

As he wheeled the SUV up the ramp and onto the street, he decided that he would have to come up with some sort of explanation for his behavior tonight. And while everything about the idea appeared stupid, even ludicrous, he couldn't help thinking that there was a sliver of hope to be found somewhere. After all, he had been in Dr. May's office for a scheduled appointment. It had been Fresno and Cook who broke down the door and wrecked the place. It had been the two FBI agents who drew their guns with wild eyes and shot at him for who knows what reason. Temps was innocent in the matter, a patient in need of medical attention trying to defend himself and his honor as the senior detective working the Auto Theft table at the Topanga station.

He hit a red light, mulling it all over.

His explanation sounded like bullshit. He needed to get rid of his gun. And he needed to come up with something that accounted for what Dr. May would say the minute she called 911. Still, she had spent most of the time hiding in the closet. The lights in the office had been out. How much could she have really seen? If asked about who punched her in the face, Temps could claim that he was confused at the time, then turn it around with a barrage of questions. Why had the FBI broken into an office owned and run by the LAPD? If the FBI wanted someone's personal medical file, what was the process? Wouldn't they have to get a warrant signed by a judge? And what about the Police Protective League? Wouldn't they jump in and save his rotten soul just like they had last time?

A man in the car behind him hit his horn. Temps's mind stopped streaming, and he noticed that the light had turned green. When he grabbed the steering wheel and pulled forward, he glanced at his right hand and saw the blood on his fingers. Too much blood.

He looked down at his chest, and then his belly. Blood was oozing through his shirt an inch or two below his ribs.

He'd been hit.

FORTY-FOUR

Traffic heading downtown on the Santa Monica Freeway was unusually heavy. Matt switched on the radio, found KNX News, and waited for an update. But tonight the radio signal seemed weak, and he couldn't hear the announcer through the static. Even more irritating, there was something wrong with the media screen on the dashboard. The video image kept fading in and out and appeared degraded, the feed ghostlike. When he tried another radio station, and still another, the static got worse, and the media screen went blank.

He turned off the sound, wondering if it might be a satellite issue or even the work of that would-be car thief who ran off. Maybe he shorted out the electrical system when he was messing around with the door lock.

Matt took a deep breath and tried to let it go.

But then his cell phone started ringing. Not through the audio system in the car but in his pocket, as if the Bluetooth connection had been broken as well. Matt slipped his hand beneath the seat belt, wrapped his fingers around the phone, and took the call.

"Matthew?"

It was a woman's voice—a familiar voice—but he couldn't place her.

"Who's this?"

"Julie."

"Julie?"

"Dr. May," she said.

Matt's attention bolted to the surface. She had never called herself by her first name before, and she sounded terrified.

"What's happened?" he said quickly. "Are you okay?"

She lost it. She started weeping.

"Talk to me, Julie. What's going on?"

She didn't say anything. He could hear her trying to pull herself together. After several moments, she spoke in a soft, shaky voice.

"There's been a shooting. I need you."

"Where are you?"

"In my office," she said. "Hiding in the closet."

Hiding in the closet.

Matt's head lit up as the picture formed. "Hold on," he said. "I'm only fifteen minutes out."

He slipped the phone into his shirt pocket, set his LED light bar on the dash, and plugged it into the outlet below the audio system. When the lights didn't come up, he yanked the cable out and tossed the unit onto the passenger seat.

What the hell was going on with his car?

He tried to reel in his anger and chill. But after hitting the hazard lights, he swerved into the left lane and gunned it. Drivers working their car horns followed his wake. In the end Matt ignored them, pressing forward and bulldozing everyone in the left lane out of his way.

Within ten minutes he had reached the city. Within another five he had arrived and was speeding down the ramp into the parking garage. The elevator seemed hopelessly slow but finally made it to the sixth floor. When the doors opened, he hurried down the hallway, then came to an abrupt stop.

The lobby door was standing wide open, the room dark.

Matt waited and listened and drew his .45. The sound of the silence in the lobby appeared heavy. But there was something else going on in the background. When he began to realize that he was listening to Dr. May weeping, he raised the pistol, stepped into the gloom, and found his way around the reception desk.

The door to her office had been broken off its hinges but still covered the entrance. Matt used his gun to push it away from the frame, then ducked underneath and stepped inside.

Despite the darkness, he could see the dead bodies on the floor. There were two of them. And through a thin layer of smoke he could see the closet on the other side of the room. He could hear her better now, and it hurt more.

Matt rushed around the pools of blood, crossing the room and ripping open the closet door. He found her on the floor in the gloom. She was trembling and weeping and afraid to look up.

"It's me, Julie. It's Matt. You're safe now."

He knelt down beside her. When she turned, he could tell that his gun frightened her. Returning it to its holster, he gathered her into his arms.

"It's okay," he said. "You're okay, do you understand?"

She nodded.

"I wanna get you out of the closet."

"There was a shooting," she whispered.

Matt switched on his phone and looked her over in the dim light. He could see it in her face and in her eyes now. Either she had a concussion, or she was in shock.

"I wanna get you over to the lounge, but I want you to keep your eyes off the floor."

"Why?"

"You know why," he said. "Now let's go."

She grabbed his arm and wouldn't budge. "How many are there?"

"Two," he said. "Let's go."

He helped her get to her feet, then guided her over to the same lounge that he had spent so many hours on during their sessions. Once she lay down, he pulled the desk chair over. Her face and body appeared to be glowing from the ambient light spilling in through the windows.

"Would you hold me?" she said in a quiet voice. "Just for a little while."

He met her eyes, then leaned over and felt her arms wrap around his shoulders. As he pulled her closer, he could feel her chest contracting with the weeping, but it seemed to have become easier. He ran his fingers through her hair and then began rubbing the back of her neck.

"It's important that you don't fall asleep," he said. "But you're a doctor and probably already know that."

She nodded again, then whispered in his ear. "I was scared, Matthew. All the way until you got here."

A moment passed, quietly. Gently.

"I need to turn on the lights," Matt said finally. "I need to see what happened. Are you okay with that?"

"Yes."

Matt lowered her to the lounge and crossed the room to the wall switch by the door. When he turned on the lights and gazed at the two bodies on the carpet, he knew that his own world had just gone a shade or two darker. Fresno and Cook were dead. Not by a single shot but with a spray of bullets.

It was a tell. A sign that implied emotion. It was the kind of killing that revealed anger, like everyone involved knew each other and something personal had been going on.

Matt knew that he would be the lone person of interest. The first name on the list of people who would have wanted the two agents out of the way. No one would believe that he hadn't shot them.

"You look like a ghost," Dr. May said. "What is it, Matthew? What's wrong?"

Matt walked over to Fresno, rolling him onto his back with his foot.

"I'm fine," he said. "These guys are Feds. They worked for the FBI."

"Are they the same men you used to talk about?"

He turned to her and nodded. She was leaning on her arm looking at the two corpses. Her gaze seemed to have cleared some.

"Are you in trouble?" she said.

"Probably."

As he thought it over, he stepped around the pools of blood and sat on the edge of Dr. May's desk. "You said you were hiding in the closet. Did one of these guys hit you?"

Her eyes drifted from Fresno to Cook. Turning back to Matt, she shook her head.

"There was someone else here?" he said. "Who?"

"A detective. A patient."

"What's his name?"

"Jack Temps."

It hung there, in the room with the spent gunpowder still lingering in the air, and it felt like a slap in the face.

This was Matt's fault. He owned it.

He could have prevented it. If he had confronted Temps at the governor's house, none of this could have happened. But there was a brutal irony to it as well. If he had stopped Temps in the Palisades, he wouldn't know where Emily Kosinski and her little boy had been killed.

"How long has Temps been your patient?"

Her eyes flicked from the filing cabinets to Matt as he sat down in her desk chair and moved closer.

"It lasted for about two minutes," she said. "A first visit, or a way to get to me after hours. It turned out to be all about you. He wanted your personal file. He wanted to know how much you'd told me about the case you're working on. When I said nothing, he wouldn't believe me."

"And so he hit you."

She nodded again. "When I woke up, these two guys were trying to break into the office. Temps turned off the lights, and we hid in the closet. They must have found your file because he walked out and confronted them. Then the shooting started."

Matt looked back at Fresno's corpse, then Cook's mangled body in the corner. If they had found Matt's medical file, that could only mean that Temps had taken it away from them.

Temps.

Matt rolled the chair even closer and leaned over her face. "You're gonna have to call this in," he said.

"I will."

"You're gonna have to call nine-one-one. The police need to know what's happened, and you need medical attention, okay?"

She met his eyes and held the look for a long time.

"And you can't be here," she said finally.

He nodded. "I can't be here. But that doesn't mean anything as far as your statement goes. Tell them the truth, Julie. Tell them everything."

"Would you hold me again? Just for a little while?"

He smiled at her and stroked his doctor's cheek with his fingers. "You need to make a phone call," he said.

FORTY-FIVE

Matt pulled over and gave the house in Canoga Park a long look. It was a small run-down ranch-style home in a neighborhood of other run-down ranches where few people bothered to cut their lawns. Temps's place was dark. As if in a rush, he had pulled the Interceptor into the front yard and left the driver's side door standing open. The gate beneath the carport was open as well, and Matt could see a backyard so small it might have been called a patch. The house next door belonged to a fortune-teller named Dora, the neon sign by her front door indicating that she was still open.

It had taken an hour and a half to get here—plenty of time for Matt to catch his breath. He could remember how difficult it had been to leave Dr. May alone. Yet he could also remember the moment he noticed the trail of blood on the hallway carpet leading to the emergency stairwell beside the elevator. He had missed it on his way in—too jacked up to spot it. Now, looking at Temps's place, he realized that the man had been wounded in the shootout. And he'd lost a considerable amount of blood but decided not to go to a hospital. Instead, he was inside his small house with the lights out.

Matt circled the block and parked on the street beside the fortune-teller's corner lot. He checked his .45. After returning the pistol to his belt holster, he slipped a couple of extra mags into his pocket and got out of the car. There was a cool breeze tonight, the moon up but waning, and Matt took a few minutes to let his eyes adjust to the darkness. While he could hear a dog barking on the next block, it was the distant sounds of motorcycles street racing, cut against waves of police sirens, that filled the night here in the Valley.

He let it go and turned back to the fortune-teller's house. The curtains were drawn, the narrow backyard not fenced in. As he considered the possibilities, he figured that Temps had to know someone would be pursuing him tonight. Because he had killed two FBI agents and was wounded, Temps would probably be desperate. Most likely he was sitting in the living room keyed in on the front door with a gun in his hand.

Matt remembered the size of the magazine on that pistol. Seventeen rounds plus one in the chamber.

It was a grim image. Nothing about the way in would be easy.

He glanced at the empty streets, then crossed into the fortune-teller's backyard. He walked silently, keeping to the shadows and melting into the darkness behind the house. As he passed the kitchen window, he peeked inside and saw a middle-aged woman with a cat on her lap watching TV in the living room. It seemed so peaceful that he had to force himself to turn away and keep moving. He stepped around the corner and through the side yard, following Temps's fence until he reached the driveway and passed through the open gate.

Temps's backyard had the look and feel of a dump. Several old appliances were stacked in the corner beside a refrigerator that was lying on its side with the door off. Piles of debris lined the rear of the property instead of bushes or trees. Off the back porch, a small space had been cleared of junk to make room for a cheap table and two chairs. Beside the table, a portable gas grill had been set up on a cinder block and, despite the rust, still looked as if it was used once in a while.

Matt turned to the house. When he noticed that the back door was cracked open, he stepped closer feeling uneasy about it. He peered through the glass above the door handle, but it was too dark inside to see anything other than his own reflection staring back at him. He tightened his jaw. He could still hear those motorcycles racing in the streets and the chaotic wave of police sirens. Somehow, they seemed closer now. More disturbing, and in his way.

He tried to slow his heart down. He tried to quiet his breathing as he eased the door open, waited a beat, then stepped into the dark room.

He found himself standing in the kitchen. The sound of an old refrigerator laboring to avoid the trash heap outside appeared to dominate the entire house. He was attempting to locate Temps by his wheezing. But when he managed to filter the sound of the refrigerator out of his mind, the heater switched on and filled the room with more white noise.

He turned and looked at the dishes stacked on the counter beside rows of dirty glasses. The plastic trays from countless microwave dinners were stuffed into a plastic trash bag. And then there was the wretched smell of the place. The foul odor of rotting food, sweaty sheets, and a house that may not have been cleaned since Temps moved in. A fly entered the room. Matt watched the insect land on a glass in the sink and drink a single drop of water.

He turned away, sickened, and started across the kitchen. He could see the living room in the gloom. The front door was coming into view. A picture window over a couch with dim light from the street filtering in.

And then a crushing blow to the back of his head.

Matt collapsed onto the floor.

Before he had time to react, Temps began kicking him in the head. Matt fought through the blows and grabbed hold of the man's leg. Yanking him down to the floor, he got to his knees and flipped him onto his back. Temps seemed to panic with the move, his fingers reaching out of the darkness for Matt's face and throat. But he wasn't fast enough. Matt straddled his body and sent three hard fists into his face. The blows stunned Temps for a moment. When he seemed to come to, he rolled onto his belly and tried to squirm away. Caught by surprise, Matt pulled him back and managed to get to his feet. He threw Temps onto the kitchen table, the sound of everything crashing onto the floor horrendous. Temps made another try for the door and still wasn't quick enough.

Matt could see that things were beginning to slow down in his mind and knew inside himself that he was thinking of Dr. May now. What Temps had done to her. What role the detective may have played in the governor's two killing sprees.

He saw Temps trying to get away and felt a load of adrenaline scream through his body. Lunging forward, he seized the man by the belt and shirt collar and lifted him off the ground like a toy. And then he swung him through the air and tossed his body onto the counter. Temps let out a groan. Glasses and plates shattered as he slammed against the wall, bounced back, and tumbled off the counter onto the floor.

Matt watched the man's body begin shuddering. As he lay facedown on a carpet of broken glass, he started twisting his neck and moving his arms and legs. Matt was about to cross the room and cuff him when Temps suddenly jumped to his feet and made a third try for the living room.

Caught by surprise, Matt could see him sprinting away and gaining distance. He could see him reaching for the front door and yanking it open.

And that's when Matt hit the light switch and froze.

The man vanishing through the front door wasn't Temps.

FORTY-SIX

Matt watched the front door slam shut—stunned.

It wasn't Temps.

It had been Alan Fontaine, the governor's personal attorney and fixer.

Worse still, Matt suddenly became aware that he wasn't alone in the room. Someone else was here. His shoulders tightened, and he turned to his left very slowly.

Temps was sitting in a chair by the TV. His eyes were open, and he'd dropped his gun on the floor. Blood had begun to radiate across the beige carpet, forming a large pool.

If there was something past death, another exit after the final stop, it looked like Temps had made it and paid the toll.

Matt felt a chill ripple up his spine as he eyeballed the corpse and stepped closer. By all appearances Temps had tried to mend the gunshot wound himself. But the color of the blood was almost black. He must have known that he had been hit in the liver and anything he might have tried on his own would have been pointless.

He must have known that he was dying.

Matt took a deep breath and exhaled, glancing at the front door and thinking about Fontaine. Why would he drive all the way out here? Had Temps become a risk? Did Fontaine want to clean things up before his killer client announced his campaign for the presidency tomorrow night? Did the governor's fixer come here to fix Temps?

Matt gave the room a hard look all the way around. His medical file and the envelope with the photographs were nowhere to be seen. Yet Fontaine had left empty handed. Matt was certain of it.

He looked back at Temps. From the impressions in the blood-soaked carpet, it seemed like the chair had been turned to face the couch and picture window. And when Matt followed the dead man's morbid gaze, it appeared to stop on the SUV parked on the front lawn.

Matt ripped open the front door, checked the street for Fontaine, then rushed over to the Interceptor. He noticed the keyless remote starter in a cup holder but didn't see anything on the seats except for a grocery bag filled with small bottles of Irish whiskey. Searching under the driver's seat, he spotted an old .38 revolver and wasn't surprised to find that the serial numbers had been removed. As he stuffed the handgun behind his belt, he stretched his left arm over the console and reached underneath the passenger seat. He could feel a canvas bag there. It was small and flat and about the size of a book bag. When he pulled it out and opened the flap, he saw his medical file and the manila envelope inside.

Matt raced back into the house, locked the front door, and sat down on the couch. After weighing the envelope in his hand, he unfastened the clip and slid out the pictures.

And then his stomach turned, and he became very still.

The murders of Emily Kosinski and her three-year-old boy had been photographed.

He glanced at the dead man staring at him and that chill came back. Colder this time—deeper. And he could feel the hairs on the back of his neck standing on end.

Once he regained his composure, he set the stack of pictures on the coffee table and began paging through them. The crimes had actually been documented. It was a photographic study of the depraved.

Governor James D. Hayworth, a war hero, roughing up his intern and forcing himself on her. Governor Hayworth wielding a long knife that easily could have been a bayonet. Governor Hayworth screaming with a madman glint in his eyes and blood all over his face and mouth like Hannibal the Cannibal. Governor Hayworth on the bathroom floor with his victims in a scene too gruesome to even imagine.

Murder, like rape or even forced sex, was ultimately about power. Matt could remember his mentor at the academy talking about it.

Power.

A governor running for—

Matt glanced at Temps again, then turned back to the pictures.

All of the images appeared to have been taken from the same angle. As Matt chewed it over, it occurred to him that the alarm sensor in the ceiling had to include a hidden camera. The governor probably wanted pictures, maybe even a video and keepsakes, so that he could get off on the murders over and over again.

How could anyone anywhere under any circumstances cross that far over the line of human decency? How could anyone who experienced such a deep psychological breakdown want to remember the moment with pictures?

A bead of sweat dropped onto the manila envelope. Matt's mind jolted to the surface, and he froze.

It was the sound of those police sirens. They had changed direction. They weren't in the distance any longer. They were approaching.

Matt slid the pictures into the envelope and stuffed everything into the book bag. Then he raced across the room and hit the light switch.

Moments later, he could see them out the picture window and returned to the couch for a better view. Two police cruisers from the Topanga station were roaring down the street with their lights flashing. When they skidded to a stop in front of the house, Alan Fontaine slipped out of the shadows like a weasel, waving his hands in the air and showing the four cops his ID. Matt counted three men and a woman, and he could hear Fontaine shouting at them. He was telling them that he was the governor's personal attorney. That Jones was a cop killer. That Jones had just shot and murdered one of their own. A detective from the Topanga station.

Matt knew that they were buying Fontaine's story by the look on their faces. But even more, three of them were drawing their guns while the fourth reached for his radio mic and appeared to be calling for backup.

Jack Temps. The Topanga station's pride and joy.

Matt guessed that nothing about who Temps might have been a few minutes ago would matter for the next couple of hours. And he could feel the terror chasing him as he bolted through the kitchen and out the back door. He could hear the police radios now, the squawk between transmissions from the front of the house. The dispatcher updating the progress of incoming grunts and the hopelessly misinformed.

He looked at the open gate and knew that he would be seen. Climbing on top of the refrigerator, he straddled the fence, dropped onto the other side, and sprinted through the fortune-teller's backyard.

He could see his car parked across the street. He could hear the approaching sirens getting louder. The sound of his lungs pumping air in and out of his chest. His ears ringing.

He started across the sidewalk. And then, as if being pulled back, he stopped and turned and looked directly at a man standing in the middle of the street one block down the hill. It was Alan Fontaine, staring at him with a big grin on his face. He wasn't calling out for help. And he didn't appear to be afraid or even in a hurry. The governor's fixer was just standing there with an evil smile on his face.

In many ways it felt like a break in time. But then it ended with Fontaine climbing into a Lincoln Town Car and driving off.

Matt rushed over to his own car, totally spooked. Tossing the book bag on the passenger seat, he got the engine started but noticed that his hands were shaking violently. The radio came up, along with the static, and he turned it off. As he pulled away from the curb, he glanced at the media screen on the dashboard and watched it flicker, then go blank.

He picked up speed, wiping the sweat off his brow.

He was passing a long line of cop cars now, all racing in the opposite direction with their lights and sirens screaming. For some strange reason, all he could think about was a swarm of killer bees whizzing by with their stingers cocked and loaded.

He let it go. And then he let more of it go, his hands still trembling.

After they passed, he checked the rearview mirror and began to relax some. But as he left the neighborhood behind and crossed through an intersection, he noticed the smell of something burning inside the car. It was an electrical fire, coming from somewhere behind the dashboard. He could see smoke billowing into the cabin—an acrid, bitter cloud, so dense that he swerved off the street and jumped out. Using the flashlight on his cell phone, he panned the beam of light underneath the audio system.

And that's when he spotted the wires that shouldn't have been there.

He turned and started running down the street and over a fence into a field. He was sprinting faster and faster and faster still. He could feel the dread chasing him—the Grim Reaper reaching out with his long fingers.

Alan Fontaine's vile grin.

That man dressed in black standing by his car outside the governor's house.

And then something snapped, and the world felt like it stopped and broke and shut down. The flash of light was so bright that it could have been high noon, the sound of the explosion deafening.

The ground started shaking, and he lost his footing and fell down. The smell of gasoline was everywhere, and he could see flames rippling through the dry grass and racing by his body until they reached the top of the hill.

He glanced back at what was left of his car—the pictures, the evidence, his case—the blaze eating up the night and beginning to surround him.

He watched in horror as his shirtsleeve burst into flames from the sheer heat. When he couldn't wipe the fire away with his hand, he ripped off his shirt and struggled to get back on his feet. He tried to fight through the confusion, the terror, and maybe just get to his knees.

He knew that he needed to run. He knew that he needed to get away.

But then he gazed upward. Something on fire was falling toward him from the sky. It didn't look like a tire or a car door. As he realized that it was the front seat, he thought he could hear the sound of a man quite like himself let out a hideous scream.

FORTY-SEVEN

Matt gazed at his watch, wiping his eyes and trying to focus on the numbers. Somehow the past thirty minutes had been lost. When he woke up, he found himself in the bushes three doors down from Temps's house. His feet hurt as if he had been walking or scrambling or running a great distance. All he really knew was that he had managed to avoid being crushed by the front seat of his car and that the explosion had caused a massive wildfire.

He could see it from here. The entire ridge was engulfed in flames a mile or two off. And even though it sounded like firefighters were already on the scene, the winds blowing in from the desert had picked up.

He turned back to Temps's house. Five black-and-white cruisers were parked at the curb, with crime scene tape strung along the property line. But what really mattered was the Interceptor and the keyless remote starter Matt remembered seeing in the cup holder. The SUV had been moved onto the street behind the cruisers to make room for the evidence collection truck and the coroner's van. Two cops were knocking on doors and interviewing neighbors. Everyone else seemed to be inside the house.

Matt kept his eyes on the two cops knocking on doors. They were working their way toward the other end of the block. When they reached the corner house and stepped up to the door, Matt slipped out from behind the bushes and rushed over to the Interceptor.

The keyless remote was still in the cup holder.

He jumped in, turned off the auto headlight switch, and started the SUV. After giving Temps's house another quick look, he shifted into neutral and let the car glide in reverse down the hill into the intersection. Then he shifted back into drive and idled through the darkness onto the next block.

He lowered the windows and listened.

Silence never sounded so righteous. No one had seen him. No one had noticed.

Switching on the headlights, he tried to keep cool and quietly drove off. Unfortunately, the freeway was on the other side of the wildfire. Within a few miles, he had passed what was left of his car, along with the fire engines and emergency vehicles that were still arriving but seemed too late. The trees and bushes were burning on both sides of the street here. It was like streaming through a fire tunnel, and he could smell the foul odor of the SUV's tires beginning to melt. When he saw a grove of trees burst into flames just off the road, he flinched and gasped but barreled forward like there was no turning back.

He had lost a lot in the car explosion. But what he missed most right now were the meds he kept in his laptop case. His shoulder, his feet, the burns on his arms, the wounds from the four gunshots he had taken in the fall—it all seemed like it was dialing in at once.

For the first time in his life it felt like he was alone. Like he was circling the drain. Like Dr. May had been right when she warned him that he could reach a point where there was no way back.

Why hadn't he listened to her? Why hadn't he played it safe and sat this one out?

He knew the answer without thinking about it. Still, the ride through the burning forest seemed endless. He turned on the police radio, not really listening as much as playing back the last few days in his head. As the past seemed to rush forward into the now, he began to realize that he was finally breaking through the fire wall. He could see the freeway entrance buried in the clouds of smoke. A traffic sign pointing west, and another leading east just ahead.

What if neither one of them made sense anymore?

He thought about the way forward. He knew in his gut that the fire wasn't really behind him. That what lay ahead would probably be his undoing. He also knew that he had to see someone.

He needed to make sure that they knew what had been found tonight. But also what had been lost.

It took an hour and a half of hard driving before he pulled off the 134 Freeway in Pasadena and wound his way back to North Grand Avenue. He spotted the chief's security team in a Chevy Suburban at the corner and guessed that they had called the chief the minute they saw him approaching. As he drove down the block beneath the canopy of branches and leaves, he checked the time on the dash. It was late, too late to wake up an LAPD chief. But when he pulled over and climbed out of the burned-up SUV, there he was sitting on his front porch in a bathrobe.

Chief Richard S. Logan. The man with eyes the color of a semiautomatic pistol.

Matt walked up the steps and could see the chief measuring him.

"What the hell happened to you, Jones?"

Matt shook his head without saying anything.

"Where's your shirt?"

"It burned up."

"Come over here," he said. "Take this chair next to me."

Matt strained to cross the porch and sit down.

The chief met his gaze. "Would a drink help, son?"

"I don't think so," Matt said. "But thanks for asking."

A car idled by the house, the sound muffled by the tall oak trees. Matt watched it closely, suspiciously. When it pulled into a driveway near the end of the block, he turned back to the chief.

"He did it, Chief," he said in a lower voice. "The governor murdered his intern and then killed the boy."

"You sound so certain."

"I am because he took pictures of himself committing the murders."

The chief remained quiet for a while. When Matt read his face, he didn't see shock—just disappointment and pain.

"Do you have these pictures?"

Matt shook his head. He could barely say it, or even admit it. He could barely maintain his composure.

"They were in my car when it blew up," he said in a shaky voice. "Everything burned. Everything's gone. All I have are these."

Matt pulled out his cell phone and showed the chief pictures of the blood spatter he had recorded at the governor's house in the Palisades.

"Where were these taken?"

"In his bedroom."

The chief passed the phone back. "You realize that these were illegally obtained? That you've committed a crime? That if anyone ever found out you entered his home and took these pictures without a warrant, it would blow the entire case?"

The chief's words settled in. Matt wiped his chin, reeking of gasoline.

"I took them for myself, I guess. I took them because I needed to know if it was true or not."

"That's not a good-enough reason. No reason's good enough. You broke the law."

Everything the chief just said was righteous, and Matt knew it. He had followed Temps to the governor's house. He had watched the detective commit a break-in, then steal an envelope filled with pictures that he had found hidden in the master bedroom. If Matt had been in control of himself, if he hadn't been so jacked up, he would have confronted Temps on the street. But he blew it.

The chief cleared his throat. "I've got bad news, son. Real bad news."

Matt leaned closer. "What could be worse than what's already happened?"

"Topanga reported the explosion. They thought that you were killed until they realized Temps's car had been stolen. The manhunt's on again. I'm sure you're safe for a while, but I wouldn't go home tonight."

Matt was surprised. "They still think I shot Temps?"

The chief nodded. "It's complicated. The Feds don't believe Dr. May's story. They think she's covering for you."

"What about Temps's gun? The rounds he fired in her office? They have to match."

"His pistol was found by his body and is on its way to the lab. But the tech who entered it into evidence claims that it looks brand new. He doesn't even think it's ever been fired. They found the box it came in on the kitchen floor by the trash."

"But Temps was there. Security cameras would have picked him up. And it's a matter of record. He made an appointment to see her."

"He was there, the Feds were there, but it was dark. It's tough to say who shot who or even what time it was. Dr. May says Temps knocked her out. She doesn't remember looking at her watch when she woke up. According to the investigator from the coroner's office, Temps's wound is a through and through which they believe shattered a window. They don't have a bullet. Your story, or even the timeline, can't be verified."

Matt thought it over. His examination of Temps's corpse hadn't been any more thorough than a quick look. He hadn't noticed the exit wound.

"Why would Dr. May be covering for me?" he said finally.

The chief mulled it over before speaking. "During the interview with the FBI she used your first name. She did it more than once. They think the two of you are having an affair—that you mean more to her than a patient. It's no secret that Fresno and Cook have been on your back from the beginning. A witness, a sous-chef at the Biltmore, claims he saw them rough you up in the kitchen. The Feds think you shot Fresno and Cook, then wounded Temps. When Temps got away, you followed him home and let him bleed out without calling for help."

Matt added it up.

Two dead FBI agents and a dead LAPD detective who once had a decent reputation. Matt Jones, Jersey Boy—Cop Killer.

It sank in like a judge reading the word *guilty* in a courtroom.

Guilty.

Matt wiped the sweat off his forehead.

"It gets worse, son," the chief whispered.

Matt gave him a look. "How could it get worse?"

"The DNA," the chief said. "Speeks called with the results. The semen they found in Emily Kosinski's body doesn't match the governor's. And the governor's DNA doesn't match the boy's."

Matt started to get up like it was time to run. The chief grabbed his arm and pulled him back into the chair.

"Listen to me," the chief said. "The boy's DNA doesn't even match the mother's."

It doesn't seem possible, Your Honor! Something happened! Something's wrong!

Guilty as charged. Take him away.

"But I saw the pictures, Chief. With my own eyes—I saw them. The governor killed these people. Not just his intern and her boy. Ryan Brooks and his wife and daughter were murdered exactly the same way. Brooks figured out who the governor was before I did. Madina says that the bite marks are an exact match, as good as a fingerprint. The governor's a madman. He's killed two families. He's murdered two kids. He's a psychopath. So what happens next? He walks?"

The chief sat back in his chair. Matt could see him chewing it over with his eyes turned inward. When he spoke finally, still thinking it through, his voice was deathly quiet.

"He walks," the chief said. "And then he claims that we were out to get him. That there was never any evidence that he had any relationship with the girl. That somewhere out there is the real killer. That we made it all up. That we lied. That we manipulated the evidence. That all it ever was or ever will be is a conspiracy theory. An attempt by the LAPD to destroy his good name and outstanding career."

FORTY-EIGHT

His good name and outstanding career . . .

Matt pulled into the lot behind the Hollywood station, burying Temps's burned-up Interceptor in the rear aisle with twenty-five other Interceptors. Then he found his unmarked sedan and waited for two narcotic detectives whom he knew and liked to park and enter the building. Once they were inside, he pulled onto Wilcox trying not to think about how much he had let his friends down.

How much he had let the chief and the department down.

It was late, and the marine layer had swept in off the ocean. Traffic was thin to none, and in less than an hour, Matt had reached the metered parking lot on the beach in front of Ryan Brooks's house. The truth was, he didn't know where else to go. And he needed time to get cleaned up and think.

He turned off the headlights and sat in the car for ten minutes, keeping an eye on things and devouring a Double-Double with fries that he'd ordered at the In-N-Out Burger over on Venice Boulevard. He hadn't eaten in what felt like days, and the piping-hot coffee tasted pretty good, too. When he finished, he tossed the bag on the passenger-seat floor and gave Brooks's house another look through the eerie mist.

The death house. The place where, at least for him, this catastrophic nightmare began.

It seemed so odd given the depravity of the murders that had occurred here. But in all this time, Matt hadn't seen a single cop pass by on either Manhattan Beach Boulevard or Ocean Drive. He had noticed the same thing earlier in the week when he realized that the house and property hadn't been sealed with crime scene tape. This was an exclusive beach community. It felt like no one wanted to be reminded that an entire family had been killed here. Instead, the investigation had been handed over to the Feds so that the entire neighborhood could pretend it had never happened.

And then what? They became beautiful again? They could look at themselves in the mirror and think that life was what?

Good? Fair? Just?

Matt got out of the car and made his way up the path through the fog. When he reached the house, he climbed over the fence into the side yard, passed through the privacy gate, and opened the front door with the key he had removed from Cindy Brooks's key ring.

Enough ambient light was feeding in through the windows that he could find his way around without a flashlight. As he stepped into the kitchen, he noticed that the rank odor of rotting blood was beginning to fade into the background. But the silence of the place, the absolute stillness, was more oppressive than ever. Everything looked exactly the way it had looked when Brooks and his family were alive. Matt could see the pot still on the stove. The box of pasta on the counter. The table set for a simple dinner.

The finality of it all cut deep enough to spawn more than a few nightmares.

He looked away, trying to ignore it. Then he climbed the stairs, grabbed a towel from the linen closet where Sato had found Brooks's file, and walked into the bathroom off the nursery. There was no blood here. Nothing really to worry about except for the windows.

After a careful glance outside, he peeled off his jeans in the darkness and stepped into the shower. Standing under the spill of warm water almost seemed overwhelming. Washing away the smells of the wildfire—the gasoline clinging to his skin and strewn through his hair—felt even better. When the hot water ran out, he toweled himself dry and entered the master bedroom. He could see the bloodstains on the carpet and moved around them to the closet. Matt imagined that he and Brooks were about the same size and build. As he got dressed, he tried not to think too much about what he was doing.

Still, it was there in the mirror, reflecting back at him like a mark on his forehead. There he was standing in the gloom—clean and fresh and wearing a dead man's clothes.

He shook off the bad vibes and checked the master bath. It was too bloody to enter, and he hoped that like most people, Brooks kept emergency medical supplies in the kitchen. He hurried downstairs and found them in the cabinet beside the stove. A small first aid kit that included Band-Aids and a tube of Neosporin. Behind the kit he saw a large supply of vitamins and sorted through them until he spotted a bottle of ibuprofen. Prying the cap off, he shook the caplets out and counted only three. Not enough to kill the pain but as many as he needed to get started.

Matt swallowed all three pills with a glass of water from the sink, then pulled out his cell phone and stepped down the foyer into Brooks's study. Checking the couch for fingerprint powder before sitting down, he paged through his recent call list and hit "Enter."

Dr. May picked up after the first ring.

"Are you alone?" he said in a low voice.

She cleared her throat lightly. "Yes."

"Where are you?"

"In bed," she said. "Where are you?"

"Still out and about."

"Out and about?"

"Sort of," he said. "You know you've had a concussion. You're not supposed to fall asleep."

"I'm not feeling very sleepy."

A moment passed. And then another. Matt lifted his legs onto the couch and lay back.

"They think I'm in love with you," she whispered.

More silence. Matt could feel his stomach churning. His heart beating. He checked the cell phone's battery. It was low. If it died right now, he might die with it.

"Are you?" he said.

"Am I in love with you?"

"Yeah."

He could hear her breathing. He could see her naked body in the sheets.

"I'm your doctor, you know."

"But that doesn't really answer the question," he said.

"Tell me what you've been doing since I saw you last."

"Do I call you Julie, or do I call you Dr. May?"

"Julie," she said. "That much I'm sure of."

"I'm in trouble, Julie."

"The FBI told me that you murdered three people. I tried to tell them that you weren't even here at the time, but they wouldn't believe me."

Matt tossed it over. "They didn't want to believe you. That's the way some cops are."

"Normal people, too, Matthew. Sometimes they only see what they want to see."

Matt rolled onto his side, staring through the doorway into the kitchen. "I've let a lot of good people down."

"Is it over?"

"Close."

"But close isn't over," she said. "Close only means close."

He saw the lights bouncing off the walls and froze. Lights from a patrol unit, then flashlights.

"I've gotta go," he said quickly.

"Are you okay?"

"Company," he said. "I've gotta go."

He switched off the phone and scrambled to his feet. He could hear voices now. They were coming from the other side of the front door. Three men. Inching toward the foyer, he could see them peering through the two windows. Two cops in uniform—one older, the other young—with a man whom Matt guessed was a neighbor.

"What did you see?" the older cop asked.

"Nothing really," the man said. "I thought I heard someone moving around in there."

"You didn't see any lights?"

"No, but it sounded like the water was running."

Matt heard the younger cop check the lock on the front door, then saw him start around the side of the house. He seemed like the nervous type, and Matt wondered if he might not be trigger-happy. Still, Matt left his .45 holstered and crossed the room to the window. Through the slats in the blinds he could see the cruiser in a cloud of fog parked on the street. A second unit had just turned into the metered lot on the beach, passing Matt's car and parking at the end by the bike path.

If they didn't have a key to the house, he would be okay. But that didn't make watching them any easier. They were on the deck now, checking the locks on the sliders and peering into the great room and then the kitchen.

"Maybe all you heard was the ice maker," the older cop said.

"No," the man said. "It was longer than that. And I thought I heard someone talking."

"What if all you heard was someone on the beach?"

The man shrugged. "What about the running water?"

The older cop frowned and gave his partner a look. "Let's go back to the car and call it in."

They walked down the steps to the beach, then waved the second unit over. Matt returned to the window and watched all five of them walk up the path to the cruiser. Despite the marine layer, he could see the older cop sit down in the passenger seat and grab the radio mic. Everyone seemed edgy and spooked and kept their eyes locked on Brooks's house.

The murder house had become a problem in their neighborhood again.

Matt thought it over. If they didn't have a key to the front door, they were about to get one. He guessed that he had less than five minutes to bolt. The front door was too out in the open. Even worse, the rear deck was too well lighted.

Matt ran into the kitchen and opened the window over the sink. Lifting away the screen, he climbed through and lowered himself to the ground. Once he got the window closed and the screen back in place, he rushed down the narrow side yard and peeked around the deck. The lights were flashing on the second cruiser, but the car still appeared empty.

Matt raced across the bike path onto the beach. After passing three or four houses, he looked back through the fog and saw a third cruiser making its approach down Ocean Drive. But the house was empty now. And Matt had reached the hard sand by the water's edge. He was on the run, sprinting through the clouds and into the darkness. Again and again, into the wind.

FORTY-NINE

Matt saw the Biltmore half a block up the street but took a moment to gaze at the skyline just as he had earlier in the week. Downtown LA had changed so much since he'd moved here, and just the sight of the tall buildings, the lights, even the people filling the sidewalks helped steady his nerves.

He wasn't sure who said that the shortest way to nowhere was straight ahead, but he'd spent the past few hours mulling things over, and the phrase sounded good enough to roll with tonight.

As he started up the sidewalk eyeballing the hotel, he gave his belt a tap just to confirm that he had left his .45 behind. The governor's limo was already parked in front of the doors to the lobby, along with a procession of motorcycles, cruisers from the Sheriff's Department, and more than ten unmarked SUVs. Two areas had been roped off and were waiting for the media, and Matt guessed that a lot of planning had gone into making the governor's exit appear presidential on TV.

Every winner needed a motorcade.

He pulled himself together as he entered the hotel, badging his way past security and stepping into the main ballroom. The place was already packed with hundreds of the governor's supporters, holding their seats and chanting along with the music that was playing. At the head of the room, fifty American flags lined the stage before a huge banner that read JIMMY D.

Hayworth for President—Fighting for Us, Rebuilding Our Dreams. In the back by the entrance, the media had set their cameras on a stage of the same height to ensure clean shots over the heads of the crowd.

Matt could feel the electricity in the room. The anticipation and excitement that came with the governor's long-awaited announcement. But he could also feel the stares he was starting to get as he made his way down the center aisle toward the stage.

The Feds were here in all their glory and seemed eager to make the arrest of Detective Matthew Trevor Jones. LAPD detectives in plain clothes were here as well and easy enough to spot. Yet something was holding them all back. Two men wearing uniforms. And when they turned and started walking toward him, Matt realized that it was Chief Logan, along with Matt's supervisor, Lieutenant McKensie.

Their faces were grim. Stonelike. Fierce with determination.

Matt continued walking to the side of the stage as they reached him and, without a word, traded hard looks. Through the doorway he could see the governor wearing a smock and seated before a makeup table and long mirror while a woman touched up his face before doing his hair. His wife, Lisa, was seated right beside him, wearing a smock as well and watching a second makeup artist unpack her kit. Alan Fontaine was leaning against the wall with a smirk on his face and a sheaf of papers in his hand.

This was the night. The moment.

And then Matt stepped through the doorway with the chief and Lieutenant McKensie following him into the room.

"How's it going, Governor?" he said. "Big night tonight?"

They turned. All of them. Their eyes bright with shock and awe. Fontaine bolted forward.

"What in the world are you doing here, Jones? It's over. All the way over."

Matt nodded. "You're right about that. You win, I lose, Counselor. I just thought I should stop by for a few minutes to wish the governor luck."

"Luck?" the governor bellowed. "What is he doing here, Chief? Why hasn't this man been arrested?"

"We'll get to that later," the chief said. "Until then, he's with me."

"And with me," McKensie added.

Matt took a moment to size up the governor. "Before you walk out on that stage, Governor, I'd like to hear you explain yourself. It's the decent thing to do, don't you think?"

"Are you out of your mind?"

Matt shrugged. "I think you need to clear the air. You owe us that."

"For God's sake, I don't owe you anything."

Matt glanced at Lisa, saw that she was upset, then turned back to the governor. "I think you do. I think you owe me. And I think you need to tell all of us about the affair you had with your intern, Emily Kosinski."

It hung there. The unsaid and the unspoken. In the middle of the room with everyone staring at each other.

Matt moved closer. "You remember her, don't you?" he added. "The young woman who worked in your office, Governor? The one who disappeared?"

The governor shook his head, aghast. "I don't even know what you're talking about! Alan, get rid of these people!"

Fontaine took a step forward, then stopped dead in his tracks when Matt flashed his teeth and waved him off. Matt was staring at the governor now and tossing things over. He had to admit that the governor's thin skin surprised him. Despite the makeup, he could see sweat beginning to bead on his forehead. He had already noticed the choppy cadence in the way the man was speaking. Those nervous blue eyes flicking back and forth. Matt knew that he should have been thrown out of the room five minutes ago, yet he was still here, plunging forward. Maybe Julie May had been right when they spoke on the phone last night. Close didn't necessarily mean that he'd reached the end. Close only meant that he was close.

Matt let the thought go and took another step forward. "We're not going anywhere, Governor. And you know exactly who I'm talking about. Emily Kosinski had everything going her way. She was young, smart, and went to a great school. She had looks, style, and a bright future. You had an affair with her, sir. You were in love with her."

The governor started shaking, then pointed a finger at Matt's chest. "I never had sex with that woman!"

Matt traded looks with the chief and McKensie, then turned back to the governor. "Is that how you're gonna explain yourself? Is that the best you can do? *I never had sex with 'that' woman?* Why do you think those words sound so familiar?"

A moment passed, the air in the room doubling in weight. The governor was staring at his wife, beckoning her for help. Then Lisa turned to Matt. She seemed shy and nervous, and when she spoke, her voice was just above a whisper.

"Does this really have to happen tonight, Matty? Couldn't it wait until morning, or at least until we have more privacy. The media's out there. Hundreds of people are waiting. It seems so embarrassing to do it this way. So needlessly unfair."

The chief glanced at the two makeup artists, pointing them toward a second door in the back of the room. Matt waited for them to scurry out and then turned back to the governor's wife. He didn't want to hurt her. He didn't want to violate the memory he had of his best friend's sister when he lived in New Jersey. The teenage girl who had looked after him as a boy.

"I'm sorry," he said. "You don't know how sorry I am that it has to be this way. That it has to happen tonight. But if everything your husband just said is true, no one will ever know." Matt's eyes rocked back to the governor. "How'd you put it again, Governor? *I never had sex with 'that' woman?*"

The governor started nodding. "It's the God's honest truth, Jones. I swear it is. Not with that woman. I never did, and I never would. She was cheap. Disgusting. Below my station in life."

Matt leaned into the governor's face and met his wild eyes. "You had a love child with that woman, Governor. A little boy whom she named after you."

Matt's voice was soft and steady, but it reverberated throughout the small room as if it had been shot from a gun. Fontaine and Lisa cringed while the governor shook his head back and forth and sank into his chair.

"You have absolutely no proof of this," he said. "No proof at all. You're ruining everything. The whole goddamn night! Alan, what am I paying you for? Do your job!"

Fontaine tossed the roll of papers on the table and turned to the chief. "They're right, Chief. No matter what's happened, this doesn't have to be like this. You're standing in front of the next president of the United States, and you're spouting what? Theories. Opinions. Or is it worse than that? Best guesses based on a maybe or a what-if? Everything that Jones has just said amounts to nothing more than political dirt. And you're pulling this stunt with all those cameras out there. All those people waiting to hear him speak. Listen to them cheering. Do you realize what kind of a lawsuit we could bring to the table? You don't have a single piece of evidence. We know that, don't we, Jones? All you have is a hunch!"

Matt met Fontaine's eyes. "A hunch, Counselor?"

Fontaine looked around, then lowered his voice, seething. "I know what you're inferring. Everybody here knows what you're inferring."

"And what's that?" Matt said.

"This has nothing to do with the affair the governor had with Emily Kosinski, or even the boy. You think that he murdered them."

Lisa let out a gasp. The governor turned, his eyes big and glassy.

"My God, Alan," he said. "What have you just done?"

FIFTY

"**You killed her,**" Matt said.

The governor sank deeper into his chair, shaking his head with his eyes closed. "No."

"You killed your own son."

"No."

"You can't hide it, Governor. There may have been a lab error with the first DNA test we ran, but another is underway right now. It began this morning and there's nothing you can do to stop it or defile it. We'll have the results tomorrow morning by nine a.m."

"But it won't prove anything," the governor said quickly. "Even a match proves nothing."

Matt leaned into the man's face. "It proves everything, but that's not your biggest problem right now."

"What's his biggest problem?"

Matt turned. It had been Lisa who asked the question. He could see the pain in her glassy eyes. The disappointment and fear showing on her face. Matt wished that there could have been another way forward.

Any other way.

"The autopsy reports," he said as gently as possible. "The bite marks that were discovered on Emily Kosinski's body and the ones found on Cindy Brooks. They're a perfect match. According to the medical examiner, they're just as good as a fingerprint."

Matt looked back at the governor, measuring him carefully. The man appeared lost inside himself, and Matt wondered if he wasn't replaying the murders in his head.

"You did it," Matt said finally. "You stabbed them to death. And you couldn't help yourself. When you were done, you murdered a three-year-old boy. Your boy, Governor. Your own flesh and blood. And when a reporter started asking questions and you thought you were gonna get caught, you killed him as well. You murdered Ryan Brooks and his wife. But even that wasn't enough for you. Even that wasn't enough to satisfy your demented appetite. You killed them and then you stabbed their two-year-old daughter to death. An infant. Emma Brooks. She weighed less than twenty pounds, Governor. You killed her in her parents' bathtub with a ten-inch chef's knife."

The governor's body started trembling and he pounded the table with a closed fist. "Okay," he said in a loud voice. "Okay, I did it! Are you happy? I did it! I've been holding it in for three goddamn years! Holding it in and trying not to explode! I stabbed them to death! Emily and David! But not that reporter, or his wife, do you hear me? And not the little girl!"

Matt grimaced. "Stop playing games. I just gave you the results from the autopsies. The medical examiner called the bite marks a lock."

"But you don't understand, Jones. You still don't get it! I loved Emily! Do you hear me? I loved her! I didn't want to hurt her! Jesus Christ, I didn't mean to do it!"

Matt glanced at Lisa. The pain he'd seen just a few minutes ago had become agony now. The fear more like terror. Her lips were quivering. He looked back at the governor.

"You didn't mean to do it?" Matt said. "Is that what you just said? You loved her?"

"I did," the governor said in a weak voice. "I was in love with her."

"You fell in love with Emily Kosinski?"

The governor nodded, unable to speak.

"Then why did you stab her forty-seven times?"

The governor pounded the table again. "But I didn't mean to do it. The whole thing was a blur. My wife wasn't supposed to be in town. She was supposed to be in Sacramento. And then all of a sudden she walks in and catches us in bed together. I was beside myself. I loved Emily. I loved her—but not now! No, no, no! Not ever again! Now I hate her! Now I hate everything about her! That bitch ruined me! That's right—I said it! She ruined my life!"

Matt traded looks with the chief and McKensie again, then turned back to the governor, whose eyes had begun tearing.

"She ruined your life, Governor?" he said quietly.

The man nodded slightly without speaking. Matt leaned closer.

"What do you think you did to hers?"

The governor wiped his cheeks, his hands still trembling, his chest heaving. "She ruined everything."

A long moment passed. Bitter and acidic and radiating a grim darkness. Matt took a step back and gave the man another long look.

"How did the bodies end up in a parking lot in Pico Gardens?" he said finally.

The governor paused to think it over, still shaking, still wiping his cheeks, still confused. "Like I said, the whole thing was a blur. A nightmare. When I came out of it there was blood everywhere. All over the sheets. All over me. I thought I was gonna have a heart attack. I dropped the knife and called Alan. Temps owed him a favor, so Alan brought him in, and he became the lead detective. Temps wanted a lot of money. Once we came to an agreement, they cleaned up the place and dumped the bodies on the other side of town."

Matt glanced at Fontaine, who had begun fidgeting in the corner. "Did you make up the counterfeit IDs, Counselor?"

"That was Temps," Fontaine said in a low voice. "He knew somebody who could do it quickly."

"You're an attorney," Matt said. "You had to know what you were doing."

"Emily was a good kid," he said without emotion. "I knew about the affair almost from the beginning. When she had the baby, it didn't take much to guess that the governor was the father. Still, it was a secret. No one knew, and I never mentioned it—not even to him. But after three years, all that changed. The baby was beginning to look more like a boy every day. You could see the resemblance in his eyes and face, and everybody started talking about it. Eventually the governor realized that his secret was out of the bag, and he freaked out. Then we had a problem."

"You call a double homicide a problem?" Matt asked.

Fontaine winced. "There was a lot at stake, Jones. A lot at stake for everyone."

The governor mumbled something. Matt gave him a look.

"Did you say something, Governor?"

The governor stared back at him—the madness, the insanity beginning to glow in his eyes.

"You bet I did," he said after a while. "I would've made a great president. The greatest of them all!"

FIFTY-ONE

Matt glanced at the chief. "We should probably move this down to headquarters," he said. "We'll need statements from everyone."

"May I ask for a favor, Matty?"

Matt turned to the governor's wife, who despite the shock still seemed to be holding herself together.

"It depends on the favor, Lisa."

"The ballroom's filled with people, reporters, cameras," she said. "Is there any chance we could leave out a back door?"

The chief stepped forward. "There's a way through the kitchen," he said. "It leads straight to the loading docks in the garage."

"Could we leave through the kitchen then, Chief?"

He nodded. "I think it would be better for everyone. I'll make the arrangements."

Matt glanced at the governor, who still appeared to be deep inside himself. He looked worn out and frail—almost as if he had aged twenty years in less than an hour.

"Okay," Matt said as he turned to check on Lisa. "We'll walk out through the—"

He stopped.

He was watching her pull the smock away from her dress. He was watching her pull her hair back when he noticed the brooch pinned to her chest.

At first, he couldn't believe what was happening, or what he was seeing, or even thinking. He let his mind skip back through the days to that morning when he showed up for a meeting with Brooks and found everyone in the house dead. He could see the family portrait on the wall above the lamp and table in Brooks's study. He could see Cindy Brooks on the pier holding Emma on what he had guessed was their first trip home after the child's birth. He could hear Vince Sato telling him what kind of a woman Cindy had been. A talented architect who, after having a child, went back to work and suddenly became a huge success. She got hot was the way Sato had put it. Her business really took off.

He tried to control his breathing as he thought about that family portrait. He felt dizzy and grabbed hold of the table.

The chief rushed over from the door. "What is it, Jones?" he was saying. "What's happened? Are you okay?"

Matt didn't answer. He could feel everyone in the room staring at him. In an instant, the entire world had been tossed off its axis and shot through a black hole.

Lisa Hayworth was wearing the brooch.

The replica of the Library Tower that Sato had been searching for.

The piece of jewelry that Cindy Brooks's father had made by hand and given to her because she was an architect and loved the building. The brooch that she never seemed to take off. The one that she had been wearing in the family portrait.

It was a singular piece of jewelry. Like the building, a one-of-a-kind work of art.

And Lisa Hayworth was wearing it. Lisa Hayworth, the governor's wife. Lisa Tillman, the teenage girl who had looked after Matt as a boy.

What it implied rattled Matt's bones.

Now he knew why the kids had been murdered. It had never really made sense before. Even after considering the possibility that the governor might be insane. It had never made sense until this moment. Until he saw the brooch pinned to Lisa's dress.

"Chief," Matt said, "I'd like to ask the governor a few more questions before we leave. If you wouldn't mind, maybe we could set up the walk through the kitchen a little later."

"What is it?" the chief said.

"A few more questions, that's all. Before I forget."

Inside he was reeling. Inside everything was tumbling through a horrific vortex. He tried to make the spinning stop. He tried to focus as he faced the governor.

"Do you see the brooch that your wife is wearing, Governor?"

The governor glanced at his wife without interest, then turned back and shrugged.

Lisa stepped away from the makeup chair. "What's this about, Matty? Listen to the people in the ballroom. Can't we talk about this at headquarters?"

Matt kept his eyes on the governor. "I was just wondering where the brooch pinned to your dress came from, Lisa," he said. "Did you give it to her as a gift, Governor?"

The man shook his head. "I've never seen it before tonight."

"Hey," Lisa said in a louder voice. "What's going on here?"

Matt ignored her question, still staring at the governor's face. "What about the pictures I saw?"

"I don't know what you're talking about," he said.

"Sure you do. The pictures you kept. I saw them. In some you're having sex with your intern. In others, you're holding a knife over her head. The shots of you with the dead bodies are too disturbing for me to describe, but I will if I have to."

The governor clamped his eyes shut and cringed. "Someone is sending them to me."

"Are you saying that you didn't take them as a way of remembering the night?"

"Remembering the night?" he said, stammering. "Who would want to do that?"

"Most mass killers collect keepsakes, sir."

The governor met Matt's gaze. "I told you before, Detective. I've been living with this impossible situation for three years. It's been killing me. I was in love with her."

"You claim the pictures are being sent to you. Are you saying that someone is blackmailing you?"

The governor shook his head. "They never ask for anything. Every once in a while whoever it is sends me a new one. I shudder every time I see the envelope because I know what's inside. They're disgusting. I've destroyed every one of them. I burn them in the fireplace."

Lisa took a step closer with her eyes glued to the chief. "I don't know where this is going, Chief. But I think it should stop right now."

The chief glanced at her. "Have a little patience, Mrs. Hayworth."

"I'm the governor's wife," she said. "I don't need to have patience. This has to stop right now. I'm ordering you to stop it right now."

The governor shook his head at Matt and seemed confused. "I don't understand why you're asking me these questions either."

He started to get out of the makeup chair. Then Fontaine walked over and eased him back down into the seat. There was a knowing glint in Fontaine's eyes, and he seemed more than focused right now.

"What are they doing, Alan?" the governor whispered to his attorney. "Why is Jones asking me about Lisa's brooch?"

Fontaine patted his client's hand. "Hold on, Jimmy. I think it's in your best interest to sit tight and listen to what the detective is saying right now."

Matt took Fontaine's place as the attorney stepped away. "You should follow his advice, Governor. Just a few more questions, I promise."

The governor waved his hand through the air as if disgusted by it all. "Go ahead," he said in a weary voice.

"When I asked you about the murders a few minutes ago, you called the whole thing a blur. A nightmare. A bad dream. You said in your own words, and I quote, 'When I came out of it, there was blood everywhere.'"

"What's the question, Detective?"

Matt leaned closer and lowered his voice. "Do remember having a headache at the time? When you came out of it, Governor, did it feel like a hangover?"

"What are you trying to get at?"

Matt gave the governor a long look. "Is there any chance that you might have been drugged?"

"Shut up, Jimmy!" Lisa shouted. "Keep your mouth shut!"

Matt couldn't be certain, but it may have been more of a shriek than a shout. There were shades of desperation in her shrill voice, and she appeared frenzied.

Matt met the chief's eyes and caught the slight nod. When he looked over at McKensie, he thought he detected the faintest of smiles. The door was about to open—all the dots aligned and connected for everyone to see. All those harsh loose ends were clipped and trimmed and ready to be tied off into knots.

She'd slipped, and it was a tell.

Matt watched her back across the room until she bumped into the wall.

"You knew about the affair, Lisa. You're the one who took the pictures. They were hidden in your bedroom."

"So what?"

"I'm gonna guess that you knew your husband had been having sex with Emily Kosinski for a long time."

"Maybe I did," she said. "Maybe I even came down from Sacramento and watched. Maybe I'd been doing it for months."

The governor looked at Matt with glazed eyes and seemed more confused than ever.

"What does this mean?" he said. "Are you trying to trick me?"

Lisa let out a gasp. "Shut up, you stupid man," she said. "I do all the work, and all you've done is screw everything up!"

The governor turned to her, still bewildered but now surprised. "What did you say to me, Lisa?"

"You had sex with that slut," she said in a raised voice. "You did it in our home. In our bed. For God's sake, Jimmy, you had a baby with her, and you named him David! That's your middle name!"

The governor looked at Matt for help. "What's going on, Detective? Please tell me."

Fontaine took the governor's hand and squeezed it. Lisa stepped away from the wall, glaring at her husband.

"I'll tell you what's going on, you idiotic man," she said. "I killed them! I stabbed that whore to death! Your lover! I did it! And then I murdered your child! I killed your son!"

Matt could see the hate redrawing the shape of her face and infecting her eyes. "And what about the Brooks, Lisa?"

She laughed. "You should have seen the look on that reporter's face when he opened the front door. He knew why I was there! He knew he was done!"

"But why kill the babies? The infants?"

A tremor moved through her body, and she shivered as if overcome by the Furies. Once she pulled herself together, she narrowed her eyes.

"Because neither one of them was mine!"

Her words settled into the room like a cloud of noxious gas. Everyone was staring at her. And now everyone finally knew. But Matt was wrestling with the images in his head—shot after shot of the woman swinging the knife into human flesh. He could hear her cackling as she killed every member of both families one by one. He could see her biting Emily Kosinski, then biting Cindy Brooks, in a fit of absolute madness. He could feel her insanity as she broke from the world of all things human and stabbed these innocent people again and again until they were long past their final breath.

After several moments, the governor got out of the makeup chair and faced his wife.

"Is this true, Lisa?" he said in an odd voice. "You murdered these people? You murdered Emily and David? You drugged me? You faked the pictures after you killed them? And for three years you've made me think that I did it? For three years I've had to endure this pain and live in terror. You duped me and Alan and everyone else into thinking that I murdered these people whom I cared so much for?"

She laughed at him again. "Three years," she said. "For three years I've watched you twist in agony. When you needed prodding, I'd send you a picture so you might remember what you'd done to me. You betrayed me. You cheated on me! You fell in love with this nobody after all I'd done for you! A stupid slut! I hate you! I hate everything about you!"

The governor kept his eyes on her. From where Matt stood, the man looked as if he was struggling to bridle his anger and rage and losing the battle the hard way. He pointed a finger at his wife. Matt couldn't help noticing that his hand was rock steady.

"You murdered Emily because you found out that it was more than an affair. You killed her because you spied on us and realized that I'd fallen in love with her."

"Ha!" she said. "You're pathetic, Jimmy! You just told everybody in this room that you hated the slut! Which is it, Governor? I'm your wife, and I'd like to know! Did you love her, or did you hate the stupid bitch?"

The governor closed his eyes again. He was rolling his neck in a circle and appeared to be muttering something. A prayer, a chant—Matt couldn't tell. When he opened his eyes finally, they ripped through the air and pinned themselves to his wife like a set of darts. A moment of complete stillness passed. Complete darkness. Complete clarity. And then the governor suddenly lurched forward, swinging his right fist at his wife's mouth. It was a powerful blow. A blow that Matt guessed had been building ever since Emily Kosinski was murdered. And when it hit its mark, the spine-tingling sound it made echoed through the room. Lisa had been caught off guard and howled as blood sprayed all over her face and the governor's. Before Matt could reach them, the governor wrapped his hands around his wife's neck and thrust her body through the door into the ballroom like a rag doll. People waiting to hear the governor announce his run for president could be heard squealing, then screaming in horror as the couple landed on the floor.

Matt raced through the door and saw the audience and media hovering over them. Cameras were rolling. Strobe lights pounding. Matt struggled to part the mob, but no one would budge. When he finally broke through the crowd and reached them, he could see the governor banging his wife's head into the floor with his hands still clamped around her neck.

"But I loved her," the governor kept repeating through clenched teeth. "Don't you understand, Lisa? I loved her."

Matt tried to pry the governor's hands away from Lisa's neck, but the man was too amped up and filled with fury. In the end, it wouldn't have made any difference. Lisa's eyes were open, her face drenched in blood. But it was her neck that had taken the beating. The woman was obviously dead. Still, the governor never stopped, even when he began weeping.

ALSO BY ROBERT ELLIS

The Girl Buried in the Woods

The Love Killings

City of Echoes

Murder Season

The Lost Witness

City of Fire

The Dead Room

Access to Power

ABOUT THE AUTHOR

Robert Ellis is the international bestselling author of *Access to Power* and *The Dead Room*, as well as two critically acclaimed series—the Lena Gamble novels *City of Fire*, *The Lost Witness*, and *Murder Season*, and the Detective Matt Jones Thriller Series, which includes *City of Echoes*, *The Love Killings*, *The Girl Buried in the Woods*, and *City of Stones*. His books have been translated into more than ten languages and selected as top reads by *Booklist*, *Kirkus Reviews*, *Library Journal*, *Publishers Weekly*, National Public Radio, the *Baltimore Sun*, the *Chicago Tribune*, the *Toronto Sun* (CA), *The Guardian* (UK), *People* magazine, *USA Today*, and *The New York Times*. Born in Philadelphia, Ellis moved to Los Angeles to work as a writer, producer, and director in film, television, and advertising. He studied screenwriting with Walter Tevis, author of *The Hustler*, *The Man Who Fell to Earth*, and *The Color of Money*, and went on to ghostwrite the final draft of *Nightmare on Elm Street 4: The Dream Master* before becoming a novelist. Ellis's books have won praise from authors as diverse as Janet Evanovich and Michael Connelly. *City of Echoes* received a "Best Book of the Month" award from Amazon.com.

For more information about Robert Ellis, visit him online at:
https://www.robertellis.net

Printed in Great Britain
by Amazon